About the Author

Susie Murphy is an Irish historical fiction author. She loves historical fiction so much that she often wishes she had been born two hundred years ago. Still, she remains grateful for many aspects of the modern age, including women's suffrage, electric showers and pizza. A Class Apart is her first published novel.

ISBN-13: 978-1-915770-01-1

www.susiemurphywrites.com

Join the Susie Murphy Readers' Club
for updates and free stories:

https://bit.ly/susie-murphy-readers-club

A Class Apart

A Matter of Class, Book One

Susie Murphy

Also by Susie Murphy

A Class Entwined
A Class Forsaken
A Class Coveted
A Class Reunited
A Class Inherited

For Nana and Granda,
who always asked when I would write my story.
And for Aoife,
who showed what it was to have tremendous courage.

Chapter 1

Bridget twisted in her seat as the horse-drawn carriage reached the top of the avenue and the familiar edifice of warm red brick came into sight.

'There it is!' she exclaimed, heart soaring with emotion.

In the seat opposite, her mother squared her shoulders and gripped her fan tightly, her knuckles straining the material of her glove.

Bridget pressed her nose to the window, striving to take in as much as she could through the dust-streaked glass. All the servants had congregated in the open space before the manor house, waiting to greet their mistress on her return. As the carriage lumbered to a stop, wheels crunching on gravel, Lady Courcey fixed her gaze upon her daughter.

'You shall maintain absolute decorum, as befits a proper lady,' she said in a low, measured tone.

Bridget deflated in an instant but there was no time to respond because a liveried footman had already opened the door of the carriage, letting in a breath of air which alleviated the stifling heat within. He offered his hand to assist Lady Courcey and the lady stepped out. Then he reached for Bridget's hand and she too emerged blinking into the May sunshine.

Oakleigh Manor rose before her. The immense, elegant building remained unchanged, save for the ivy creeping further across its walls. A sea of servants' faces floated in front of it but impeding this view was the form of her massive-bellied uncle, Lord Walcott, three or four small dogs yapping around his ankles. Just behind him stood the butler, Mr Buttimer, who had been in the family's service for several decades. His back and shoulders were as straight as if he were about to receive instructions from a military commander.

Lord Walcott's voice boomed out in welcome. 'My dearest Constance!' He waddled forwards under the weight of his great bulk and stooped to kiss his sister's proffered hand. 'Your journey was comfortable enough, I trust?'

They had spent the past couple of days travelling more than sixty miles south from Dublin but, despite the heat, had dined well at the inns where they had stayed and had suffered no wheel-related misfortunes.

'It was an excruciating necessity,' said Lady Courcey.

Lord Walcott chuckled and turned to bestow a similar kiss upon Bridget.

She curtseyed in response. 'How do you do, Uncle Stuart.'

Mr Buttimer stepped up next. He bowed without disturbing the rigidity of his posture and said, 'Your ladyship, you are most welcome back. The estate has not been the same in your absence.' Still bent over, he cast a hasty glance in Lord Walcott's direction. 'That is to say, it has been well managed, but of course we all prefer to see a Courcey in the family seat. Ahem, I don't mean to imply—it goes without saying that his lordship has been a fine substitute—not my intention to demean—'

'Thank you, Buttimer. My daughter and I would like some refreshment after we have settled back into our chambers.'

'Indeed, a luncheon is already being prepared, my lady.'

The butler seemed on the verge of expanding on this subject but Lady Courcey cut him off with a nod and a beckoning gesture of her fan to Bridget. Her mouth was a thin line as she turned towards the red-bricked manor. While for the most part a very happy place, Oakleigh was also the site of some painful memories and plainly those were the ones she was choosing to remember upon their arrival. Bridget felt the poignancy too but it was not enough to quell her joy in coming home at long, long last.

They headed towards the front entrance of the house, making their way through a gap in the neat rows of maids, footmen, stable hands, gardeners, and even some of the local farmers and cottiers. Lord Walcott, who appeared to have taken no offence to Mr Buttimer's babbling, ambled along in their wake, calling his dogs to heel.

Bridget's gaze roamed to either side, recognising familiar faces from her childhood. She was not far from the front steps when she spotted Cormac in the last row, his fair hair standing out among the rest. His presence took her by surprise – she had not thought of him in so long, but when she had it was never to imagine him as a servant. His eyes, like the others, were cast respectfully downwards but as she passed by he glanced up. Startled, she turned her head at once so as not to be caught looking herself.

Somewhat flustered, she climbed the broad, stone steps to the front door and crossed the threshold, the barking of her uncle's dogs shrill in her ears. The enormous entrance hall was pleasantly cool after the sweltering heat outside. Its dominating feature was a sweeping mahogany staircase which rose in splendour to the next floor. At the foot of the stairs stood Mrs Walsh, the housekeeper, a ring of keys hanging at her waist.

'Your ladyship, Miss Muldowney. I am delighted to welcome you both home.'

Lady Courcey sniffed. 'Ryan should be following shortly with the luggage. Send her up to me as soon as she arrives.'

She made for the staircase and Bridget followed, eager to reach her bedchamber, which she entered with a sigh of nostalgia. She had been a girl of only twelve when she had last set foot here but nothing seemed to have altered. The four-poster bed was still decorated with burgundy-coloured curtains, at its foot lay the same sheepskin rug into which she had loved sinking her bare toes, and her old hairbrush rested on the dressing table as though she had just left it there that morning. It even smelled the same, of wood polish and fresh linen and something comforting which she could only label as 'home'.

On the far wall hung a long, silver-framed mirror. A glance into the glass made her pause. Here was the one thing in the room that had wholly changed: her own reflection. She had grown up since the last time she had looked into this mirror and for a moment she did not recognise herself. Her dark brown eyes stared back, struck by the transformation that seven years had wrought upon her, and she looked away, disconcerted.

She turned to the window, which offered a prospect vastly different to the one she could see from her bedchamber in Dublin. Merrion Square, its street busy with passing carriages, had been a sight she had initially hated, then become accustomed to and in the end rather fond of, but it could never replace the view out of any window of Oakleigh Manor, with its endless expanse of nature on every side.

She looked down upon the space in front of the house, where the workers were dispersing back to their duties. The window was open and their voices drifted up to her. Although the rustic Carlow accent was as disparate from the polished intonations of the aristocracy as it was possible to be, the distinctive brogue charmed her now as much as it ever had.

The stable hands remained to see to the carriage and its horses; Bridget saw Cormac grasp a bridle and rub the horse's neck. A donkey and cart laboured into view at the top of the avenue, the back of the cart loaded with large trunks. Ellen Ryan, Lady Courcey's freckled lady's maid, sat beside the driver. She hopped down from the cart and said something to Mr Buttimer who clicked his fingers at his footmen and the stable hands.

Bridget moved away from the window and rang the bell pull. When a breathless maid scuttled into the room, she said, 'Please bring me some water for washing. I would like to freshen up before going down to luncheon.'

The maid curtseyed and scampered out again. Bridget's gaze landed once more on the sheepskin rug and, overcome by an impish urge, she sat on the bed and hitched up her skirts to take off her ankle boots and stockings. She sighed as her feet escaped their sweaty imprisonment, then stood on the rug and buried her toes in the wool. A feeling of contentment settled over her like a blanket.

Footsteps came tapping smartly down the corridor and through the open door she saw two footmen pass by bearing a trunk bound for her mother's room. Close on their heels was another pair who stopped outside her own chamber.

They weren't footmen but stable hands. She let her skirts fall to cover her exposed feet as Cormac and a lanky boy carried the trunk into her room and set it down by the wardrobe with a muted thud.

They both headed back towards the door but some inexplicable impulse made her say, 'Please wait a moment, Cormac.'

After the barest hesitation, he said to the other lad, 'You go on, Liam. I'll be right behind you.'

Liam shot him a quizzical look but left nonetheless. Cormac turned around to face her. At these close quarters, she could see that he had changed too, physically at least. He was much taller now and the skinny frame of his boyhood had developed into the sturdy body of a young man used to hard work. His skin was tanned and his fair hair was longer than it used to be, falling into his eyes, which she perceived were still that astonishing shade of blue.

'I...' She didn't know what to say next. Why had she even called him back?

He saved her by offering a smile. ''Tis good to have you home.'

'It is good to be home,' she said, smiling in return.

'Might you be back for good?' he asked.

'Mother says it is just for the summer, but I am hopeful we shall stay much longer than that.'

He glanced over his shoulder as the two footmen, who had deposited her mother's trunk, passed by again. 'I'd best be going.'

'Yes, of course. Thank you for...' She gestured towards the trunk.

'No trouble,' he said and disappeared out the door.

The maid returned moments later with a pitcher of water and Bridget set about washing the sticky heat from her skin.

Chapter 2

One particular aspect of living in the countryside which Bridget had forgotten, and very soon remembered, was just how obsessed one could become with the weather. In Dublin, the weather presented a mild inconvenience; a shower of rain might signify a muddy hem on the way to visiting an acquaintance, or a warm day increased the heat inside a ballroom. In the country, the weather conditions entirely dictated the pattern of daily life.

After the sunny day that marked their homecoming to Oakleigh, there followed two solid weeks of rainy, windy misery. Bridget maintained an optimistic outlook to begin with as it gave her an opportunity to explore the house of her childhood through adult eyes. She chose different books from the shelves in the library, admired the paintings on the walls with greater discernment, and relished playing the grand piano in the drawing room with a far more practised touch. She especially loved going down to the kitchens and chatting with the cook, Mrs Kavanagh, something which she had never felt at liberty to do in the Merrion Square townhouse.

However, the more she gazed out of Oakleigh's windows, the more she longed to be outside, and the more it poured. Mrs Kavanagh said it was the wettest month of May she had ever seen.

'And I've seen my fair share of Mays,' she said, her big bosom shaking as she chuckled.

But now June had arrived and with it came the promise of a real summer. The sun had emerged at last, the clouds were feathery white ribbons in the sky, and the green, lush outdoors called to Bridget.

And her mother insisted upon her performing yet another recital in the drawing room.

After the third movement of a Mozart piano sonata, Bridget could bear it no longer. She played the closing chords with an air of finality and, when her mother and uncle's polite clapping had died away, said, 'Mother, it is a fine day to go for a ride, don't you think?'

Lady Courcey folded her hands in her lap. 'If the weather holds, we shall take the opportunity to ride across the estate tomorrow.'

Lord Walcott let out a rumbling laugh. 'That's a mighty big "if" in this country.'

Bridget wholly agreed. She pressed her fingertips to her forehead. 'Do you mind if I retire to my bedchamber for a little while? I feel a headache growing. Perhaps it's from the heat.'

Her mother gave a brusque nod. Bridget shut the lid of the piano and made her escape.

***

Cormac slipped through the green-painted door of Oakleigh Manor's walled apple orchard and followed the winding path among the trees, saw dangling languidly at his side. It was shady beneath the canopy and a bird sang somewhere in the branches above his head, its serene melody adding to the peacefulness of the place.

He kept walking until he reached the clearing at the centre where the apple trees subsided and a solitary oak towered over all else. His purpose in coming hung precariously from the oak tree: a branch about four feet long that was close to breaking off. The new under gardener was supposed to have seen to it but the lad was still finding his feet so Cormac had taken it upon himself to complete the job, given that he had the tools to do it.

He pressed his palm to the ancient tree's weathered bark, recalling the first day he had come upon it. At five years old, his thirst for mischief had known no bounds and he had trespassed on the grounds of the big house with no regard for the consequences. More interesting than even the stables or the hay barns had been his discovery of the orchard with this most excellent tree for climbing. He had been perched in its gnarled branches when the sound of singing drifted near and a girl entered the clearing below him. Unable to resist such a prime target, he had plucked an acorn from the tree and dropped it on her head. Even now, he could recall her yelp of surprise and her high voice reverberating around the clearing in indignation.

'I know there's someone up there, I can see your toes!'

Wiggling them had produced a reluctant laugh on her part. He had swung down and greeted her as affably as though the offending acorn was not present between his bare feet and her dainty shoes, and she had found it within her to forgive him. After establishing names (of which hers made no sense to him at the time: 'I'm a Muldowney but I'll be a Courcey when I grow up if Mama and Papa don't have any sons...') and an understanding that acorns must never be tossed onto people's heads, there ensued an education on the topic of climbing trees. She had been a novice but determined not to show fear and the lesson had ended in laughter, two grazed knees and a rip in the hem of her dress.

When they heard her governess calling, she had turned to run, but not before asking hopefully, 'Will you come back tomorrow?'

'I will,' he had promised.

Fourteen years had passed but that chance meeting remained vivid in his memory. Only for this oak tree, they might never have crossed paths at all.

He turned his attention to the broken branch. As thick as a man's leg and still partly attached to the tree, it drooped in the throes of its demise, a few leafy twigs jutting from it like flailing arms. After scrutinising the height of the branch and its angle to the ground, he decided he was better off tackling it from above and climbed nimbly up into the tree. He braced his back against the trunk, secured his grip on his saw, and attacked the branch. It had been nearly ready to fall; the wood snapped and the branch split from the trunk, settling on the leaf litter beneath the tree with a creaking sigh.

'Oh!' said a female voice.

He swivelled in surprise, teetered on his perch, and slung an arm over the branch above his head to catch his balance. Bridget stood in the clearing staring up at him. The irony of their positions did not escape him and he suppressed an impulse to laugh.

Concern filled her face. 'The tree isn't dying, is it?'

'Not at all,' he said. 'Just a weak branch. Otherwise 'tis the finest.'

Her shoulders slumped with relief. 'That's good.' She glanced about, clasped her hands together in front of her, tucked them behind her back, then left them swinging by her sides. 'I came outside for a walk. I had been playing the piano for my mother and uncle but this weather was too lovely to resist.'

'The piano?' he repeated. 'You always used to hate that thing.'

She flushed. 'I know, but I applied myself to proper study of it when I went to Dublin. It is actually an enjoyable pastime.'

He tilted his head but made no further remark on it. He descended from the tree, taking care not to cut himself on the saw's blade, and landed lightly, fallen leaves crackling underfoot. Instead of continuing on with her walk, Bridget lingered where she was.

'It's hard to believe how long it has been since I was home,' she said tentatively.

Fishing a length of string from his pocket, he used it to secure the saw at his waist. 'Seven years,' he said.

'And three months,' she added.

He knelt next to the broken branch and set about stripping twigs from it, glancing at her out of the corner of his eye while he did so.

She looked so...changed. Gone were the wild curls he remembered, the scuffed elbows and knees, the rosy cheeks. In their place stood a docile girl – no, *lady* – whose chestnut brown hair had been tamed into tidy ringlets and whose skin was as pale as porcelain. She radiated such an impression of cleanliness and daintiness that it was difficult to believe she had ever climbed a tree in her life.

She took a few steps closer, her posture a little more relaxed. 'I tried to write, but my mother found me out, even when I attempted to sneak letters to Ellen. Mother burned them all.'

That did sound like Lady Courcey.

'I would've written,' he said, 'but Mrs Walsh wouldn't give me your address. She didn't believe I was able to read.'

'Well, we know better, don't we?' She smiled. 'Do you practise anymore?'

He shrugged, a guilty student. 'Don't have much reason to. Just a few letters from my sister, Mary, but her writing's even worse than mine.'

'Is she still away taking care of your aunt?'

'My aunt passed over a year ago but Mary wrote to tell us she'd found a position in Dublin and she'd send us some money soon.'

He neglected to mention that no money and no more letters had come. Instead, he asked, 'What was Dublin like? Did you hate it there?'

She laughed. 'For several years, yes. I was a demon, steadfastly refusing to do anything or go anywhere. I drove my mother to distraction every single day. But when I eventually came out into society I discovered that attending balls and wearing fancy gowns was not so appalling as I thought and I began to enjoy myself.' She seemed aware of the frivolity of her comment and rushed on, 'And how have you been? You are a stable hand now?'

'I am,' he said, straightening and wiping his hands on his clothes. 'And I do some carpentry as well, whenever 'tis needed.'

'Just like your father! He must be proud of you.'

He hesitated. 'He...was.'

She blinked. 'Was?'

'He died. Three winters ago.'

'Oh, Cormac!' she exclaimed. 'I am so very sorry, I did not know.'

He felt the force of her empathy. She knew what it was like to lose a father.

'I lost my brother too. They died within weeks of each other. Just before Christmas.'

Her hand flew to her mouth. 'How did this happen?'

He looked away into the gloom under the apple trees beyond the clearing. 'D'you remember the bridge we used to cross over the Sruhawn to go to the Tullow horse fair? There was terrible flooding that December. My father was returning from the fair when the stream burst its banks and swept the bridge away, taking him and his horse with it. His body was found downstream two days later.'

Her eyes brimmed with tears. 'What a grievous loss for you and your family.' She shook her head in disbelief. 'And your brother?'

'Patrick died in a fire in the stables. It might've been started by something as stupid as a neglected rushlight, no one knows for sure. Almost the entire structure burned down. We lost two lads and four horses that night.'

She was aghast. 'Your poor mother. How is she coping?'

'As well as can be expected.' Two and a half years had passed but how could his mother ever get over the loss of her husband and her eldest boy?

Without warning, Bridget reached out and clutched one of his hands in both of hers.

'Please pass on my condolences to her,' she murmured, 'and tell her I shall visit her soon.'

When she let go, she could not seem to meet his eyes. She turned and touched the tree trunk, her fingertips tracing the letters they had carved into the bark so many years ago.

'Do you still have that rusty old blade?' she asked. 'You never went anywhere without it.'

'I only keep it for nostalgia's sake. I use my father's tools now he's...gone.'

She gave him a compassionate look, then stared upwards into the branches above her.

'I have not climbed a tree in years,' she said, her tone almost wistful, 'but I spent half my childhood sitting at the top of this one.'

'We had fun, didn't we?' he said. 'Climbing trees, picking apples...'

'Playing hide-and-seek in the quarry,' she contributed. 'Throwing hay in the fields. Wheedling hunks of cheese from Farmer McKinty's wife.'

'D'you miss it? The way it was back then?'

She sighed. 'I miss the simplicity of it all. Life in the city taught me that becoming an adult is a complicated matter. There were so many times when I was obliged to be a prim and proper lady and converse with people I detested, and all I wanted was to be back at Oakleigh with my best friend.'

His skin tingled at the sincerity of her words. 'I wish you hadn't been taken away against your will. Seven years is a long time to be so unhappy.'

She gave him a reassuring smile. 'You have no need to be concerned on my behalf for I did not suffer in perpetual misery. I found much contentment in Dublin. In fact, I have some very happy news to impart.' Her smile widened. 'I am engaged.'

It took a few seconds for her pronouncement to sink in. 'Engaged?'

She bobbed in effervescent affirmation.

He glanced down at her hand. 'But there's no ring on your finger.'

'There isn't,' she acknowledged. 'The proposal was quite spontaneous. He did not have a ring ready at the time.'

She was still beaming. With effort, he schooled his expression into one of pleasure and said, 'My congratulations to you. Who's the lucky fellow?'

'Mr Garrett Lambourne. He is an English gentleman but his father has property in Ireland and they have spent a great deal of time in Dublin over the past couple of years. He is heir to the viscountcy of Wyndham.'

His internal wince matched her visible one, though he had no idea why she would feel reason to react like that. Perhaps the title came with a substantial debt.

'Is he in Dublin now?' he asked without much enthusiasm for the answer.

'No, he was obliged to go back to England for a brief spell as he and his father had business to manage in London. But he is due to return within the month. We are expecting him for a visit here at Oakleigh.'

No doubt Mr Lambourne would be an avid rider and spend half his days at the stables. Cormac felt an urge to hurry the conversation along to its conclusion. 'You must be looking forward to that very much. If you'll excuse me, 'tis past time for me to be going.'

He rolled the broken branch into an easier position for picking up.

'I'm sure I'll see you again soon,' she said.

'Next time you need your horse saddled, I expect.'

Silence fell between them, broken only by the light rustle of leaves overhead. 'What do you mean by that?'

He swallowed. 'I mean we shouldn't be talking like this. It would've been fine when we were children but not now. Not when I'm your servant.'

'I don't think of you that way at all,' she said, and there was absolute sincerity in her dark brown eyes.

'I'm a servant at Oakleigh, you're the heiress to Oakleigh. I'm your servant. More to the point, I'm your *male* servant.'

'Oh, for heaven's sake,' she said, even as her cheeks reddened.

'You're alone with me here in a deserted orchard. I can't say I know much about society rules but I know 'tis enough to ruin a young lady's reputation.'

She caught the tip of her tongue between her teeth, a gesture of anxiety that was so familiar to him from their childhood. 'But we are just old friends, there's nothing else to it.'

'There probably isn't another soul on the estate who'd see it like that. And neither would your future husband.'

Her blush spread all the way down to the neckline of her dress. 'I-I suppose you're right.'

He stooped and hefted the branch onto his shoulders with a grunt.

'I hope you've a happy summer at Oakleigh,' he said and hurried from the clearing.

CHAPTER 3

The following morning, Bridget took breakfast with her mother and uncle. As Lord Walcott returned from the sideboard with his third stacked plate of bacon and eggs, he said, 'Another fine day, ladies. How very fortunate. When you go out riding later, you must take note of the design of the stables.' He sat heavily in his chair and puffed out his vast chest. 'I oversaw the reconstruction of them after the fire, an excellent opportunity to indulge my architectural interests.'

Lady Courcey tapped the top of her soft-boiled egg, saying nothing. Bridget remembered Cormac's brother and laid her spoon down, her own egg untouched.

'And if you go as far as the quarry,' Lord Walcott continued after devouring two forkfuls in quick succession, 'you will see that it is prospering since I ordered excavation to begin there again. The limestone is a valuable resource and the workers are very satisfied with progress.' He belched as discreetly as he could behind his napkin.

'I don't believe we shall make it that far today,' Lady Courcey said and added with the faintest hint of derision, 'You set great store by the workers' satisfaction levels, do you?'

Bridget's attention drifted away from the conversation, her confused thoughts returning to her encounter with Cormac in the orchard. Talking with him by the oak tree had brought back so many vivid memories of their friendship that she had actually begun to think they might be friends again. Until he had made some very valid points on the matter.

She could try to convince herself that everyone knew what staunch companions they had been as children and that it was clear their intentions were nothing but innocuous, except for the fact that a world of difference existed between twelve and nineteen. If they had been discovered, there would have been uproar; it was so far from prudent behaviour, particularly when she was meant to be in her bedchamber trying to soothe a headache. Furthermore, she had a strong hunch that her fiancé would not be pleased at the idea of her partaking in any sort of acquaintance with a stable hand beyond the basic requirements.

She felt a surprising sense of loss. Mr Garrett Lambourne was to be her future but Cormac held a link to her past that no one else did. He had been with her at her father's passing and through every other event of her childhood, meaningful or trivial. The one thing that had consoled her during those awful early years in Dublin was that they would return to each other someday. But then over time she had ceased to view her life as a tragedy and hence her longing for Oakleigh and the people there had lessened. Of course, it had helped to be courted by a gentleman who had swept her off her feet with his charm.

She cringed when she recalled her declaration that Garrett was heir to a viscountcy. What had possessed her to say that? It had played no part in her decision to accept his suit – though it had been a substantial source of satisfaction for her mother – and it had sounded shallow of her to mention it. Much as the upper classes praised the virtues of ascending the social ladder, she despised the notion of marrying a man for his title. She was fortunate that theirs was a love match.

'I beg your pardon?'

The tone of her mother's voice drew her attention back to the breakfast table. Though Lady Courcey had used an expression of politeness, it was suffused with a chilliness which indicated she would rather be anything but civil. Lord Walcott was not the kind of man to wilt before a glare but even his massive frame seemed to shrink a little when faced with his sister's hostility.

'Can you repeat that?' the lady said, very quietly.

Lord Walcott cleared his throat. 'Now, Constance, I vow that it was an outstanding decision on my part. The tenants are content with their lot which means the estate is flourishing like never before.'

Lady Courcey dabbed her napkin at the corner of her mouth. 'Indeed. If it has been such a success, then why did you choose not to inform me of it?'

He waved an airy hand. 'You had more pressing issues to occupy you. Marrying off your daughter, for one.' He threw a theatrical wink in Bridget's direction.

'I would consider this issue as pressing as the marriage mart,' said Lady Courcey, 'if not more so, because it pertains to the excessive spending of estate resources.'

Bridget's head swivelled from her mother to her uncle. To what lavish levels could Lord Walcott have overspent that her mother was so displeased? Mrs Kavanagh had mentioned that he had been fond of inviting guests to Oakleigh but no mere party of extravagance would cause Lady Courcey to react like this.

'If you speak to Laurence Enright, he will assure you of the soundness of my claim. He interacts with the tenants on a daily basis and tells me they are deeply grateful for the arrangement. The tithes were an insufferable strain upon them.'

'A strain which you have incurred upon the estate, and my daughter's inheritance, instead.'

'Oakleigh can afford it. And I am confident Bridget will not even notice the expenditure when she is living on a viscount's income.'

'What tithes?' Bridget interjected, exasperated by her ignorance.

Her mother's lip curled. 'If you are so uninformed as to be unaware of their existence, then you are in grave need of an education this summer.'

Exhibiting a greater degree of patience, Lord Walcott said, 'The tithes are taxes paid by the tenants to support the Church of Ireland.'

Bridget frowned. 'But the Church of Ireland is not a Roman Catholic establishment. Why would the tenants be required to fund its upkeep?'

'Seems unfair, doesn't it?' agreed her uncle. 'I elected to absorb the tithes into the outflow of the estate, given that Oakleigh is the only non-Catholic residence for miles around. The tithes are but one of many hardships suffered by the Irish people, hardships which have only multiplied since 1798.' He shook his head. 'Their rebellion lasted no more than a few months but they have endured its ramifications these past thirty years. They have borne the tithes even longer and I deemed this to be a benevolent gesture to encourage goodwill. Your mother's agent helped me facilitate it.'

'A liberty you took without consulting me and which you have purposely kept concealed until now,' said Lady Courcey, the words barely making it past her clenched teeth. 'When I gave you authority over the estate in my absence, I did not expect you to be so wasteful with it. I intend to discuss this further with you and Mr Enright.'

Bridget could tell that 'discuss' meant 'abolish', and in short order. Lord Walcott gave a resigned shrug.

'I counsel you to embrace a philanthropic attitude on this matter,' he said, 'as they will respect you for it and work all the harder. Do take time to deliberate upon it before making a decision. For now, ladies, good morning to you.'

He heaved himself up from the table and gathered the final few scraps of food from the breakfast dishes on the sideboard into a handkerchief: treats for his pets who under no circumstances were permitted to be present at mealtimes while Lady Courcey was mistress of the house.

As he toddled towards the door, Bridget marvelled at the revelation of his generosity. Several years spent in rural Ireland had made a significant impact on him because the uncle she remembered had thought of nothing but his belly and his dogs. She glowed with admiration at his retreating back and resolved that, if her mother chose to eradicate her brother's altruistic deed, she would reinstate it as soon as Oakleigh came into her own possession.

***

Cormac opened the back door into the kitchens and was greeted by a wave of heat as fierce as the June air outside. Steam issued from a huge pot of water boiling over the open hearth. His two sisters, Margaret and Bronagh, stood at a long table in the centre of the kitchen, their faces red as they sliced vegetables. At the far end of the table, Mrs Kavanagh and Mrs Walsh sat on a bench, the cook counting off items on her fingers while the housekeeper made notes on a piece of paper. Mrs Walsh looked up sharply at his appearance.

'What is it, Cormac?' she said, her tone only a touch short of abrupt. She presided over the household with a will of iron as unyielding as the set of keys hanging at her waist.

'I just wanted to check if there are any scraps for the horses?'

Mrs Kavanagh gesticulated towards the two girls chopping vegetables. 'Not yet, you'll have to come back later.' She turned back to Mrs Walsh, pointing at her notes. 'Make that four dozen, better to have too much than too little. Lord Walcott has shown no sign of leaving yet and he's not shy about asking for third helpings.'

Cormac gave the cook a deferential nod. She was a tyrant in the kitchens but she could be softened if one knew how; well-timed offerings of charm had on occasion won him a mouthful of fresh bread or a bite of leftover cake, never mind treats for the horses.

He stepped over to his sisters at the table. Both were younger than him and dark-haired and grey-eyed like their mother, whereas he had inherited his fair hair and blue eyes from their father. Bronagh continued to slice her onion, glancing covertly in Mrs Kavanagh's direction; her eyes were watering so much that, had Cormac not known she was the sort of girl who never cried, he would have been worried that there had been another death in the family. Margaret, the older of the two, laid down her knife and half-chopped carrot and gave him a wide smile.

'Good to see you, Cormac!' she said. 'Is everything well with you?'

He made an effort to grin. 'All's fine. How are you two?'

'Worn out! 'Tis been chaotic for the past two weeks. But 'tis nice to have the family in the house.' Margaret nudged Bronagh, who was wiping her eyes with the corner of her apron. 'Isn't it?'

Bronagh shrugged. 'Way I see it, it just means more work.'

'Don't mind her. She's in a bad mood 'cause she got in trouble with Mrs Kavanagh this morning for burning the servants' porridge. That's why she's stuck with the onions.'

'Don't tell Ma,' Bronagh said to Cormac.

'Cormac McGovern, have you quite finished taking up my maids' time?' came Mrs Kavanagh's voice from the other end of the table. 'Those vegetables won't get chopped by themselves, lad.'

'I'm leaving now,' he said and beat a hasty retreat.

The kitchens were situated at the rear of the big house, facing onto a cobbled courtyard which was bordered by the stables on one side and the orchard on the other. He crossed the cobblestones, entered through the open double doors of the stables and commenced with the task of mucking out one of the stable stalls. Lost in his thoughts, he was startled when he heard his name called and looked up to see the stable master, John Corbett, leaning over the half door of the stall.

The small, wiry man joked, 'Why so down? I know 'tisn't roses you're smelling, but 'tis nothing you haven't smelled a thousand times before.'

Cormac plastered another grin on his face. 'You're right about that,' he said, and started whistling to prevent further questions.

He had no right to be looking glum. After all, he had harboured no expectations of a renewed friendship upon Bridget's homecoming – he had understood very well that the nature of their situation would be infinitely different from that of their youth. But perhaps there had still been the trace of a twelve-year-old boy inside him who had hoped he would get his childhood friend back in some limited fashion. However, their chance meeting in the orchard had established that that kind of familiarity was out of the question.

His whistling faltered. She was *engaged*. The more he thought about it, the more he wondered how he had not seen it coming. She had lived for seven years in the city, maturing to the optimum age of marriage for a young woman and attending balls which would have been frequented by dozens of single men. Looking at it from that viewpoint, he was surprised she was only betrothed and not already married.

He didn't allow himself to speculate about what might have happened had she not been forced to depart from the estate. The appearance of Mr Garrett Lambourne, or some other fellow like him, would always have been the inescapable outcome.

He was once again jolted out of his reflections by a clipped English voice outside the entrance to the stables. 'Fetch the stable master to me and prepare our horses. My daughter and I are going to ride across the estate.'

He heard a murmur of 'Yes, m'lady,' followed by footsteps running to do her bidding. Seconds later, Liam's anxious face appeared above the half door of the stall. 'Will you help me, Cormac?' Though he had started working at the stables a year or so after Cormac and was more than capable, the lad looked daunted by the idea of serving the two ladies of the big house by himself.

'For sure. You go tell John her ladyship wants him and then take care of her horse. I'll look after Bonny.'

Liam nodded and hastened away. Cormac dropped his pitchfork and went into the next stall which housed Bridget's glossy, white mare, a gift from her father on her twelfth birthday. Bonny whinnied at him in greeting.

This encounter presented him with a challenge: how ought he to behave when he saw Bridget? Clandestine meetings were unacceptable but he could envisage no harm in being amicable on accidental occasions such as this.

After grooming and saddling her horse, he grabbed a mounting step and led the mare out of the stables. It was a glorious day, the sky a ceiling of pure blue and a gentle breeze blowing.

John appeared to be praising the design of the new stables to the ladies. The clip-clop of Bonny's hooves made them turn as one but while Bridget's expression lifted, her mother's went sour. The stable master seemed to interpret this as dissatisfaction that her own horse was not yet ready and muttered, 'The lad's thorough but slow,' before hurrying back inside.

Cormac guided the horse up to Bridget, trying to ignore the fact that Lady Courcey walked away with a sniff of distaste. Bridget's uncertainty was plain on her face – she too was unsure how to act.

He decided to take the lead. 'Bonny's happy to see you, Bridget,' he said in a light voice, hoping to convey that friendliness, if not friendship, still existed between them.

He might have said more, only for the exclamation of outrage that intruded upon them.

'Insolent boy,' Lady Courcey snapped, spinning on her heel. 'That is no way for a servant to speak to his superior.'

Bridget looked shocked. 'Mother, please, I took no offence.'

The lady paid her no heed, levelling a ferocious glower at Cormac. 'You shall address my daughter in the appropriate manner, or not at all.'

He could almost feel her disgust burning into his skin. 'Begging your pardon, m'lady,' he said through gritted teeth. 'My apologies, Miss Muldowney,' he added to Bridget, as it was the only thing he could say.

She mumbled something unintelligible, mortification flooding her face.

He set the step on the ground and offered his hand to help her mount. She took it in her own gloved one, climbed onto Bonny and squeezed before letting go. At the same time, Liam scurried from the stables leading Lady Courcey's horse and the lady mounted, her lips pursed.

Cormac stepped back and the two ladies trotted off, their horses' hooves striking the cobbles in rhythm. Humiliation coursed through him, and not a little loathing which he aimed in Lady Courcey's direction. Every line of her figure was rigid, from her straight shoulders to her stiff perch in the sidesaddle. Even her hair, the same chestnut shade as Bridget's, was severely styled under her hat, unlike the softer curls around her daughter's face. She radiated inflexibility and disapproval.

It came as no surprise. She had despised him from the moment they had first met. At the time, he had been just seven years old but he had also been Irish and a stable hand's son and in Bridget's presence, and his bare feet had been standing on a luxurious rug in the big house's library where Bridget was showing him how to read letters. 'I want this vagrant out of my house this very minute!' were the loudest words he had ever heard the lady utter from that day to this. He had been unfamiliar with the term 'vagrant' but its meaning had been unmistakable. Only for Lord Courcey's timely appearance and Bridget's desperate plea for intervention, he would have been driven from the building.

They had taken care to stay out of Lady Courcey's way after that but she could not fail to notice how much time they spent together. It had galled her to be overruled by her husband on such a matter, which had only caused her dislike of Cormac to strengthen. And it transpired that the passage of seven years apart had done nothing to dull the detestation – on both sides, he had to admit, as he gave her turned back a glower as good as the one she had given him.

Just before the ladies rounded the end of the big house, Bridget looked back over her shoulder at him, an apology in her glance. He nodded to show he understood and then they disappeared around the corner.

Chapter 4

'Bridget, are you paying attention?'

She dragged her gaze from the window, through which she could just make out a young gardener struggling with the weeding of an elaborate flower bed in the manor gardens, and met with three censorious stares.

'Yes,' she said guiltily.

'I feel obliged to remind you,' said Lady Courcey, 'that these proceedings are for *your* benefit.'

The lady was seated behind a large writing desk spread with various papers. Mr Buttimer and Mrs Walsh hovered by her elbow, trying not to look too reproachful – Bridget was a grown woman, after all, and no longer a child to be reprimanded for misbehaviour.

'I understand,' she said, folding her hands in her lap. 'Please continue.'

Since their return to Oakleigh, Lady Courcey had taken to conducting any necessary business in the wood-panelled chamber that used to be Lord Courcey's study and her primary task of the summer now seemed to be extending her daughter's education. Thanks to her ignorance about tithes, Bridget had been forced to endure almost a fortnight of gruelling lectures on a range of subjects relating to the estate and manor household, including how to keep accounts, assess crop yields, evaluate the rates of rent, and hire and discharge servants, as well as learning which domestic issues were pertinent to the butler and which to the housekeeper, the particulars in relation to having guests to stay, and the finer points of hosting social gatherings.

Most of her instruction came from Lady Courcey, but Mr Buttimer and Mrs Walsh also offered their perspectives (long-winded sermons from the former, succinct footnotes from the latter). Even Lord Walcott attempted to contribute advice, but his sister discouraged this based upon recent evidence which indicated, in her opinion, his lack of sound judgement. There had been no further developments on that dispute as of yet but a meeting with the land agent, Mr Enright, had been scheduled. Bridget hoped she would be expected to attend – perhaps three voices would be enough to drown out Lady Courcey's contention.

'Bridget!'

She bit her tongue and sat up straight. 'I was thinking about estate matters, I promise!'

Her mother nodded a dismissal to Mr Buttimer and Mrs Walsh. 'I think we shall finish for today.' After they left the study – with an aggravated cough from the butler implying he was either unhappy with Bridget's attention span or suffering from the onset of a chest cold – she turned back to her daughter. 'It is in your interest to absorb these valuable lessons. In a twelvemonth from November you will reach the age of twenty-one, at which point you will legally inherit Oakleigh. All of this,' she waved a hand at the desk, 'will become your responsibility.'

Bridget gulped. 'I know that,' she said, even though she had never given it much consideration. She recalled some fuss after her father's death relating to the line of inheritance specified in his will because hers was the first in four generations where the baron had fathered no boys. All manner of strangers popped up out of nowhere claiming to be the last surviving son of a distant cousin of a younger brother and wasn't it obvious from the portrait in the drawing room that he had the same colour eyes as the 1st Baron? However, in a rather uncommon proviso, the estate had been entailed by male-preference primogeniture, which meant that, in the absence of any male progeny, the eldest of the female offspring in the family would become the lawful heiress. Thus, Lord Courcey's only daughter would inherit his title, property and assets in her own right, but not until her twenty-first birthday. In the meantime, her mother had been appointed to act as guardian of the estate.

At the age of twelve, nine years had seemed a lifetime. Now her birthright dangled over the not-too-distant horizon.

Lady Courcey sighed. 'Of course, it is unlikely that you will need to put any of this knowledge into practice as you will soon have a husband who will handle the estate for you. But it is wise to prepare for the worst. After all, I intended to live to old age with my husband at my side.'

Bridget gaped at her mother. Her shoulders drooped and her eyes were sad, like they were looking at something that wasn't there. But then she snapped to attention again.

'So do endeavour to focus on what we are telling you. It may prove useful.' She shuffled some of the papers into a neat pile. 'I place no further demand on your time for now. I have letters to write which I wish to do in solitude.'

Bridget made a swift departure from the study. She supposed she could write some letters of her own – no doubt Madeleine and her other friends in Dublin would be eager to hear how she was adjusting back to country life – but that could wait. In truth, she wanted to seek out Cormac which, having been so confined to the house, she had had no opportunity to do since the day her mother had rebuked him in the courtyard.

Regardless of their resolution not to meet on familiar terms, he deserved a proper apology for the way he had been treated.

Still, there was something else she had to do which took higher priority. It was time she visited her second mother.

She donned her sturdiest boots before emerging outdoors. While the afternoon had clouded over and the air had turned muggy, it did not look like it was going to rain yet. A circuitous series of lanes presented the long way round to her destination, which most dignified ladies would choose to take, but crossing the fields was the more direct course and today did not strike her as the day to break a lifelong habit.

She couldn't help glancing about for Cormac as she passed the stables and the paddock but she caught no glimpse of him, though there were other stable hands who saluted her. Beyond the paddock lay the boundary to the first field, known locally as the Gorteen. She slipped through the gate and proceeded at a sedate walk to the far end where she entered the next field via a stile in the hedge. Then, when she was certain there was no one around to see, she hoisted her skirts up past her ankles and bounded across the grass, relishing the feel of the solid turf beneath her feet. Granted, it would have been far more liberating to sprint in the riding breeches her father had acquired for her back when she had learned to ride astride, but she was well past the age where such clothing, or such a position on a horse, could be deemed decent. She ran until she became out of breath, halting at last to draw in deep lungfuls of fresh air, a herd of curious cows her only witness to her indiscretion.

After that, she continued along the once well-trodden route at a more comfortable stroll. Most of the landscape triggered cheery memories of childhood jaunts, but she shivered as she crossed one particular field featuring a natural, three-pronged rock formation which jutted up out of the turf like a giant's clawed hand. Cormac had in the past divulged far more of its dreadful history than she had wanted to know. On their braver days, they had played morbid games about rebels and hangmen beneath its shadow, but more often than not they had steered clear of the rocky outcrop. She quickened her pace now and gave it a wide berth.

A few fields further on, she found another stile in the hedgerow, this one leading out into the neighbouring lane, where a round, brick-lined well stood at the opposite side. Someone had been assiduous in trimming back the thick hedge and no brambles tugged at her dress as she clambered over the stile. She followed the lane for a minute or two until a small cottage came into view at the side of the road. It was thatched and whitewashed and a horse shoe hung over the door. Adjoining it was a modest plot of land for growing potatoes, while a patch of woods extended behind it. A column of smoke streamed from the cottage's chimney, a box of wildflowers rested on its one window sill, and two or three hens pecked at the ground in front of it. Everything about the dwelling was familiar and welcoming and she felt a rush of gladness; how blessed she was to have two places in her life which she could call home.

She went up to the door of the cottage, the hens flapping away at her approach. The top half of it was open so she leaned over it and peered into the gloom. 'Is there anyone here?'

An exclamation of astonishment and delight came from the depths of the room within. 'That's never Bridget Muldowney!'

She smiled as a woman appeared at the door. 'Good day, Mrs McGovern.'

'Arrah, none of that now,' said Cormac's mother. 'You always called me Aunt Maggie and I hope that hasn't changed.'

Pulling back the bottom half of the door, she ushered Bridget inside. She had dark hair and light grey eyes but there were more white streaks and wrinkled lines than Bridget remembered.

The cottage, on the other hand, was the very same as when she had visited it as a child. Thanks to Jack McGovern's skills as a carpenter, Cormac's home boasted more furniture than the typical cottier's abode. A well-scrubbed table occupied the centre of the single room, with a bench on either side. There was a rocking chair in one corner and a spinning wheel in another. A simple dresser stood against the back wall and next to it a ladder led up to the loft, where the family slept at night.

A fire glowed in the grate despite the heat of the day; she inhaled the smell of the burning turf with satisfaction. Sitting before the hearth was a bare-footed little girl whom she did not recognise. She held a hen in her lap and stared at Bridget with big, round eyes.

'Of course, ye two have never met before,' said Maggie. 'This is Orlaith, my youngest girl. She's only five.' She crossed over to her daughter. 'Orlaith, this is Bridget. She's a good friend of your brother's. She lives in the big house.'

Cormac must not have told his mother about the incident in the courtyard and Bridget was glad of it; she would have been horrified if Maggie had tried to address her as 'Miss Muldowney', given that the same woman had been the one to pacify her at age eleven when she had found blood on her undergarments. That level of intimacy transcended any prospect of formality.

'It is nice to meet you,' Bridget said but Orlaith just gazed back solemnly.

Maggie winked. 'Don't worry, she's like that with everybody, our quiet little one.' She waved her hand at the table. 'Do sit down. 'Tis wonderful to see you! Would you like a cup of milk?'

'That would be lovely,' said Bridget, seating herself on one of the benches.

Maggie bustled over to the dresser, picked up a cup, and went outside. Bridget supposed the pail still stood in its same shady spot behind the cottage. She looked over at Orlaith and tried to catch her eye but the little girl was absorbed in stroking the feathers of her hen and humming softly to it.

When Maggie returned, she set a full cup of milk in front of Bridget and then took a seat opposite her. Bridget sipped from the cup and smiled. 'I feel like I am six years old again.'

Maggie chuckled. 'I remember it so well, the first time you came to visit us. Pouring out of the heavens it was, and that daft boy brought you across all those fields. You were soaked through when you got here, poor craythur. But an hour or two in front of the fire with a blanket and some warm milk and you were fine again.' She gazed at Bridget with affection. 'You've grown up so much since then. Look at your beautiful hair! It must've been some ordeal to get that wild mane under control.'

'Yes, my mother regards it as one of her greatest achievements.' This time they both laughed, recalling the many occasions when Bridget had come blazing to the cottage to recount yet another argument she had had with her mother over her untamed hair.

'I was hoping you might come to visit me once you got settled back,' said Maggie. 'When Cormac told me you'd returned I said to him it was only a matter of time before you showed up here.'

'Of course. How could I not come by? I have always considered this cottage my second home and its inhabitants my extended family.'

In an instant, Bridget's jollity died away.

'Maggie,' she said, reaching across the table and clasping the other woman's hand, which was rough and calloused. 'I want to offer my deepest condolences about Jack and Patrick. I grieved to hear of it. My heart goes out to you.'

Maggie's eyes dimmed. 'Thank you, dearie. That's kind of you to say.'

'It is one thing to lose a parent, but to lose a husband and a child and then be left raising the remaining children by yourself...' Bridget glanced at Orlaith, who would have been only two when her father died. 'I cannot imagine how you have coped.'

'I'd never have managed without Cormac. He's the man of the family now and he's looked after us all without a word of complaint, though he's had to deal with so much himself, poor boy.'

Bridget's forehead creased. 'What do you mean?'

'Didn't he tell you? What made their deaths so hard for him was he was there when they happened. He watched his father and his brother perish and there was nothing he could do.'

Bridget experienced a fresh wave of sympathy for Cormac. 'Oh, how truly awful.'

Maggie cocked her head towards the hearth. 'Orlaith, will you fetch me some water from the well? I'll need it for the supper later.'

'Yes, Ma,' the little girl said and hopped to her feet.

'Don't wander from the lane, and make sure the rope isn't tangled before you lower the bucket,' Maggie cautioned as Orlaith disappeared outside, her hen squawking behind her. A call of assent floated to them over the half door.

Maggie turned back to Bridget. 'Her little ears don't need to hear this.' Her voice became faint as she supplied the details her son had omitted. 'Cormac was accompanying his father home from the horse fair. Jack could see the bridge was weak and said they should cross it one at a time, so Cormac was waiting on the bank when the stream burst. It was a narrow escape. He nearly got swept away himself.' She took a shaky breath. 'And he was sleeping in the stables the night of the fire. The stable hands woke with flames and smoke all 'round them. It was chaos trying to save themselves and the animals. When Cormac realised his brother was still inside he tried to go back in but John Corbett grabbed him just before the loft caved in. Only for John, I might've lost both my boys that night.'

Bridget was horror-struck. Cormac had brushed with death twice and she, in her pretty dresses attending fancy balls, had never known. The very idea of him dying, even though it had not come to pass, filled her with distress. She clutched Maggie's hand all the harder.

'We struggled to survive after that, although Cormac did his best to support us all. I had my spinning and we bartered the eggs, but it wasn't enough. I had to send Margaret and Bronagh out to find employment. Fortunately, your uncle had taken to inviting guests so often that Maura Kavanagh was willing to hire new scullery maids.'

'They must have been very young,' Bridget said, thinking the girls could only be in early adolescence now.

'They started work on Margaret's twelfth birthday. Bronagh was just after turning ten. They're gone over two years now.'

Bridget shook her head. That was too soon to leave a mother's skirts. 'I have seen them on a few occasions when I've gone down to the kitchens. They seem to be reasonably content, especially Margaret.'

'Maura tells me they've shown promise and she sometimes entrusts them with kitchen maid duties, though I gather Bronagh gets demoted more often than promoted.' Her lopsided smile revealed she expected no less from that particular daughter. 'Margaret, at least, hopes to become a proper kitchen maid by next year. They sleep in the servants' quarters at the top of the big house 'cause they rise so early and get to bed so late, which means they don't come home much beyond their afternoons off. I believe they're happy enough but I do wish I could see my girls more.' She sighed. 'Let's speak of more cheerful matters. Tell me about your stay in Dublin.'

'Cheerful? Then I had better leave out the part where I sat on the floor of my bedchamber in my riding breeches and refused to move while my mother and the maids tried to get me to put on a decorative gown.' It was such a trivial thing to say, in light of the McGoverns' hardships, but it made Maggie's eyes crinkle.

'Ah, my dearie. You didn't adjust too well to city life?'

'That is an understatement of the situation.' Bridget folded her arms. 'Once we were out of mourning, my mother wasted no time in announcing she intended to have me presented as a debutante at Dublin Castle as soon as I turned sixteen. I railed against her for as long as I could, and we struggled and quarrelled day after day, until she threatened to take me to the London season instead.'

'London?' Maggie looked mystified by the notion, as though Lady Courcey had suggested taking Bridget to the moon. 'You wouldn't have liked that at all.'

'Precisely,' said Bridget with an emphatic nod. 'So I conceded defeat. And then, after my coming out, I discovered that I had been making a fuss for no reason. I thought it would be nothing but cups of tea and monotonous conversations in drawing rooms and, yes, there was some of that, but I also met the most amiable girls and forged fervent friendships with them. The biggest surprise of all was I learned just how much I love dancing. It transpired that the city was in fact an agreeable place to live once I allowed myself to be happy there.' She twisted her lips. 'It was far from a smooth transition though. I was so tongue-tied in company at first. Mother faced quite a task in teaching me how to dress, speak and behave like a lady. Sophistication is a hard-earned trait, but essential if one wishes to be deemed eligible for marriage.'

She found herself blushing at this. Maggie plucked fondly at her chin.

'You achieved success in that area. Cormac told me about your engagement. My hearty congratulations. A nice gentleman, is he?'

'Oh yes, exceedingly charming. We began courting during last year's season and he has been ever so attentive since then.'

Maggie leaned forwards. 'Do tell me about him.'

Her eagerness spurred Bridget to divulge the full narrative of her courtship with Mr Garrett Lambourne; after all, she was as good as a fifth daughter in this family and heaven knew the unfortunate woman needed some pleasant news to lift her spirits.

'...and in March I was seated in our drawing room when he burst in and said he had been called away to England on urgent business but could not leave without ensuring my hand in marriage first!'

'How romantic,' marvelled Maggie.

'Apart from the fact that it was so impromptu he did not even have a ring,' Bridget said with amusement. 'But he means to bring one when he returns to Ireland. He will be coming to visit Oakleigh soon.'

'I'm sure you'll enjoy showing him 'round your home.'

'If I can find the time. Mother seems to think that every moment of the day should be filled with learning the duties of a lady in charge of her household.'

She went on to describe the regimen Lady Courcey had imposed upon her and the lectures to which she had been subjected; her depiction of Mr Buttimer's pompous pronouncement that he by no means had any responsibility for the chamber pots drew a genuine laugh from Maggie. It was good to hear it.

At length, Bridget swallowed the last of her milk and stood. 'I must go now, but it was lovely to see you again. I am so sorry about Jack and Patrick. I do hope that your grief will ease over time.'

Maggie made a visible effort to look optimistic. "Tis been difficult but I still have the rest of my family to be grateful for. And we've our horse shoe over the door. It'll bring us good luck, I'm sure of it.'

They hugged warmly. As Bridget left the cottage, Orlaith materialised with a full bucket of water swinging at her knees, its rope wound in neat coils around her arm. Bridget bid her farewell but the little girl edged past with her eyes fixed on her toes.

Head and heart full of her conversation with Maggie McGovern, Bridget set off on her return journey across the fields. The sky looked a good deal more ominous than it had upon her departure and she began to worry that she would not make it back to the manor before a deluge came down.

She reached the Gorteen just as the first, fat drops of rain started to fall.

CHAPTER 5

'D'you have potatoes for eyes, boy? Get out of my sight and don't come back to me 'til you've the intelligence to spot a flower from a weed!'

Cormac looked around for the source of the shouting. He was crossing the cobbled courtyard from the kitchens to the stables, bearing a basket of carrot peelings for the horses, and a slender youth was striding from the manor gardens in his direction. Beyond the boy, he distinguished the formidable form of the head gardener, Fintan Kelly, brandishing a rake.

When the lad marched into the courtyard, a black look on his face, Cormac recognised him as Malachy, Fintan's grandson and a new worker at Oakleigh, just shy of two months in his position as under gardener. Cormac had heard from John Corbett that the old man held high hopes he would eventually be succeeded by his grandson in managing the upkeep of his beloved gardens, but the evidence at hand suggested his hope might well be misplaced.

Malachy checked at the sight of Cormac, assumed an air of nonchalance, and grinned.

'Damn grumpy codger,' he said, jerking his thumb towards his grandfather, who had turned away and was stumping back into the gardens, the rake swung over his shoulder.

The lad had to be lacking in wits to defy that redoubtable old man. Once, and once alone, had Cormac trespassed into Oakleigh's gardens as a child and he had received a brutal wallop of a spade on his backside for his efforts. He could not ride a horse for two days after it. Even now, Cormac treated Fintan Kelly with a deep respect tinged with wariness.

'Still got a bit to learn with the gardening?' he said, thinking the boy might be in need of some encouragement. 'You'll soon get the hang of it.'

Malachy, who could be no more than fifteen, laughed. He had shoulder-length, greasy hair which he pushed out of his eyes with a careless flick. 'Ah, I know the difference between a flower and a weed. But I've learned if I pull up too much of the wrong thing, I'll get the rest of the day off!' He looked pleased with himself.

Cormac raised his eyebrows, unimpressed. 'And what d'you plan to do with your free time?'

'Might pop into the kitchens, see if I can pinch some bread from that cook. She's large enough that she must be scoffing it herself all day, but maybe there'll still be some lying about.'

Liking him less and less with every word that came out of his mouth, Cormac said, 'Best not talk like that in front of her,' although part of him hoped Malachy would ignore his advice just so he could hear the whack of the cook's rolling pin on the boy's shins.

Malachy shrugged and sauntered away towards the back door of the kitchens. Shaking his head, Cormac stepped inside the stables just before the skies opened and the rain started to lash down.

He had scarcely deposited some of the carrot peelings in the first occupied stall when a figure came barrelling through the open double doors, desperate to escape the downpour. She gasped upon reaching the shelter of the stables and then again upon spotting Cormac. Her hands flurried as she attempted to smooth the waist of her dress and tuck back wayward chestnut curls, but she couldn't hide her sorry state. His lips twitched because she was embarrassed and yet he thought she looked the finest she had since she'd returned to the estate – a little dishevelled was how he had always known her.

'Out for a walk in this weather, Miss Muldowney?'

The formal address was for the benefit of John Corbett who, currently wedged into the tiny room opposite that served as his personal workspace, was within both sight and earshot through his open door. Cormac could see it bothered Bridget but she couldn't very well object to it in public.

'I didn't anticipate the rain,' she said.

'Most folk could tell 'tis been threatening since morning.'

'Yes, well, perhaps I don't have the same intuition as "most folk".' It was the kind of teasing that might have offended someone else but she took it on the chin; at least her sense of humour hadn't been impaired by her stint in Dublin.

'I recommend the kitchens as the swiftest route indoors,' he said, turning to carry his basket to the second stall.

'Please wait.' He stopped and she took a step nearer to him. 'There's something I wish to say.'

Wary, he glanced around. John appeared engrossed in a sheaf of papers, not seeming to notice there was anyone ten feet beyond his threshold. Down at the further end of the stables' central aisle, Liam sat on a stool, elbows and knees sticking out as he cleaned a saddle. They were in full view but not under scrutiny. 'What is it?'

'I want to express my regret at my mother's behaviour,' she said, her voice low. 'She was downright rude to you that day and, regardless of your position, she had no right to speak to you in that way.'

He was astonished that she still felt the urge to apologise for that, even though it had happened nearly two weeks ago. 'Don't fret about it at all.' He wanted to add that it was no more than he expected from the harridan, but figured that would be a degree past courtesy.

She sighed. 'Mother has such a frightful disposition these days. She was not always like this. I do have vague memories of her laughing once upon a time.'

He would wager they were very vague.

'At any rate, I needed to assure you her perspective was not my own. And I'm sorry I couldn't tell you before now. She has kept me practically incarcerated indoors ever since in order to acquaint me with the never-ending list of duties of an heiress.'

Privately, he speculated that Lady Courcey's demand on her daughter's time had an ulterior purpose beyond the obvious. The more occupied Bridget was in the house, the less opportunity she would have to wander around the grounds and bump into, say, a stable hand.

'Least you got the afternoon off today,' he said.

She nodded. 'I've just been to visit your mother.'

He was touched. 'Thank you,' he said with feeling. 'That'll have meant a great deal to her.'

Bridget's face filled with emotion. 'She told me—'

She broke off as, at the far end of the stables, another stable hand slithered down the ladder from the loft and started making loud conversation with Liam.

'You should go inside and get dry,' said Cormac, thinking it was perilous to allow the conversation to continue, when her dark brown eyes glistened like that. 'I'll find something for you to shelter under as you cross the courtyard.'

Tucking the basket under his arm, he unearthed a saddle blanket from one of the stalls and shook it out.

'It mightn't be the cleanest,' he said awkwardly.

She took it and breathed in. 'It smells good and horsey to me.'

'Just leave it in a corner of the kitchen so and I'll collect it later.'

She dithered for a moment and then, swinging the blanket over her head and shoulders, she ducked out into the rain.

His long working days at the stables meant it was more convenient for him to sleep on a bed of straw in the stable loft than trek home each night to his family's cottage, but he still made the effort to go back two or three times a week for his mother's sake. In view of Bridget's afternoon excursion, he decided that tonight he would head for home.

After he had completed his final tasks that evening, he dropped by the kitchens to retrieve the saddle blanket and see if Margaret and Bronagh had any messages or mending for their mother. The blanket was neatly folded on a stool; he draped it over his forearm and went to look for his sisters in the scullery, where he found them up to their elbows in dishwater. Mrs Kavanagh was giving out to Bronagh as usual.

'If I see another pot come back to me in that state, you'll regret it, girl. I have no qualms about keeping you here until two in the morning if necessary. What do you want, Cormac?'

'I'm just checking if my sisters want me to bring anything home to our mother.'

Mrs Kavanagh's countenance changed at once. 'Dear Maggie, I do wish I could see her more often. Here, I've got something you can take to her, lad.' She led him back into the main kitchen, wrapped a few buns in a cloth, and handed the parcel to him. 'Mind you bring the cloth back to me. I'll be needing it again.' She cast a sharp glance at Margaret and Bronagh, who had followed them. 'Do you have anything for him?'

Bronagh declined but Margaret said, 'I do. May I run up to my room?'

'Fast as you can,' Mrs Kavanagh said in a much kinder tone than Cormac had ever heard her use with his younger sister. Even as Margaret scampered through the door to the servants' staircase, the cook barked at Bronagh, 'See, she has her wits about her. No shoddy work or mooning over boys. You'd do best to follow her example.'

This was peculiar, considering Margaret had always been the romantic sister and Bronagh as tough as nails. Cormac was about to remark upon it – she deserved a fair defence, after all – when the inner door that led to the family quarters above stairs opened and Mr Buttimer appeared in the gap. Mrs Kavanagh bristled; relations became strained between butler and cook whenever the latter believed the former was interfering in her domain.

'How can I help you, Mr Buttimer?' she said with barely disguised antagonism.

For once, he did not retaliate in a similar attitude. His expression was sombre as he held out a note to her.

'This just arrived for you. The messenger was quite urgent about its contents so I thought it ought to be delivered to you without delay.'

It was perhaps the shortest speech he had ever made. The fact that he had chosen to convey the message himself indicated the gravity of what he believed to be inside. Mrs Kavanagh's ruddy face paled and she accepted the note with a trembling hand. Cormac exchanged a glance with Bronagh; neither of them was used to seeing the formidable cook in any state of vulnerability. Bronagh hid her look of vindictive satisfaction poorly. It was not a quality he liked to see in his sister but she did receive an awful lot of abuse from the woman.

Mrs Kavanagh opened the letter. She scanned its contents, crossed herself, and sat heavily on the kitchen bench.

With uncharacteristic compassion, Mr Buttimer said, 'I hope it is not too grim.'

'I-it's from my sister,' she stammered. 'There's been an uprising on the Rathglaney Estate.' She stared at the letter, eyes round with distress. 'A gang of tenants tried to burn down the big house and Lord Fitzwilliam was injured in the attack. M-my sister is unharmed but her son and husband have been captured. Lord bless us and save us, it's likely they will both be hanged.'

This was serious indeed. It wasn't the first rumour of unrest to reach Oakleigh – there had been sporadic disturbances in other counties during recent years, despite the failed rebellion against English rule in 1798 – but to hear of one with such a personal connection made a profound impact. The Rathglaney Estate lay only over the border into Wexford.

Margaret chose that moment to burst back into the kitchens with a bundle under her arm. Cormac tactfully drew her and Bronagh out the back door to give the cook some space to process the terrible news. The earlier rain had diminished to a soft drizzle and it beaded on their hair as he filled Margaret in on what they had just learned.

'Oh, poor Mrs Kavanagh,' she exclaimed. 'How dreadful.'

Bronagh did not look quite so sympathetic but she kept her opinions to herself.

'I'm going to head on now,' said Cormac. 'I'll tell Ma about this. She'll want me to pass on her sympathies. Anything else ye need brought home?' he added, shifting the saddle blanket and buns to take the bundle from Margaret.

They shook their heads and he turned towards the stables to bring the blanket back before setting out across the fields. As his sisters re-entered the kitchens, the sound of quiet sobbing drifted out.

The drizzle was the kind that hardly seemed to be falling and yet soaked into his clothing so thoroughly that he was drenched by the time he reached the cottage. He pushed open the door to find the room lit by the fire in the hearth and a solitary rushlight in a holder on the table. Orlaith had fallen asleep in front of the grate, a hen tucked under one arm; the other hens roosted on a rafter above her head. His mother sat darning a shirt in her rocking chair, pulled close to the table to avail of the rushlight's illumination. She rose at the sight of him, her face full of pleasure.

'*A mhac*, I wasn't expecting you. God above, you picked a dreary night to come home.'

She began speaking in Irish – 'son' – but slid into English out of habit. After the rebellion thirty years ago, Bridget's straitlaced grandfather, the 2nd Baron, had prohibited the use of Irish within the boundaries of the Oakleigh Estate and, while her father had relaxed the ban and Lord Walcott had been lenient with the occasional slip of the tongue, Lady Courcey had made it clear she would not tolerate it. Cormac had learned the language from infancy, when Lord Courcey had been in command of Oakleigh, but had seldom ventured to speak it since gaining employment at the big house.

He shrugged in what he hoped was a casual manner and dropped the sodden bundle he carried on the table.

'Mending from Margaret,' he said before taking off his wet boots and slinging them into a corner of the room.

He accepted the rag his mother offered him and wiped his face and the outer layer of moisture from his clothes, then hung it on a nail by the fireside to dry. As he warmed his hands, he perceived his sister's hazardous position beneath the hens' rumps and gently tugged her to one side, which prompted her companion, indignant at the intrusion, to flutter from the dresser to the rafter to join the others. Orlaith mumbled in her sleep but did not wake.

'Are you hungry?' Maggie asked. 'I can make you some stirabout.'

He would have preferred potatoes to the oatmeal-and-milk mixture but the new crop wouldn't be ready until autumn. 'No need. I've something even better,' he said and produced Mrs Kavanagh's buns from his pocket.

There were three hidden within the folds of the cloth. Maggie's eyes lit up.

'Nothing beats Maura Kavanagh's baking,' she said with appreciation.

They sat beside each other at the table and shared one each, saving the third for Orlaith, who could have it in the morning – it would be a bit hardened by then but still a rare treat. As they ate, he related the dire news which the cook had just received up at the big house. His mother blanched, letting her half-devoured bun fall to the tabletop.

''Tis happening again, isn't it?' she said. 'Oh, how I've feared this. The country's too fragile for the folly of revolutionaries. They need to leave well enough alone. Those *damned men*!'

This burst out of her with such unexpected vehemence that Cormac glanced at the hearth to make sure it hadn't roused Orlaith.

'You don't need to w—' he started to say but Maggie cut in.

'Of course I need to worry. If it can happen in Wexford, it can happen in Carlow. What's to stop the tenants rising up here?'

'Oakleigh's different. That's plain as day when I meet other folk at the horse fair. There isn't the same level of poverty here as on other estates. The land's thriving, and we're not paying the tithes. 'Tis that as much as anything else that gets people so angry.'

'That may be so but they'll find any excuse to revolt. There are still English landowners on our soil. That's what caused the rebellion last time, and look what it did, it decimated both sides of this family. 'Tis why you've no grandparents left alive.'

While he personally believed that fighting English rule was a just cause, he appreciated that his mother only wanted peace after the atrocities of the past. So he said, 'The tenants learned from '98. Oakleigh won't suffer Rathglaney's fate.'

He gave her a reassuring, one-armed hug and she subsided, eating the rest of her bun in silence. When she had finished, she crossed to the dresser and pulled a string of rosary beads from one of its drawers. Draping this around her neck, she returned to the rocking chair and picked up her darning again. She glanced over at him as she moved the needle in and out. 'I had a visit from Bridget Muldowney today.'

He lifted his eyebrows as though this was news to him.

'The craythur, she's pale as a ghost and not a pick on her. Did they not feed her in Dublin?' His mother didn't seem to expect an answer to that, just muttered something about a good appetite not being fashionable in the city.

'What did the two of ye talk about?'

'This and that. She told me about her time away. And her fiancé.'

He frowned at the last bun nestled in Mrs Kavanagh's cloth. He had no particular inclination to discuss Mr Lambourne.

'She sympathised regarding your father and brother too. You hadn't told her your part in all of that. She was terribly shaken to hear of it.'

He tilted his head. Was that what had distressed her so much?

''Tis been seven years but she still cares for you. I could feel it in the way she clutched my hand. Truth be told, I sometimes wondered about you and her. Ye were so close as children that I thought ye might develop a deeper bond when ye got to a certain age.'

He murmured something indistinct, growing warm despite his damp clothes.

'But it wasn't meant to be, once she was taken away. Arrah, it was a fanciful idea in any case, given your backgrounds. Nothing but a silly mother's daydream. Besides, she seems quite smitten with her Mr Lambourne.'

That was more than enough to bring his flight of imagination plummeting back to earth.

Maggie looked pensive. 'She's changed a great deal but I don't think she realises it herself. And I'm not talking about her pretty ringlets, I mean her demeanour. Did you notice? She's so elegant and composed now, a proper lady. The fiery girl we knew is gone.'

'Her mother finally got her claws into her,' he said with a bitter sense of loss for his best friend.

'It was bound to happen. Think about it from Bridget's point of view. 'Til she was twelve, she ran wild 'round the estate and her sole companion was a boy just as wild. When she went to the city, her companions became sophisticated girls who knew more than her about everything. It was only natural she'd feel out of place and turn to her mother to be taught how to fit in. Moving to Dublin must've changed their relationship altogether.'

'It changed her relationship with me too. If she'd stayed...'

Maggie let out a sigh. 'No one can say what would've happened if she'd stayed but it mightn't have been as straightforward as you believe. Her mother would've succeeded in interfering sooner or later. We all know she never approved of your friendship.' She paused. 'There's no place for you in her life anymore. You realise that, don't you?'

He turned his face away. 'I do.' He had already known it, and now both of their mothers had made it plain too.

Maggie got up from her rocking chair again and slid onto the bench next to him, taking his hand in hers. 'Sometimes special people are only meant to be part of our lives for a little while,' she said, and it seemed as though the shadows of her husband and her other son fell over the table. 'You'll get over this disappointment, I know it.'

For her sake, he said, 'I'm sure I will.' He kissed her on the cheek and stood. 'Goodnight, Ma.'

He crossed to the hearth. 'Come on, chicken,' he murmured and, hoisting his sleepy sister over his shoulder, carried her up to bed.

CHAPTER 6

Bridget entered her father's study – now her mother's study, she supposed she must allow – to find Lord Walcott pacing before a pair of empty wingback chairs and Lady Courcey standing at the window, lines of tension in her shoulder blades.

'What's happened?' Bridget asked, on the alert at once.

Her mother turned and handed her a letter. 'Rathglaney.'

She skimmed the note with a degree of difficulty; it looked like it had been dashed off without scruples for ink smudges or punctuation. Its author, Lady Fitzwilliam, wrote that the Irish savages had committed the most unspeakable of acts and attacked their property and her husband's own person. Bridget's blood ran cold as the lady's message sank in. An uprising.

She looked up. Her mother's lips were so tight they had all but disappeared; it was a wonder she could still form words as she said, 'Lady Fitzwilliam felt the need to warn as many neighbouring estates as she could. Her advice is unambiguous: get out while we still can. As soon as Lord Fitzwilliam is recovered, they will leave the estate for good. They plan to go to Dublin or even London. Anywhere, so long as it's far away from these delinquents.'

Lord Walcott made a tutting sound. 'Another absentee landlord. It will ruin the Irish countryside.'

Lady Courcey turned an incredulous gaze upon her brother. 'You think *that's* the urgent issue?' She sniffed. 'I feel compelled to remind you that while you reside here you are an absentee landlord at Lockhurst Park in England.'

He inclined his head. '*Touché*.'

'Are you worried, Mother?' asked Bridget.

Lady Courcey deliberated before replying, 'I shall see what Mr Enright has to say on the subject first.'

The land agent was due to arrive any minute, with the ostensible purpose of discussing general estate matters, but everyone knew the topic on Lady Courcey's mind was the paying of the tithes. And now insurgent rebels could be added to the list.

Bridget's role was to make a written record of the proceedings, a dull task which she had offered to take on to ensure her presence at the meeting. She had just assembled her paper, pen and ink on a small table at the end of the large writing desk when a knock came at the door and Mr Laurence Enright was shown in. He gave off an odd air of brawny and bookish, with his muscular build and a pair of spectacles perched on his nose. She was pleased to see him – she fondly recalled how she and Cormac had dogged his heels while they went through a phase of play-acting as land agents, so much so that he had been obliged to shoo them away on more than a few occasions. His manner was serious but, when he acknowledged her, there was a twinkle in his eye that suggested he remembered those times too.

Lady Courcey settled behind the writing desk but Lord Walcott took a more discreet seat in one of the wingback chairs, deferring to the lady's reinstated authority. Bridget dipped her pen and Mr Enright commenced his delivery of a series of reports on the state of the accounts, the collection of rents and arrears, and improvements to estate property, with a meticulous memory for figures and details which could only impress. Even Lady Courcey had no reason to offer a single objection – until the agent asked her if she had any queries.

'Yes, indeed,' she said, her tone dangerously calm. 'I wish to discuss the matter of the tithes.'

Bridget had a suspicion that Lord Walcott had managed to forewarn Mr Enright because he didn't bat an eyelid.

'Which aspect of them do you wish to discuss, my lady?' he said.

'Their irrelevance. They are a church tithe and of no concern to this estate.'

He touched the bridge of his spectacles. 'It is true that the Church of Ireland reaps the benefits of the tithe collections. There is no monetary gain to Oakleigh by covering the tithes on the tenants' behalf.'

'My precise point,' said Lady Courcey, as though her argument had already been won.

'That is not to say there is no other form of gain, however,' he continued. 'This course of action has eased a burden on the tenants. Though they are by no means affluent, they do perceive themselves to be in a better position than their peers in neighbouring estates. I wouldn't go so far as to say they are happy, but their level of satisfaction has been enough to encourage a higher work rate and a deeper allegiance to this estate than might otherwise have been possible.'

Bridget tried to keep up with her note-taking while sneaking furtive glances at her mother. Lady Courcey had been looking smug but, after this last speech, her expression curdled.

'What evidence is there of that?' she bit out.

'I am in regular contact with other land agents who struggle to acquire rents and maintain order because their tenants continue to live under the rule of harsh, and often absentee, English landlords. The rebellion may have been quashed in

1798 but the fire that started it still burns in the people's hearts. However, there is no such disloyalty on the lands of Oakleigh, thanks to the payment of the tithes. Despite their lack of education, the folk comprehend the magnitude of the gesture.'

Lady Courcey had no response for this.

'It is my understanding that the tenants on the Rathglaney Estate were particularly hard done by. The Fitzwilliams supported the procurement of tithes by force if necessary, and in the past twelvemonth also instructed their agent to raise the rates of rent. It was beyond the people's capacity to tolerate such mistreatment. While I do not condone their behaviour, I do appreciate the cause of it.'

At this point, Mr Enright's work was done and it became clear that Lord Walcott and Bridget would have no need to contribute their own voices to the dispute. Lady Courcey was a shrewd woman; she perceived as well as anyone else in the room that the current situation was best, though a faint pink in her cheeks showed how annoyed she was to have been thwarted by unassailable logic.

And so the agent left the study with the instruction that the tithes arrangement should remain unchanged.

Lord Walcott, quietly exultant in victory, departed next to take his dogs for a walk, leaving the two ladies alone. Emboldened by the success of the meeting, Bridget decided it was time to act upon her own campaign of appeal. Following her visit to Maggie McGovern, an idea had taken root in her mind which she now wanted to put forth to her mother. It was difficult to gauge how the lady might react but she had proved once already today that she could be persuaded by rational motivation, if it was in Oakleigh's interest.

Lady Courcey had reached for the notes on Bridget's table and was perusing them with an attentive eye.

'Mother, may I have a word?'

Her mother lowered the pages. 'Yes?'

Bridget cleared her throat. 'I have been speaking with my uncle on matters of labourer appointments, in order to further my knowledge on the subject. While Oakleigh was his responsibility, he had to oversee the hiring of several new workers due to some unfortunate circumstances.' She swallowed. 'There were the two boys who died in the stable fire. A man drowned in the Sruhawn returning from trade at the horse fair in Tullow. And there have been numerous injuries at the quarry since it reopened which, while not life-threatening, have rendered some of the men incapacitated to work. I was wondering about these people and their families. Uncle Stuart said that no compensation was provided to them.'

'What of it?'

She bit the tip of her tongue. 'Don't you think there ought to be? These injuries and deaths happened to Oakleigh workers on Oakleigh land. It seems only fair that the estate recompense the victims or their families in acknowledgement of their sacrifice.'

'Most of those incidents happened a number of years ago. It is too late to offer remuneration now. Not to mention the people already enjoy the privilege of not being required to pay the infernal tithes.'

'Oakleigh's payment of the tithes does not equate to reparation for loss of life, and I don't believe the people would ever feel it was too late to receive what they justly deserve. I imagine their gratitude would spread to the other tenants, spurring them to work even harder for an estate that treats them with such benevolence. Oakleigh can only benefit from this deed.'

She was riding the coattails of Mr Enright's more eloquent reasoning but she didn't care so long as it achieved the result she desired.

Lady Courcey sat back in her chair. 'You advocate quite the resolute standpoint on this.'

Bridget made her voice light. 'You have been teaching me to develop the acumen of an astute landowner. This is the consequence of my education.'

There was a glint in the lady's eye and a rare lift at the corner of her mouth. 'Indeed. I am glad to witness it. I shall look into your proposal.'

'No need to trouble yourself with the details,' Bridget said quickly. 'Uncle Stuart has the records and I am certain I can put together the figures with his help. It should be a simple matter of signing your name to them.'

She only hoped her mother would not notice the name 'McGovern' on the list or her goodwill would evaporate in an instant.

Chapter 7

June ended with two more days of rain but the first day of July brought a break in the wet weather. Determined not to waste the opportunity, Bridget entered the stables in her riding habit, where she received a warm greeting from John Corbett.

'Going for a ride, miss?'

'Yes,' she said and added, 'A proper one.'

He gave a chuckle of appreciation. Her last mounted excursion had been a sedate trot in the company of her mother, but today she intended to ride to the full extent of her capabilities. John had been her tutor when she had learned the skill as a girl and he had always said she was a natural on horseback.

He himself went to prepare Bonny for her. As she followed him into the stall, she cast a surreptitious glance around for Cormac but he was nowhere in sight. She felt disappointed; their last encounter had left her with an unsettled sensation, like there was more to be said between them.

'And where are you off to this afternoon?' John asked as he groomed her horse.

'I mean to seek out my old haunts,' she said. 'My favourite track will lead me to Ballydarry and then across the fields to the woods. I might even go as far as the quarry if I have enough time.'

'D'you require an escort? I can get young Liam Kirwan to accompany you if needs be.'

'Not at all. I am amply familiar with the terrain.'

'You know the quarry's in use again? Best stay out of the men's way as they'll be working with the rock. 'Tis a more dangerous place than the deserted hole you remember.'

'I shall take due care,' she promised.

His solicitousness was touching and it occurred to her that, had her mother not extracted her from the bosom of Oakleigh, John may well have become a father figure of sorts after her own father's death. Or, perhaps even more likely, that charge may have fallen to Jack McGovern. Moving to Dublin had consigned her to an exclusively female sphere of influence, when a masculine presence would have better suited her tomboyish nature. Still, she had to become a lady sometime.

Even as that thought crossed her mind, she trailed after John into the harness room and threw a longing look at the standard saddles hanging on the rack. However, she made no objection when John lifted up the sidesaddle, though he too seemed to regard it with a faint air of distaste. She hid a smile at their shared unconventional leanings.

After mounting, she bid him farewell and rode out of the courtyard, around the corner of the manor house and down the gravelled avenue. The recent rain had cleared the mugginess, creating the impression that the world had been soaked in a tub of water and left out to dry. Moisture dripped from the trees lining the avenue and the dusty gravel had been rinsed to a clean, dark grey. She gulped in mouthfuls of wholesome air with satisfaction. This experience was unattainable in Dublin, except maybe in the very heart of Phoenix Park.

Negotiating the lanes leading to Oakleigh's local village proved to be a challenge. The ground was muddy beneath Bonny's shoes and flooded in some parts, so they were forced to keep to a slower pace than Bridget had intended. She would have to save the thrill of the canter for the open fields and hope that the grass would not be too slippery.

Rounding a bend in the lane, she spotted two men on foot ahead of her. As she drew nearer, she discerned their uniforms and arms and realised they were members of the constabulary. They turned at the sound of Bonny's hoof beats and stepped to the side of the road at Bridget's approach. One looked old enough to be her father, the other so young as to barely merit the label 'man'.

'Afternoon, Miss Muldowney,' said the older constable. The younger one saluted, then seemed confused over whether he ought to have done so.

It didn't surprise her that they knew who she was; there was no other upper class family living in the immediate vicinity. What did surprise her was their presence. Hadn't Mr Enright only three days ago communicated that Oakleigh was a peaceful estate? Surely these constables would be better off occupying themselves on Rathglaney lands rather than strolling about the serene countryside here. She eyed their rifles and bayonets dubiously as she stopped to greet them.

'Good afternoon...' she said with an enquiring eyebrow.

'Constable Quirke at your service,' supplied the older man. 'And this is Constable Tierney. You appear to be alone, miss. May we have the pleasure of escorting you to your destination?'

'Thank you for your kind concern,' she said, 'but I would be loath to detain you from your duties.'

Whatever little they had to be doing. She offered them a civil nod and rode on.

Just a little way beyond, the road went into a gentle, downhill slope, which gave her a broad view of the village of Ballydarry. It was a small settlement – two streets meeting at a crossroads with a scattering of dwellings and a drinking house – but it was dominated by its pair of churches: St Canice's, the Church of Ireland establishment at the nearer edge of the village, and St Mary's, the Roman Catholic church further down by the crossroads. She had only ever attended Church of Ireland services in the past but Cormac had on a few occasions brought her into St Mary's and taught her some Irish prayers while they sat in the deserted pews.

She and Bonny proceeded into the village at an easygoing pace. All was quiet and she saw no people until she passed through the crossroads and approached the site of the drinking house. Here, a sign depicting a man wielding a pike swung above its door and three of its patrons lounged on a bench by the entrance. When they saw her coming, they nudged each other and straightened up.

'Fine day, miss,' one of them hollered.

'Fair one to be outdoors,' another agreed, jumping to his feet. He was the only one wearing a cap and he swept it off and down to his knees in an elaborate bow.

She smiled and halted. 'Indeed, it is so fresh after all the rain.'

The third man came up and rubbed Bonny's neck. 'She's a top quality beast. I'm quite the horse lover myself.'

'Only 'cause nothing else will lie with you,' the first man said with a throaty laugh.

The man with the cap gave him a whack on the arm. 'Manners, Joseph Hayes.'

Joseph shot Bridget an apologetic grin.

''Tis parched work, all that riding,' the man with the cap said. 'Will you quench your thirst before heading on? I can nip into The Pikeman and ask Bernie to bring you out something refreshing.'

'I'll wager he can find a carrot for this lovely lady too,' said the third man.

She had not been riding long enough to be especially thirsty but they seemed an amiable bunch – bawdy comment notwithstanding – and it would be an opportunity to engender further goodwill between the manor and its tenants.

'That would be very nice,' she said, dismounting and looping the long skirt of her riding habit over her wrist.

The fellow with the cap darted inside the drinking house. 'Bernie!' he bellowed. 'Can the young miss trouble you for a sup of water?'

As she finished tying Bonny to a post in front of the building, he returned with a balding man who was carrying the dirtiest glass she had ever seen, a brown-coloured liquid sloshing inside it. Was that supposed to be water? The Pikeman's proprietor offered it to her with an obsequious flourish and she accepted it without question, not wishing to offend, but resolved to only take the barest sip and then be on her way.

As she brought the glass to her lips, the man who described himself as a horse lover said, 'You going for a ride across all your land?'

She lowered the glass again, grateful to have avoided drinking the putrid-smelling water. 'I am. I do love the countryside.'

''Tis a fine piece of land. Solid, Irish soil, tilled by Irish hands for hundreds of years.'

This made her uncomfortable and she didn't say anything.

'Don't you think so?' he pressed.

'Y-yes, I agree.' She took a drink and it required all her willpower not to spit it back into the glass. It was grainy and sour. She swallowed with difficulty.

They all laughed.

'Can't believe she drank it,' Bernie said to the others. 'I only scooped it from the gutter out the back.'

She set the glass down on the bench; she hoped he was jesting but she wasn't going to touch it again.

Joseph levelled a narrow gaze at her. 'Aren't you going to pay for your drink?'

'I-I didn't bring any coins with me.'

He took a step closer – when had his hands become clenched into fists? 'That's typical of ye English folk. Take what ye want and give nothing for it.'

She stood her ground, though she felt intimidated by his nearness. 'I cannot imagine what you mean.'

His eyes flashed and there was a ripple of muttering from his companions. All three moved to stand next to him and this time she did step back. Fear swept over her; she wanted to flee from the situation right now.

'If you will excuse me—' she began but Joseph cut her off.

'You're not going anywhere just yet,' he said and reached out to grab her arm.

She filled her lungs to scream but, before she could expel the air, there was a bark of warning from the street and the two constables stood there, bayonets glinting.

'Let the young lady pass,' came a youthful voice – which contained only the barest trace of a waver – and the men surrounding her grumbled and fell away.

She hurried to the constables' side, feeling relief mixed with a measure of guilt. Mere minutes before she had believed them to be the objectionable party; now she was deeply thankful for their presence in the village.

Constable Quirke gestured with his bayonet and drove the irate patrons across the threshold of the drinking house, leaving the door ajar as he returned to Bridget.

'We'll deal with them in a moment, Miss Muldowney, and we apologise that they've troubled you,' he said, while Constable Tierney added, 'May one of us accompany you back to the manor house?'

She realised her fingers were trembling and interlaced them.

'Thank you, no,' she said. 'I plan to ride on. I would like to make it to the quarry and back before dinner time.'

The older constable frowned. 'With respect, I don't think that's wise. You've seen what the locals are like. You should return to the safety of the house.'

'I have never felt threatened on this estate,' she said, but a seed of doubt had been sown in her mind.

'Be that as it may, I believe we'll have to insist—'

'I can escort the young lady back, if she doesn't object.'

The three of them swivelled around and Bridget's heart thumped to see Cormac approaching. Where had he sprung from?

The younger constable set his jaw. 'She doesn't need the likes of you.'

'No, this is quite acceptable,' Bridget interjected. 'He is a stable hand at the manor. I am happy to return with him.'

She faced two expressions full of doubt.

'You've just seen how these peasants aren't to be trusted,' Constable Tierney said with an emphatic wave towards the drinking house door.

'I trust him.' They could malign the villagers, but she would brook no slur on Cormac's character. To hammer the point home, she held out her hand to him and he led her to where Bonny stood, boosted her into the saddle with her foot in his cupped hands, and untied the horse from the post.

The constables still looked dubious but made no further protest. As they turned back to the entrance of The Pikeman, she asked, with less success than the youngster at masking the quiver in her voice, 'What do you intend to do with them?'

'It will be a strong warning today,' said Constable Quirke, 'unless you wish to exact a harsher punishment...?'

Cormac gave her a sharp glance but refrained from asking any questions.

'That will not be necessary,' she said. 'My sincere thanks for your assistance.'

She directed Bonny down the street, setting a slow enough pace that Cormac could walk beside her, his hand loose on the reins. They were quiet for the length of time it took to go back through the village and reach the slope of the lane. Then he squinted up at her and said, 'What was that all about?'

She blew out her breath. 'I do believe I've had my first glimpse of just how much the Irish loathe the English.'

His countenance was grave. 'You stopped to talk to the fellows at The Pikeman?' She nodded and he clicked his tongue. 'What possessed you to do that? They're a rough bunch, for crying out loud. And if that was Joseph Hayes I spotted through the door, I can tell you he's the worst of the lot.'

Her hackles rose at his patronising manner. She knew her behaviour had been naïve but she didn't want him of all people to berate her about it. 'I have never had an uncivilised word from any of the locals in my life. How could I have anticipated such treatment?'

'Tell me what happened.'

She did, and watched his grip tighten on the reins until his knuckles grew white. He muttered something she didn't catch but she could guess its meaning.

'You think I was foolish.'

He didn't look at her. 'I do.'

'I don't see how what I did was so very wrong—'

He whipped his head around, eyes blazing. 'D'you have *any idea* what they might've done to you?'

It was the fear in his voice that made her falter. She swallowed. Despite her lack of education on such matters, she had enough imagination to envisage what four men could do to an unprotected woman. Her hands began to shake again and she had to take a few moments to compose herself before she could ask, 'Is this something I ought to have foreseen? The people were always kind to me in the past.'

His outburst over, he said evenly, 'You were a child then.'

'Why should that make a difference?'

''Cause becoming an adult means you're now held accountable.'

She felt injured at the insinuation. 'I have done nothing to hurt them.'

'You rule them, or at least your mother does. What they see is an English aristocrat who's going to inherit the land that's rightfully theirs. They hate you for that.'

She bridled, remembering Joseph's accusation. 'I consider myself as Irish as any of them! I was born on this land. My father was more Irish than English and you know it. He loved this country with every bone in his body. He gave me an Irish name, for heaven's sake!'

What her father had told her – on one of those cosy days when the rain had lashed the library windows and she had nestled in his lap by the fire to listen to him recount the native histories and legends – was that he had wanted to name her 'Brigid' after the Irish saint. Her mother had thought the spelling too ugly and they had compromised with 'Bridget'.

'Your mother's English through and through,' Cormac pointed out.

She tossed her head. 'So I am half and half. But I know which half is truer to me.' She glared down at him. 'Do you regard me as part of this reviled "English folk"?'

'Of course I don't,' he said, his denial so instant and earnest that she felt bad for having questioned him. 'And neither does anyone up at the big house. But I can't speak for every tenant on Oakleigh land, and definitely not for people like Joseph Hayes. You can make your arguments 'til you're hoarse, but they'll never hear what you say.'

She cogitated on that as they continued along the muddy lanes back to the manor. The meeting with Mr Enright had left her with the impression that circumstances at Oakleigh were almost idyllic in comparison to other estates. But unrest still existed and she had unwittingly exposed herself to it. Had the land agent glossed over the fouler details of the situation so as not to alarm her mother, or was he unaware of the extent of it himself? She understood the tenants' dislike of foreign invaders but could they not see that third and fourth generations of Anglo-Irish families, long settled on the land, were much more Irish than English?

The idea that this formed the basis of their resentment still nettled and she felt compelled to plead her case further. 'I can even speak some Irish. I learned bits of it from you when we were young.'

He was facing straight on but the corner of his mouth lifted. 'That's true. D'you recall any of it?'

Without hesitation, she launched into, '*Ár nAthair atá ar neamh, go naofar d'ainm, go dtaga—*'

'Fine, you remember the Our Father,' he broke in with a fleeting laugh. 'Well done to you. Best keep your voice down though. Irish isn't meant to be spoken 'round these parts.'

'It isn't? I thought my father revoked that edict.'

'Your mother restored it.'

That saddened her but her mind had already propelled forwards. 'Faith is another factor to contemplate. I am supposed to be a member of the Church of Ireland congregation, but sometimes I feel more connected to the Roman Catholic teachings. You acquainted me with their principles and I have found them to be a great comfort over the years.'

He looked sombre at this. 'That's a dangerous declaration to make in this country, coming from the people you do. It puts you in an awkward position. What religion will you rear your children in?'

'I-I don't know,' she mumbled.

The silence that descended between them was pregnant with many thoughts unspoken: the notion of having children, the whispers of how such things come about, the impending arrival of her fiancé to whom that future duty would fall...

Her cheeks flamed and, when she worked up the courage to look down at him, she saw that his had too.

She cast about for anything to say to end their discomfort. 'How did you happen to be in Ballydarry?'

His shoulders relaxed and he withdrew a little bottle from his pocket with his free hand. 'Mrs Kavanagh sent me to fetch some holy water from Father Macken. Not one of my usual tasks but John allowed me. We all know how worried she is about her sister.'

'Her sister?'

'She lives on Rathglaney land. Her husband and son were involved in the uprising and arrested afterwards. Mrs Kavanagh's praying their lives will be spared.'

Their conversation had come full circle. She glanced over her shoulder even though the village was now a long way behind them. 'Oh,' she said nervously.

He gave her a look of reassurance. 'Nothing like that'll come to pass at Oakleigh. Fellows like Hayes are all bluster and no action.'

Her teeth nipped the tip of her tongue. 'Didn't you just tell me how much jeopardy I was in at the drinking house?'

'That's 'cause they cornered you on your own. But no large scale revolt's likely to happen. Those men would never get a majority of the tenants behind them.'

'Do you really believe that?'

‘Absolutely. I said the same thing to my ma. You’ve nothing to fear.’

She couldn’t tell whether he meant it or was just trying to assuage her misgivings. Either way, his words of conviction appeased her, but she felt a sudden yearning for him to assure her with a tight squeeze of her hand.

His grip remained firm on the reins.

Chapter 8

On a normal day, the sweet smell of the hay barn brought pleasure to Cormac, but he was so incensed at the present moment that he didn't even notice it as he stamped in to gather a stack of hay for the stables. Twenty-four hours had been insufficient to allay his anger towards Bridget.

Her carelessness and gullibility frightened him. Suppose the constables hadn't come by? Or they had been ten minutes later? He was aghast to think that he himself had been dallying in the church across the road while the men had had her trapped. True, what he knew of Joseph Hayes was enough to admit the man probably didn't have the guts to risk inflicting real harm on the heiress to the Oakleigh Estate – death or transportation would have been the consequence. Still, someday his hatred might push him too far and, had there not been others at hand to intervene, yesterday could have been that day.

As Cormac left the barn, carrying the stack of hay and still grumbling about idiocy and naïveté, Liam came running up to him with the message that Mrs Walsh wanted to see him in the kitchens. He deposited the hay in one of the stable stalls in a hurry; the housekeeper was not a woman to be kept waiting.

Inside the kitchens, the familiar blast of heat was accompanied by Mrs Kavanagh's voice raised in fury. Bronagh stood before her with a mutinous scowl and a burnt pot. The cook seemed ready to explode but all of a sudden her face crumpled and she buried Bronagh in a big-bosomed hug.

'I'm taking my worries out on you, that's all. Bless your heart, you're a good girl. Go and wash that now, won't you?'

Bronagh looked dumbfounded as she scuttled into the scullery.

Mrs Walsh ignored the commotion and crooked a finger at Cormac.

'I have a number of carpentry duties for you to attend to.' She read the items out from a list in her hand. 'Three of the legs have cracked on a chair in Lord Walcott's bedchamber.'

The barest of pauses allowed Cormac to surmise that it was his lordship's substantial weight which had caused the chair legs to fail.

'There are two stools reported broken in the servants' quarters. And a bookshelf has collapsed in the library. The stools and the chair will be sent out to the barns for you to mend but the shelf will have to be repaired where it is. I shall alert you to an appropriate time when you can work in the library and not disturb the family.'

A footman came marching through the inner kitchen door, then stood to attention when he caught sight of the housekeeper. ''Scuse me, Mrs Walsh, Mr Buttimer sent me to fetch a stable hand. He needs one to come 'round to the front door right away.'

'Very well, Denis, I have one here.'

Denis looked pleased that his task had been accomplished so expediently when Mrs Walsh nodded at Cormac and said, 'Off you run.'

Cormac left the kitchens and trotted around the side of the house. When he reached the front, he saw Mr Buttimer standing at the bottom of the steps and bowing to a gentleman who had just dismounted from his horse. He did not recognise the tall, black-haired rider, but he guessed instantly from his handsome face and fine clothes who he must be.

Mr Buttimer caught sight of Cormac and beckoned to him. 'Look after the gentleman's horse, quick now.'

Mr Garrett Lambourne handed the reins to Cormac without even glancing at his face.

'My valet will follow shortly with the baggage,' he said to Mr Buttimer. 'Are the ladies home?'

'They are in the drawing room, sir, along with Lord Walcott. I shall announce your presence at once, if you will follow me. And might I be the first to extend you a warm welcome to Oakleigh Manor which, you may not know, has stood on this spot for four generations under the Courcey title and has been served, I am proud to say, by two generations of the Buttimer family...'

Prattling on, the butler led Mr Lambourne up the steps, leaving Cormac behind with the horse's reins in his fist and a boulder's weight in the pit of his stomach.

***

A dreary silence presided over the drawing room. Lady Courcey was perched in a straight-backed chair reading a book, while Lord Walcott had given up all pretence at decorum and lay snoozing on the sofa, his chin drooping on his chest. Bridget would have liked to play the piano, but that was not an option, given the situation of her companions. Instead, she had her latest correspondence gathered in her lap – letters from her friends in Dublin and from Garrett. These ought to have cheered her up but she was too distracted, still thinking of the danger she had narrowly sidestepped. There was no question of her telling her mother about the incident at The Pikeman; they would be in a carriage back to the city before she could insist, 'It's not the same as Rathglaney!' Lady Courcey needed no further encouragement to dislike and distrust the Irish. And on that note...

'Mother,' she said, in a low tone so as not to disturb the sleeping giant, 'is it true that the ban on speaking Irish around the estate has been reinstated?'

Lady Courcey's gaze remained on her page but her mouth tightened. 'It is.'

'May I ask why?'

The lady set her book down with an exasperated sigh. 'You are so like your father.'

A familiar sense of loss tugged at Bridget's heart. 'I don't see how that is such a bad thing.'

'It is only bad when I perceive how you share the same unfathomable blindness for that race.' Bridget expected her to stop there, shutting down as she always did when Lord Courcey was mentioned, but she carried on, 'Angus believed their primitive traditions should be preserved. It was a foolish notion. He refused to recognise that only by relinquishing such customs as that uncouth language could the creatures begin to improve themselves.'

Bridget doubted her mother was motivated by an urge to improve the Irish people; more likely, she didn't appreciate the idea of the tenants talking in a tongue she couldn't understand – after all, they might insult her to her face and she would never know.

It saddened Bridget to see how bitter her mother had become. Though always somewhat reserved in nature, she nonetheless had had a capacity for affection when Bridget was young that she hardly ever revealed now. Of course, it was easy to pinpoint when that change had happened.

In some ways, the memories were a blur to Bridget, and yet a few details stood out in stark definition. Her father's look of surprise as his horse stumbled crossing a brook and lost its footing. The horrifying crack of his head connecting with an unseen rock below the water's surface. The lack of movement in his chest when she laid her ear to it, an action she had performed countless times before to listen to his heartbeat.

She could still remember the overwhelming force of her mother's grief, the way she had crumpled at the sight of her husband's body and clutched at his hands, his face, his clothes, begging him not to abandon her. In a defiant snub to society convention, she had attended both the service and the burial, by which stage all emotion had been wiped from her countenance.

Bridget could not blame her mother for feeling bitter; she too had raged at the injustice of losing her father. But she now had a fiancé with whom she planned to share her life, while her mother still faced the coming decades alone. Had she ever considered remarrying?

Unsure whether she had the courage to voice these thoughts aloud, Bridget deemed it fortunate that Mr Buttimer chose that moment to enter the drawing room.

'My lady, Miss Muldowney, Mr Garrett Lambourne has arrived.'

Her gasp burst from her with such volume that Lord Walcott shot to wakefulness with an indignant, 'What the devil—!'

She twisted around towards the door. 'Really, Buttimer? You are being serious?'

'I pride myself in the assertion that I never joke, miss.'

And there was Garrett, striding in with a broad smile.

'You're here!' She leapt to her feet and, fighting the urge to run to him, clasped her hands together in joy.

Her mother rose with more restraint. 'You are welcome to Oakleigh, Mr Lambourne.'

'Thank you,' he said, bowing with the deepest courtesy. 'I was delighted to accept your invitation to visit.'

He approached Bridget and kissed her hand. When his hazel eyes met hers, she felt her insides dissolve and, not for the first time, marvelled that such an eligible bachelor had chosen her when he could have had his pick of any fashionable lady in London.

Lord Walcott laboured into an upright position with the least alacrity and grace of them all and the necessary introductions were made. After Mr Buttimer departed from the room in response to a summons for tea and biscuits, Garrett took a seat with the others, settling his long frame into a chair with ease.

'We did not expect you for another week at least,' said Bridget. Even though his most recent letter had communicated that he was back in the country, she had been certain a respite in Dublin would have delayed his coming.

'I must apologise for not forewarning of my arrival. I found I had not the patience to wait one moment longer to make the journey and I was in such a hurry to leave the city that I quite forgot to write ahead.'

'No apology is necessary,' said Lady Courcey. 'We judge it to be our good fortune that you have come earlier than anticipated. How was Dublin on your return from England?'

'Quiet. With the social season over, many families have retired to their country estates, in the same manner as yourselves.' He turned to Bridget. 'I happened upon Miss Madeleine Wallace in Merrion Square before I left. She told me in the most spirited language that she positively pines for you. Her family did not remove to the country on account of her mother's infirmity and she is finding the summer interminable without the company of her dearest friend.'

Bridget smiled; she could almost hear Madeleine's animated voice declaring the immensity of her loneliness. 'She disclosed the same to me in her letter. Perhaps I ought to invite her down for a visit.'

'I do believe she would kiss your shoes if you did.'

At this point, Lord Walcott, in an obvious attempt to take the measure of Garrett, asked, 'Do you like dogs?'

'Indeed, I do. I was the proud master of a faithful mastiff in my youth and my father owns the fastest pack of foxhounds in Hertfordshire.'

Lord Walcott gave a rumble of approval. 'Always happy to be acquainted with someone who appreciates animals.' The faintest sniff in his sister's direction might have been construed as an accusation but she elected to ignore it.

Garrett seemed to detect the antagonism but he hid his amusement with a good-natured nod and said, 'Dogs and horses, I've the greatest respect for both. I'm looking forward to some excellent riding on this estate.'

This prompted Bridget to experience an unexpected surge of nerves – how would Cormac react to Oakleigh's new guest?

***

'Oh, he's wonderful,' Margaret breathed. She and Bronagh were standing at the back door of the kitchens, receiving armfuls of kindling from their brother – the remains of Lord Walcott's damaged chair which could not be salvaged and would now serve best as fuel for the kitchen fire. 'He's simply...wonderful.'

'How have ye met him?' Cormac demanded.

'He's come down a couple of times after dinner to compliment Mrs Kavanagh on her cooking. 'Tis cheered her up no end. She's been weak at the knees ever since.'

Margaret pushed the door open wider so Cormac could catch a glimpse of the cook who appeared somewhat dazed as she rolled out dough on the kitchen table.

'And he took the time to thank each of the maids for doing such great work. Even Bronagh melted when he looked at her.'

Bronagh turned bright red and grabbed the firewood in an embarrassed huff.

Cormac thought it was just girls being girls. But John Corbett seemed almost as besotted.

'There's nothing the man doesn't know about horse breeding,' he said in awe. 'His knowledge is near greater than my own.'

If anyone could find fault, it would be Fintan Kelly. Cormac heard that the cantankerous gardener had become involved in a conversation with Mr Lambourne about the quality of the garden shrubs and tried to casually extract from Fintan how the exchange had gone.

Keeping a watchful gaze upon Malachy, who was being forced to trim the privet hedge with the precision of a surgeon, the old man gave an irritable cough at Cormac's enquiry, screwed up his rheumy eyes, and said, 'He's a nice chap.'

It seemed Mr Lambourne could do no wrong.

***

Bridget felt quite satisfied with her situation. She had secured an offer of marriage at the age of nineteen while many of her female companions, some several years older than her, were still unattached. She was marrying for love and not for status or wealth, although it was useful that she would gain both nonetheless. Her fiancé had amply demonstrated his charm and generous spirit by requiring a mere three days to endear himself to the full complement of family and staff at Oakleigh. It was all rather magnificent, she concluded, pushing open the green orchard door and leading Garrett into the shade beneath the apple trees.

Which made it all the more perplexing that she experienced a hiccup of misgiving as she passed under the archway.

Endeavouring to ignore it, she announced, 'This is my favourite place in the whole of Oakleigh, in the whole world,' and waved her arm in an expansive arc. Great quantities of ripening fruit hung from the branches above them; come autumn, they would fill Mrs Kavanagh's delicious apple tarts.

Garrett shook his head in amusement. 'I had no idea you were such a country girl. In Dublin you seemed happy to do nothing more than wear a pretty dress and take to the dance floor.'

That gave her pause. There had never been much occasion during their acquaintance to speak of her love for nature and the outdoors, and now his view of her as a city lady cloaked this entire aspect of herself.

'Do you like the countryside?' she asked. Apart from his early boyhood, he had resided for most of his life in London.

'I do, and I like it all the better because you are in it.' He inhaled deeply. 'I once knew a girl who said she only felt alive in two ways, and one of them was breathing the fresh, country air.'

'What was the other?'

He cleared his throat in a significant manner.

She coloured at the brazen implications of this response. 'Who was the girl?'

'You're not jealous, are you?'

She had had no inkling that he had courted another before her. Considering he was on the brink of his twenty-sixth birthday, it might have been naïve of her to assume she was his first courtship, but it still came as a shock. 'Where is she now?'

A shadow fell across his face but he grasped both of her hands and widened his eyes to convey his sincerity. 'She was nothing to me. A lump of coal compared to your bright star.'

She deliberated over whether to probe the issue further but decided against it. Whatever company he had kept before he met her was no concern of hers; she had no entitlement to that knowledge. She detached herself with a courteous smile and led the way along the path until they reached the clearing with the oak tree. Here, her discomfort increased and, to her consternation, she began to suspect the reason why. She wanted to pass through the clearing with all possible haste but he halted at the sight of the tree.

'My word,' he said, 'what an enormity.'

He stepped closer to the trunk and her heart seized at the thought of him discovering the carved initials. They were not for him to see – they belonged to her and Cormac alone. She tried to guide him on but he stopped her with a gentle tug on her wrist.

'I am glad to finally get you on your own, my darling, and in such an idyllic setting. I have been beyond impatient to give you this.'

He reached into his pocket and produced a small jewellery box. Dismayed that he had chosen this spot for the act, all she could do was utter a soft, 'Oh!' and apply the expected bashful expression to her features.

He went down on one knee with complete disregard for the leaf litter, opened the box and held it out to her, revealing an enormous ruby surrounded by a circle of pearls. It was perhaps a trifle ostentatious for her taste but she felt flattered that he would spend so much on her. She accepted the ring and murmured her admiration, angling her hand to catch the light in the gemstone.

He rose and, pulling her close, bent his head towards hers.

This was their first full kiss since he had come to Oakleigh but his lips felt alien upon hers. Guilt swept over her as she realised she was not overjoyed to receive the attentions of her handsome fiancé.

She ought to be thinking of that unforgettable moment when she glimpsed him across a heaving ballroom, of Madeleine Wallace's observation that he couldn't seem to take his eyes off her, and of the touch of his hand while he led her in the dance.

Instead, her mind insisted upon calling forth a memory wholly unrelated to the man embracing her.

She had not thought there could be anything more wretched than burying her beloved father in the cold earth, but the hours following his funeral had brought the worst news imaginable – her immediate departure from Oakleigh with no prospect of returning. Right below this very oak tree, she had flung herself into Cormac's arms and sobbed, 'How can she be so *cruel*?'

The flow of her tears could not be stemmed until he had assured her they would remain friends forever and suggested they carve their initials into the tree trunk to seal that promise. With a watery smile, she had agreed and he had taken out the rusty pocket knife that was his most treasured possession. He had scratched her initials and she his, and then they had regarded each other with the solemnity of imminent parting.

'I might not see you again before I go,' she had said. 'I screamed at Mama before I ran off. I'm going to be in a lot of trouble when I go back.'

'Stay for another minute,' he had pleaded and, impulsively, he had stepped forwards and kissed her lips.

Shy in his presence for the first time in her life, she had kissed him back before flying away through the orchard.

And, regardless of their positions now, she comprehended that she could kiss no one other than Cormac beneath the branches of this oak.

She broke from the kiss and took a nonchalant step away from Garrett, backing towards the tree trunk to conceal the carved initials from view.

'Shall we return now?' she managed to say calmly, even though her pulse pounded. 'We could go for a walk in the gardens.'

With an amiable nod, he offered her his arm and led her back the way they had come. Her shoulders slumped with relief as they left the clearing.

She would not bring him to the orchard again.

Chapter 9

Upon receiving another summons from Mrs Walsh, Cormac reported to the kitchens with his father's tool chest.

'You can come up now,' the housekeeper said, motioning him towards the door that led above stairs. 'I have informed the family that they should avoid the library for the afternoon.'

He followed her from the kitchens, up a narrow stairs and out into the massive entrance hall. The splendour of the big house never ceased to fill him with awe, from its high ceilings to the striking paintings on its walls, but what drew his gaze the most was the imposing mahogany staircase which swept up to the floor above them, a stark contrast to the modest ladder in the McGovern home.

When they entered the library, he experienced a brief wave of nostalgia as he remembered all the reading and writing lessons, Bridget looking over his shoulder while he wrote out his name on a slate in large, shaky letters. 'No,' her imperious voice drifted to him from the past, 'you need to do the R again...'

It was easy to see where his skills were needed; one of the shelves in a bookcase by the fireplace had buckled under the weight of its heavy books and collapsed into the shelf below it, which in turn was starting to bend under the extra load. A number of the books had toppled out onto the floor and the original shelf was in two splintered halves.

'I'll need to make at least one new shelf, maybe two,' he said. 'I can do that out in the barns and then bring them in here to fit them.'

'Make sure you're as quick as you can about it. And just set the books to one side. They will need to be put back alphabetically on the shelves once you are done. I can arrange them later.'

'That's fine,' he said, shrugging. 'I can read. I'll sort them.'

She raised her eyebrows and left without comment, her keys jangling.

After measuring the length and width of the shelves, he went out to the barns to unearth any pieces of wood which could serve his purpose. Aside from storage for hay, the barns represented a repository for all kinds of detritus from the stables and the house which had accumulated over time. Enough old furniture had been discarded there that, by the time two hours had passed, he had located, sawed and planed two boards of the right colour into suitable shelves for the bookcase. He hefted them onto his shoulder and carried them back to the house.

Re-entering the kitchens, he discovered Malachy Kelly lounging against the table, chatting rather cosily with a couple of the kitchen maids. The cook was nowhere to be seen.

'Where's Mrs Kavanagh?' Cormac asked the maids.

'Got a letter and ran off,' one said and the other added, 'Bet it was news about her sister's family. She looked fierce upset.'

'They've probably been hanged,' said Malachy in an offhand manner.

Speculating whether he could knock the boards into the back of the lad's head and pass it off as an accident, Cormac chose the path of temperance and settled for a sharp warning about getting back to work; raised in a home where hard graft was a chief principle of life, he couldn't stand to see such idleness. But Malachy merely gave him an impudent grin and returned his attention to the maids. At least Cormac could be thankful that neither was his sister.

Back in the library, he fixed the new bookshelves in place. He was in the process of returning the books to their proper positions, savouring the smell of them as he did so, when he heard the door open. Presuming it was Mrs Walsh coming to tell him to hurry up, he turned to say he was almost done but shut his mouth again when he saw Bridget in the doorway.

'Oh,' she said, 'I wasn't aware there was anyone in here. I came to fetch some of my piano music.' She gestured towards a bookcase against the opposite wall but made no move to approach it.

He nodded and continued with his task. Not all of the long words on the book covers were recognisable to him but he knew his alphabet well enough to arrange the volumes as Mrs Walsh wished.

When Bridget spoke again, she offered an uninspiring, 'It is a very fine day.'

''Tis,' he said, even though rain had spattered the window panes not ten minutes earlier.

'Have you met Garrett yet?' she asked suddenly.

He cleared his throat. 'I'd the pleasure of seeing to his horse on his arrival.'

'Oh. And not since then?'

He shook his head.

'I believe we are planning a ride across the estate in the coming days so I expect you will encounter him in the stables then.'

'I expect I will.'

After another short silence, she burst out, 'I do hope you will like him.'

He couldn't hide his surprise. 'I don't think I'm meant to have an opinion on him.'

She tugged self-consciously at a chestnut curl dangling at her neck. 'Your opinion matters to me.'

How was he supposed to respond to that? This sort of talk far overstepped the boundary he had established between them that day in the orchard. However, he could not help but see that Bridget's fiancé was a decent man and she was fortunate to be marrying him. Not to mention any servant would be only too delighted to be in his employment, judging by his benevolent conduct to those beneath him.

Taking a quick breath, Cormac stooped to pick up another book and said, 'By all accounts, he sounds like a respectable fellow. I'm happy for you.'

'Are you really?'

'Of course. Couldn't be happier.' He fixed his gaze on the book's spine, which displayed an author's surname beginning with D-I. That would follow D-E then. 'I hope ye'll be happy together.' He needed to stop saying that damned word.

After slotting the book into place, he met her eyes and found them wide and startled. Her lips had parted too but she closed them in a hurry.

'Th-thank you,' she said, 'that is very kind. And I wish you every happiness as well.'

She began to turn back to the door so he reminded her, 'Better fetch your music.'

She reddened and dug out a sheaf of sheet music from the bottom shelf of the opposite bookcase. 'Good day to you, Cormac.'

With that formal farewell, she left him alone in the library, where a faint scent of lilac now floated in the air.

***

Bridget sat in a haze of consternation at the dining table, taking no notice of the discourse passing between her mother, uncle and fiancé. Her thoughts were entrenched in the library, agonising over her encounter with Cormac.

What had induced her to go there? When Mrs Walsh had made it known at luncheon that the library should be avoided while the carpenter worked in it for a few hours, she ought to have accepted the housekeeper's recommendation without question, except that some strange impulse had driven her to fabricate a reason to call by. And then she had spoken to him about Garrett.

It was conceited of her to even entertain the idea. She should not make any assumptions. And yet, his cheeks had coloured, and he had avoided her gaze, and his shoulders had hunched when he had described her fiancé as a respectable fellow...

Heavens above, did he *like* her?

If he did, then her blathering on about meeting Garrett must have been cruel for him to endure. It would also explain why he had been so eager to end familiar contact between them after he learned of her engagement. An interest on his part would have made any acquaintance with her a hundred times more inappropriate.

She didn't know what to think, if she was right. Had she suspected sooner... No, she couldn't permit herself to imagine what alternative scenario might have taken place. Her future was with Garrett and there was no going back from that.

She tried to picture Cormac's future. He would remain as a stable hand on the estate for certain, but it was a good, honest placement and perhaps he might become stable master one day. Conceivably, he'd find a nice girl who would make a good wife for him. At this, she felt a pang which she did her best to overlook. Yes, he would wed and have children, and she would make her own family too, and in the years to come they would meet in passing around the manor grounds and exchange a smile as they recollected the friendship they had once shared.

That would have to be satisfactory for them both.

The removal of the second course dishes drew her attention back to the discussion around the table. Lord Walcott was reminiscing about fox hunting, a pastime which he had enjoyed in his younger and, Bridget presumed, slimmer days.

'There is nothing like the thrill of the hunt,' he declared. 'The chase, the baying of the hounds, the bolt of the fox. There can be no greater pleasure for a man in a rural situation.'

'It's a shame we're not in the season for it,' said Garrett. 'I feel I must seize every opportunity to enjoy these outdoor pursuits while I am in the country. After all, there's no possibility of going hunting in the centre of London!'

'Still, London has its attractions too,' said Lady Courcey.

'Many and varied,' he agreed. 'But it's refreshing to get away from the busy city, even just for a month or two. I do enjoy the peace and quiet here. I'll be sorry to leave when the time comes.'

Bridget attempted to follow the direction of this conversation with difficulty. What was Garrett implying with such comparisons?

'London?' she said, injured that this was the first time she was hearing about this. 'Are you planning to go back again?'

He smiled at her. 'Do not fret. You won't be left behind this time. I promise not to go without my wife.'

At least that meant he would not be leaving until sometime after they were married. Still perplexed, she said, 'Surely you have no wish for me to come along while you conduct your business affairs?'

He chuckled. 'No, indeed, I expect you will be tending to housekeeping matters in our home instead.'

His words struck her like a blow to the chest.

'Do you mean to say that we shall move to London after we marry?' she said in disbelief.

'Of course,' he said, as if it were the most obvious thing in the world.

'You never told me—!' she began but got no further as her mother cut across her.

'Speaking of outdoor pursuits,' the lady said with a touch more volume than normal, 'I wonder whether it will be fine enough for an outing tomorrow. We have been sorely lacking in sunny weather since your arrival, Mr Lambourne, and you are no doubt eager to see more of the estate.'

As Garrett responded with enthusiasm, she threw a quelling look at her daughter and Bridget refrained from saying anything else, though her thoughts had been flung into chaos. He could not have meant what he had said, could he? He had never given her the faintest inkling that he intended for them to live in London after their wedding. Her mind reeled at the prospect.

She volunteered no further contribution to the chat during the meal and maintained her silence when she and her mother retired to the drawing room afterwards. However, once the men came to join them she availed of the first opportunity to snatch a moment with her fiancé, stepping up to him by the mantelpiece where he was enjoying his glass of brandy. Lady Courcey and Lord Walcott were absorbed in their own dialogue on the sofa and would not overhear.

'Garrett, I am a little confused by an allusion you made at dinner,' she said, keeping her words measured. This may all have been a misunderstanding; she did not want to start off in an accusatory fashion.

He looked puzzled. 'An allusion to what?'

'To London. Did you speak in earnest when you said that we shall be going there once we are married?'

'Naturally. What is the matter, my darling? You are very pale.'

'You have never mentioned this before,' she said, her voice tight. 'Why must we go to London?'

He laughed. 'You didn't think we would be staying in this country, did you?'

'What reason had I to think otherwise?'

He was about to laugh again but checked himself when he saw that she was being serious. 'It would not be very practical to live in Ireland when my affairs must be managed in England.'

'But you have some property in Kildare. That is why you and Lord Wyndham came to Ireland and how we became acquainted with each other. Will you not need to be present to oversee it?'

He waved the point away. 'That estate is small and supervised by an agent. The majority of my father's assets and property is in London and thus it is by far the more pertinent place to be.'

'Can you not conduct your business from Dublin?' she appealed, desperation mounting within her. She had envisaged them dwelling here at Oakleigh once it became hers, but she would accept taking up residence in Dublin if London was to be the only alternative. 'We could stay there during the winter and just come back to the countryside for the summer months.'

'My father already relies on me to assist in the running of his estate and my involvement will only continue to increase. Soon I shall be required in London constantly. It would not be realistic to expect me to travel back and forth all the time.'

She said nothing.

'Darling, we have to be sensible. Of course we shall come back to visit, but our primary residence must be where I need to be.'

'And what about where I need to be?'

He frowned. 'What do you mean by that?'

Taking a controlled breath, she said, 'There are two of us in this relationship. Did you consider consulting me in this decision at all?'

He looked taken aback by her frankness. 'It is not a woman's place to dictate such matters.'

'But I am to inherit Oakleigh. As a baroness, my seat will be here and it will be my responsibility to see to my estate and tenants.'

'That Enright fellow will look after all that. Many rural estates in this country no longer have the owner in residence. And if there are matters to attend to, I can correspond with Mr Enright from London, so you don't need to worry about them. Not to mention, your mother will still need a place to live. If she chooses not to remain in Dublin, we couldn't very well eject her from this house.' He phrased this quite delicately but his expression conveyed that he had no desire to share a home with Lady Courcey on a permanent basis.

'Please take my viewpoint into account,' she pleaded. 'Ireland is my home. I would be aggrieved to leave Dublin, of course, but Oakleigh most of all. My seven years in the city, while pleasurable in their own way, have only served to remind me of how attached I am to the fields and the woods and the fresh air. I would be stifled in London.'

'I do not want to hear any more arguments. It will not be possible for us to stay in Ireland after we are married, is that clear?'

She was shocked into silence. Those were the first harsh words he had ever spoken to her.

Sighing, he took her gloved hand. 'I am sorry. I did not mean to be unkind. But you do understand, don't you?'

She nodded numbly.

He pressed a kiss to her knuckles and said, 'We ought to rejoin your mother and uncle now.'

He turned away from her and took a chair opposite Lord Walcott. After a dazed moment, she resumed her own seat, her hand cold inside its glove.

Chapter 10

As though Lady Courcey had conjured it, the sun nestled in a blanket of blue the next morning, promising a long, hot July day. Bridget and Garrett, confined to the manor grounds for days by unsettled weather, welcomed it with eagerness. They had already formulated a scheme for an opportunity such as this and now put it into effect, sending messages to the kitchens for a picnic basket to be assembled and to the stables for their horses to be prepared.

Bridget meant to show Garrett as many corners of the estate as she could. Her original intention had simply been to display the splendour of Oakleigh but her new motive would be to convince him that such splendour could not be abandoned for stuffy London. She would demonstrate just how content she was in the bosom of the lush countryside; with luck, this form of persuasion would help bring him around to her way of thinking. If he loved her enough, he would wish to do everything in his power to make her happy.

There was no question of them going off for a whole day unaccompanied. They had arranged that Garrett's valet, Brewer, would act as chaperone but it was solely for the sake of etiquette; Garrett was too much of a gentleman to take advantage of her in some isolated copse. Brewer would follow them at an unobtrusive distance and his immediate presence would only be needed to lay out the picnic and see to the horses when they stopped to rest.

After breakfast, Bridget dressed in her riding habit and went out to the courtyard. The horses stood waiting – Bonny, Garrett's own mount, named Commander, and an anonymous third for their chaperone – and a bulging picnic basket sat on the cobbles, appearing to contain enough food for ten people embarking upon a three-day expedition. Garrett, checking over Commander's tackle with a discerning eye, turned at her approach.

'Regrettable news, my darling,' he announced. 'Brewer's unwell. Doubled up in bed with stomach ache and headache and no doubt an ache in his elbow too. Sickly creature, he always falls ill at the most inconvenient times.'

This flippant comment, delivered with a grin, indicated that the valet was not at death's door and she need not be concerned over his continued existence. What did demand concern was the likelihood of their outing.

'Does this mean we cannot go today?' she asked, dismayed at the idea of missing out on such fine weather and the chance to champion Oakleigh at its very best.

'Fear not, I have succeeded in obtaining a substitute. The stable master said he could spare one of his hands for the day.'

'How generous of him,' she said, her dismay by no means allayed. Her luck could not be that bad, could it? Please, anyone but...

Cormac trudged out of the stables.

Her body reacted strangely at the sight of him, her stomach dropping even as her heart pumped in an erratic manner. He gave a polite nod in her direction but didn't quite make eye contact, busying himself with securing the picnic basket to the third horse. All joy at the prospect of a day-long ride leaked out of her. Already, she wanted it to be over. Could she fabricate a plausible reason to delay it to another day? No, her effusion at breakfast over the magnificent sunshine foiled that possibility. And it would cast a shadow upon Cormac's good name if she requested an alternative stable hand without explanation. They were ensnared by the circumstances.

Garrett offered a gallant hand to Bridget to assist her in mounting and then swung up onto his own horse.

'Onwards to freedom and adventure,' he said with a jovial flourish and led the way out of the courtyard, failing to perceive that his zeal met with silence.

As soon as they reached the Gorteen, Cormac allowed his mount to fall behind, giving Bridget and Garrett space and the semblance of privacy. This did little to ease her discomfort, knowing they were still in his line of sight. She hoped Garrett would not attempt to express even the barest sign of affection during the day; there would be no recovery from the mortification.

For a time, she considered feigning an ache of her own, or even boredom, but neither would serve the purpose of endearing her fiancé to the charms of the surrounding land. So, with an effort, she perked up and started pointing out notable landmarks. Perhaps she could impress him with her knowledge of crops and herds and fallow land, making him realise how suited she was to be in charge here. He did not need to know her education had been a recent acquirement.

She fell quiet as they entered the field with the giant's claw; this was one landmark she had no wish to elaborate upon. She tried to accelerate their pace but the rocky outcrop caught his attention.

'What an unusual formation. It looks rather like three curved fingers, don't you think?'

'Mmm,' she said.

'Come now, we passed an unremarkable hedgerow back there and you were able to tell me its entire history from planted seed. Surely you have a story behind this?'

'It is known as the giant's claw,' she said unwillingly. 'The locals named it. I don't know much beyond that.'

'The locals?' He flicked a glance over his shoulder. 'Do you think our companion might know more?'

She flinched. 'Oh, I doubt it. The knowledge of it likely belongs to an older generation.'

'And don't the Irish live by their storytelling? Let's try him.'

They had paused in their progress across the field, which meant Cormac had halted some distance further back. He was not looking at them directly but could not fail to notice when Garrett gesticulated and called, 'You there!'

He trotted up to them, a slight crease between his brows. 'Yes, sir?'

Garrett motioned to the rocky shape towering above them. 'Can you tell us anything of the history of this? I imagine it has a colourful past in the indigenous folklore. Perhaps it marks the site of one of your famed fairy forts?'

Cormac cast a fleeting look at Bridget and she tried to communicate her apology with her eyes. Garrett could not know how inappropriate his curiosity was.

Expression shuttered, Cormac returned his gaze to the other man. 'It has a more recent past than you'd suppose, sir, and one grislier than fairies. It played a part in the rebellion of '98.'

'Did it, indeed?' Garrett said, leaning forward. 'In what way?'

'It was used as a rallying point for the local Carlow rebels. The leaders met here to pass on information and gather arms. Sometimes they buried them in the ground at its base.'

Garrett stared down with interest, as though expecting to see indications of the churned soil disturbed thirty years ago.

'But there was an informant. The men assembled on the eve of one of the battles and were ambushed by English forces. They were hanged the following dawn, every last man. The giant's claw was the gallows.'

Bridget shivered.

'Fascinating,' said Garrett. 'It strikes me as a fitting form of justice that the hanging took place at the location of their plotting.'

Cormac's voice was very even as he replied, 'You'll forgive me if I don't quite see it the same way, sir. Both my grandfathers met their deaths here that dawn.'

'Ah,' said Garrett. He had the grace to look uncomfortable, but also a little wary. Did he wonder whether rebel blood ran through this stable hand's veins? He coughed and turned to Bridget. 'Shall we go on?'

She directed Bonny away without a word, keen to leave the place. She felt terrible that Cormac had been compelled to relive his family's painful history. Once he was old enough, his father had sat him down and related the harrowing events of the rebellion to him – she could still recall his haunted face afterwards and had never pressed him for any details beyond those which he had volunteered to give.

He waited to give them time to move ahead. When she looked back, he sat hunched in his saddle, the claw projecting above him like it would pluck him from his seat.

They rode on through the morning, sometimes at a leisurely pace and every so often cantering across the terrain, Cormac in their wake but always at a respectful distance. Bridget, leading the way, found herself shunning certain parts of the estate. She had no intention of going anywhere near the Sruhawn, which would only act as an unwelcome reminder of Jack McGovern's tragic death. She had no great yearning to venture into Ballydarry after her most recent visit there. And, while she still had not yet made it to the limestone quarry this summer, today was not the occasion for it, entwined as it was with so many childhood memories that had nothing to do with the man at her side and everything to do with the one behind her. She therefore selected a safe route across fields and through woods which, while recognisable, presented no perilous emotional links. She praised Oakleigh and Garrett admired it and both of them pretended they were alone.

When the sun was at its highest in the sky, they stopped at the edge of a large grove of birch trees to take their midday meal. Panting and sweating, they dismounted, eager to quench their thirst. As soon as Cormac caught up to them, Garrett beckoned to him to bring the picnic basket.

Bridget burned with embarrassment. 'Let me do it,' she said, reaching for the basket. She couldn't abide the idea of Cormac in such a role of servitude. Asking him to saddle her horse somehow seemed very different from allowing him to serve her food.

''Tis fine, miss,' he said, his blue eyes direct.

'Leave him be, it's what he's here for,' said Garrett, tugging at his cravat. 'My word, it's hot. I hope the wine is still cool.'

Cormac chose a flat area of grassy ground a little way into the grove, unfolded a blanket and a pair of napkins, and spread out the delicious luncheon Mrs Kavanagh had prepared. There were cold meats, bread and cheese, scones with jam, strawberries, and even two glasses carefully cushioned in cloths, but the splendid array was marked by one conspicuous absence.

'Did she provide nothing to drink?' Garrett asked incredulously.

Cormac displayed the empty basket. 'She must've forgotten to.'

'How does one forget an essential such as wine?'

Cormac's lips tightened. 'I apologise on her behalf, sir. I'm afraid she's a bit distracted at present. There's been a death in her family.'

'Oh, no,' said Bridget, clapping a hand to her mouth. 'She received word from her sister?'

He nodded. 'Her sister's son was executed but they spared her husband. He has generously been permitted to keep his position on the estate.' His inflection conveyed just what he thought of this particular brand of generosity.

She exhaled through her fingers. 'How awful.'

'What are you talking about?' said Garrett, looking from her to Cormac with a frown.

She smoothed the skirt of her riding habit with a sweaty palm. 'Our cook. Her sister lives on Rathglaney land. Do you remember I told you what happened there?'

His expression said he remembered and that he was beginning to think all of Oakleigh's servants had connections to criminals. 'I see. In any case, that does not solve our current predicament. I'm parched.'

Cormac picked up the glasses. 'I'll get ye some water. There's a stream nearby.'

'Will it be clean enough to drink?' Garrett said dubiously.

'I guarantee it'll be the best water you've ever tasted.'

He disappeared between the narrow trunks of the birch trees and returned minutes later with the two glasses brimming. ''Tisn't far. I can refill them when necessary.'

Garrett tried a cautious sip, then swallowed the rest of the contents in one gulp. Bridget took a healthy mouthful of her own; it was crisp and very satisfying as it slid down her dry throat.

'While it is no glass of wine, I do believe you are correct about its exceptional quality. It is delicious.' Garrett held out his empty glass, clearly expecting it to be replenished right away.

Bridget seized it before Cormac could even reach for it. 'I will refill them myself. Where is the stream?'

He pointed. 'About sixty yards that way. You'll hear it before you see it. I'm going to bring the horses there next to water them.'

'You should start eating,' she encouraged Garrett. 'I'll be back in a moment.'

She hurried away through the grove. Further in, where the trees grew more thickly, the merry gurgle of water drew her to the location of the stream. Her breath caught as she came upon it and she realised at once how Cormac had already known of its existence. Setting the two glasses on a flat boulder mottled with lichen, she knelt at the water's edge; it spilled over a rock shelf and splashed along a bed of pebbles, glinting in intermittent rays of sunlight. She told herself it was indispensable to wash the perspiration from her hands and neck before luncheon, but she took long enough about it that she was still there when Cormac arrived, leading Bonny between the birches. Betraying no reaction to her lingering presence, he guided the horse to a spot a dozen feet further up from her and the animal's white muzzle dipped gratefully to the running stream.

After a protracted silence, she said in a low voice, 'I have never been so mortified in my life.'

His head jerked towards her. 'What d'you mean?'

She stood, blowing out her cheeks in frustration. 'This! Your role as chaperone, Garrett's inappropriate questions, you laying out the picnic like you're—'

'A servant,' he said firmly. 'Which I am. I've no objection to it.'

'It is beyond absurd when I recall our antics here.'

He glanced at the stream. 'I wasn't sure you'd remember.'

'Of course I remember.'

'Well, it was different then. This is the way 'tis now.' His tone wasn't harsh but he said nothing else and turned back to Bonny, plainly trying to adhere to the assertion he had made that day in the orchard that there could be nothing personal between them.

She, on the other hand, surrendered to the memory. It had been her last summer at Oakleigh and a day as hot as this one, if not hotter. Roaming far across the fields, they had discovered this stream and frolicked in its cool embrace, splashing about in an exuberance of bare limbs and breathless laughter. Then, sitting on the same lichen-covered boulder, they had dangled their feet in the water and, yielding to a rare moment of gravity, talked about the future.

'My da reckons I'll start at the stables next year,' he had revealed. 'And he's going to keep teaching me carpentry. Says I show promise.'

'You really do,' she had said, having witnessed his first attempts at working wood. 'Lucky thing, you'll be outdoors a lot and always with the horses, that will be just marvellous. I, in dismal contrast, shall be stuck indoors reading accounts. Papa wants me to begin learning how the estate works once I turn twelve in November. How dull it will be.'

They had exchanged a look of realisation as they both grasped the significance of her words.

She had straightened her shoulders. 'It's no matter. We shall still find time for each other.'

'Exactly,' he had said, flicking his foot and dousing the front of her trussed-up dress.

She had shrieked and their flash of maturity had evaporated in the face of childish retribution.

What would their eleven-year-old selves have said, had they known just how far apart they would come to be. They doubtless would have scoffed at the suggestion. But then, they would never have predicted that within seven months her father would be dead.

Yesterday, she would not allow herself to envisage what might have happened had she never left the estate. Now, she couldn't resist considering the idea.

With her father's passing, she would have cleaved to Cormac and his family even more; nothing but her mother's curt manner would have awaited her at the manor house. Growing older with him at an age when boys were becoming men and objects for marriage rather than friendship, how would she have viewed him?

She sneaked a sideways glance as he hunkered down by the stream, hair falling into his eyes as he cupped his hands full of water to drink, and felt a quiver of awareness that had not been there before. Her brain ran wild for a moment and she imagined him lifting his gaze to hers, stepping towards her, touching her waist with one hand, tilting her chin up with the other...

She gulped, conscious of Garrett's presence – her *fiancé*, she reminded herself – sixty yards away.

The notion of an heiress kissing a stable hand was preposterous, all of civil society believed so. And yet, when it was her and Cormac it did not seem such an outrageous thought. Perhaps if she had stayed... But no, her mother would never have condoned it. She would have enforced their separation by any means within her power.

A jolt of shock ran through her. Wasn't that precisely what her mother had done?

His attention darted in her direction at her sudden movement. She hastened to pick up the glasses and immerse them in the running water.

When she rose again, she dared to speak her mind. 'Sometimes I wish it could be different,' she said and whisked away from the stream before either of them could say more.

What she had meant was that she wished nothing had changed. But leaving Oakleigh seven years ago had caused everything to change.

She contemplated the prospect of going to London and decided some changes ought to be fought. She refused to be taken away against her will again.

She had formulated her line of reasoning by the time she returned to Garrett.

***

Once he had watered the three horses, Cormac tied them up to graze at the edge of the grove and settled himself at the base of a tree a reasonable distance from the picnic spread. If he turned his head, he could glimpse the pair through the birches but only the faintest hum of voices came to him. It was enough privacy to be going on with. He didn't want to be any nearer, should Mr Lambourne choose to murmur loving endearments to his betrothed.

Mrs Kavanagh had slipped him some bread, cheese and a half-burnt scone when he had collected the picnic basket from the kitchens that morning. After wolfing it all down, he took out his knife and the small block of wood he had been working on over the past week. He whittled away at the shape, bringing wing and beak into clearer form.

He did not know what to make of Bridget's behaviour. Why did she struggle so much with acknowledging him as her servant? He had long since accepted it. Her resistance to the inevitability of their situation was unfathomable.

The knife scraped nimbly at the wood and the shavings drifted down into his lap like snowflakes. It was peaceful for a time, the shade of the trees a welcome relief after the baking heat of the sun. However, he soon became aware that the tone of the nearby voices had changed. They were no longer muted, with the occasional tinkle of laughter. Instead, they had increased in volume and grown sharp and heated.

The tramping of feet on fallen twigs announced that someone had been incensed enough to walk away from the picnic. Mr Lambourne came marching in his direction, shoulders stiff and mouth a disgruntled line. He looked surprised when he saw Cormac.

'Oh, it's you. I didn't know where you had gone to.'

Cormac brushed the wood shavings from his thighs and started to rise but Mr Lambourne waved him back down.

'No need.'

He expected the man to pass on by, seeking solitude to indulge in his strop a little longer, but instead Mr Lambourne folded his arms and leaned against a tree opposite him.

'Sometimes the female mind is impossible to comprehend,' he remarked.

Cormac gave a noncommittal shrug. Mr Lambourne shuffled his feet, then jutted his chin towards Cormac's hands.

'What is that you're doing there?' he asked.

'Nothing much. Just a hobby to pass the time.'

'I'd like to see it.'

After a brief hesitation, Cormac held out the wooden carving. Mr Lambourne took it, admiration growing on his face as he examined it from every angle.

'This is extraordinary. Such attention to detail. Where did you learn the skill?'

'My father taught me what he knew. After that, it was a matter of practice.'

A gleam came into Mr Lambourne's eye. 'Would you be able to replicate it? I have need to make reparation for a silly argument and a peace offering would be ideal. How soon could you make a second?'

'You can have this one, sir.'

'Are you certain? This isn't intended for someone else? Your own sweetheart?'

Cormac swallowed uneasily. 'I'd be pleased for the young lady to have it. I'll just give it a final look-over.'

He took the carving back, adjusted it with a few delicate nicks, and returned it.

Mr Lambourne gave him an approving nod. 'My thanks to you. I believe you have assisted me out of a quandary.'

With a wry twist of his mouth, Cormac watched the gentleman go back the way he had come, his step a good deal lighter.

***

Bridget knelt on the picnic blanket, shredding blades of grass into tiny pieces in her lap. Her fiancé's intransigence had come as an unpleasant discovery; instead of being open to a discussion about London, he had preferred to walk away from the confrontation altogether.

Perhaps it was her own fault. She shouldn't have raised the issue again so soon, not even twenty-four hours since their quarrel in the drawing room. He hadn't had time yet to absorb the reality that she was unhappy with the proposition. She would let him reflect on it for a while before broaching it again.

When the sound of footsteps drew near, her first guilty hope was that it might be Cormac – maybe he had overheard their altercation, seen Garrett storm away, and come out of concern. But it was Garrett weaving his way among the tree trunks. She returned her gaze to the clumps of grass on her skirt, pushing away the irrational disappointment. She ought to be glad he wanted to make peace already.

He didn't say anything. He crouched beside her on the blanket, turned her face towards his, and kissed her lips. It was a tender kiss, full of affection and apology, and she felt a tension ease inside as their ill will faded.

He pressed something into her hand and she broke from the kiss to look down at it. She gasped.

'A gift of conciliation,' he murmured. 'I hope you like it, my darling.'

She did not need to ask him where he had obtained such a treasure. She had spent hours and hours watching Cormac chip at odd bits of wood when they were young, supplying encouragement as he tried to shape them into animals or flowers or people. But the specimen in her grasp was so far beyond any of those attempts. She lifted it close to her eyes, marvelling at the delicacy of the thin legs, the texture of the layered feathers, the half-open beak as if it were about to break into birdsong. It was magnificent.

'What do you think?' Garrett asked, eager for absolution.

He didn't deserve the praise, when he had only procured it and not put the precious time and effort into its creation.

'I think its maker has the finest talent I have ever seen,' she said and then, relenting, added for his benefit, 'Thank you for giving it to me.'

He beamed and lounged back on his elbows, satisfied that all was amicable between them once more.

She stroked the wing of the wooden bird. For whom had Cormac intended it? His mother? One of his sisters? She bit her tongue; maybe he had his eye on one of the maidservants. With such care taken in its making, she felt privileged that she had been the one to receive it.

Presently, Garrett called for Cormac to tidy away the picnic spread. He came at once and set about shaking crumbs from the napkins and packing the leftovers into the basket. As he folded the blanket, he threw a quick glance in Bridget's direction. Clutching the bird so hard that its beak dug into her palm, she offered him a tentative smile and he gave her one in return.

Garrett threw back the last of his water in a long swallow and handed the glass to Cormac. Then he gestured towards the spot where the horses were grazing and said, 'Come, my darling, let us go on.'

She slipped the bird into her pocket and followed him out of the grove.

Chapter 11

The sun was setting by the time Cormac headed home across the fields, its vivid redness streaking the sky as it sank into the horizon. Exhausted, he hauled himself over the last stile into the lane, making a mental note to trim back the hedgerow again one of these days, and traipsed the final stretch to the cottage.

Despite the late hour, he found his mother at her spinning wheel and Orlaith scraping assiduously at the droppings strewn on the earthen floor beneath the hens' favourite rafter, eking out the last of the daylight with the aid of the glow from the fire. Maggie set a bowl of stirabout in front of him before returning to her work and he dug in as he listened to Orlaith, in an uncommonly talkative mood, describe a brawl that had occurred between two of her hens.

'...and then Chickie squawked and went for Henrietta and I was afraid she'd peck her eyes out!' she said, her own eyes large and round. 'But they calmed down after a lot of flapping about. I *think* they're friends again.'

He felt a swell of fondness for his little sister as she cast a maternal glance at the roosting brood above her.

'Any news from the big house?' his mother asked over the whirring of the wheel.

Knowing that Margaret had made a rare trip home two nights before and enlightened their mother on all the wonderful things

Mr Lambourne had done, he just shook his head and scooped up the last of his stirabout.

'There's some water in the rope bucket,' Maggie said with a nod towards the door.

He burped and rose from the table. Orlaith giggled but his mother raised a pointed eyebrow.

''Scuse me,' he mumbled, and carried his bowl outside.

Night had fallen clear and balmy, and the stars were out in droves. He dipped the bowl into the bucket of water by the door of the cottage and rubbed at the food stains with his fingers. Satisfied that it was clean to his mother's standards, he was straightening up to bring it back inside when he caught a sudden movement in his peripheral vision. He whirled around and saw a figure standing in the lane. It looked like the form of a young woman.

'Bridget?' he called falteringly, though there was no logical way it could be her.

The figure stepped into the dim glow of firelight falling through the open cottage door. ''Tis good to see you, Cormac.'

'Mary!'

He was flabbergasted. It had been twelve years since he'd seen his older sister – she had been sent away to live with their aunt, who was poorly and unable to afford hired help. The last they had heard from her was that their aunt had passed away and that she had found employment in Dublin. More than a year had elapsed since that communication. And now here she was, with pale hair and pale skin, emerging like a ghost from the gloom.

She was carrying a bundle, which stirred as she shifted its weight in her arms. He opened his mouth but his mother's voice rang out first.

'Cormac, while you're out there, I need you to get some turf for...' Her words trailed away as she appeared in the doorway and glimpsed her eldest child.

'God above, Mary!' she exclaimed. She ran forwards to embrace her daughter, but hesitated at the sight of the moving bundle. A faint cry from within the rags eradicated all doubt.

'This is Patrick.' Mary held the bundle out to Maggie. 'Take him. He's your grandson.'

Maggie gathered the baby to her chest. 'I see a lot of things have happened since you left us,' she said, looking down at the little face.

'Yes,' Mary murmured. 'A lot of things.'

Maggie kissed her on the cheek. 'Come inside, dearie. You're after coming a long way.'

They went indoors, where they found Orlaith hovering near the doorway, shy of this sister whom she had never met before. Sitting on a bench, Mary gave her a look of reassurance, but Orlaith remained where she was, solemn and silent.

Cormac and Maggie joined Mary at the table, Maggie still cradling the baby. There wasn't a sound for a minute or two; no one seemed to know how to proceed.

Then Mary said, 'I named him after our Patrick. I thought it was the right thing to do.' She had always been closest to Patrick; with only ten months between them in age, they had been as thick as thieves until she left.

Maggie's eyes filled with sadness but she didn't say anything.

Cormac folded his arms. 'Who's the father?' It came out more sharply than he had intended.

Mary's expression became pained and it seemed to take her a lot of effort to gather the words together. 'My husband,' she said.

She placed her left hand on the tabletop so they could all see the plain wedding band on her finger.

'Why didn't you write and tell us you'd married?' said Maggie. 'We haven't heard from you in so long and it would've cheered us to hear the good—'

'He's dead,' Mary interrupted in a cracked voice.

There was a shocked silence.

Maggie covered the ring as she clasped Mary's hand. 'You poor craythur.'

'How did he die?' asked Orlaith, speaking for the first time.

Maggie frowned in admonishment at her youngest daughter. 'You don't have to answer that now, Mary. You should take some time to settle down before you try to talk about such a difficult subject.'

'No, 'tis fine,' said Mary with a brave set to her shoulders. 'I'll have to tell yous at some point, so it may as well be now.'

Her speech had taken on shades of a Dublin accent and it occurred to Cormac that, at twenty-one, his sister had spent more than half of her life away from home. What joys and sorrows had it brought her?

She let out a slow breath. 'When Auntie died, I should've come home. But I'd been away for over ten years and what did I have to show for it? I knew how to care for an invalid and manage a house, but that was it. I wanted to experience the world while I was still out in it 'cause I'd never have another opportunity once I came back.' She raised her gaze to her mother's. 'I realise now it was shameful of me to do what I did. To take myself to the city when yous were trying to cope after Da and Patrick dying... It must've been such a hard time for yous and all I cared about was getting a taste of real life. I was too self-interested to spare a thought for my family. I'm so sorry.'

Cormac had witnessed Maggie's distress at the time – she had been devastated that her first-born had chosen to stay away when her presence and support had been so desperately needed. However, she spoke now without recrimination.

'I don't hold it against you, dearie. It was natural you should want to see the world beyond your aunt's house before being confined to home again. Of course, I would've insisted you return if I thought you were heading to Dublin with no purpose, but the fact that you said your aunt had secured you a position in a household before she passed made me feel much easier.'

Mary's lashes lowered. 'That was a lie. I had no position before I arrived there.'

Maggie stared at her daughter. 'Ah, I see,' she said and stroked the cheek of little Patrick.

It astounded Cormac that their mother could respond so calmly to this appalling news. He himself wanted to shake Mary until her teeth rattled. What had she been thinking when she went to the city with no acquaintances, no guarantee of employment, and no place to live?

She sighed. 'I got what I deserved for lying to my ma. I'd a dreadful time there in the beginning. The only work I could find was helping an old woman sell flowers on the street. I'd nowhere to stay. It was awful. If it'd been winter I think I'd have died. I thought again about coming home, but I didn't want to return a failure. I wanted to make something of myself so yous could be proud of me when I came back.'

Perhaps she had been hoping at this juncture for commendations for her fortitude but neither Maggie nor Cormac offered any. He was too angry at her abysmal lack of judgement. Her actions had been selfish and foolhardy and she did not merit an ounce of praise from her family.

She bit her lip, a tinge of pink appearing in her pale cheeks, and hastened on. 'But that was when my luck turned. I managed to find work in a bakery. It was a family business and so much more than I could've hoped for. They gave me proper wages and a room as well. At first, I just swept out the shop and ran errands for them, but in time they showed me how to make the bread myself and I was really able to earn my keep.' Her head tilted in dreamy reminiscence. 'They'd a son who was to inherit the business when his father died. Oh, he was a gentleman, so courteous, with soft, dark hair and such a charming smile. I don't mind saying I fell for him almost right away.'

Her whole demeanour brightened at the mention of this baker's son; her back straightened, her eyes shone, and her mouth curved in a tender smile.

'He fell in love with me too and we married last September. I would've written to yous but it was such a busy, exciting time, I just didn't have a moment to spare. I gave birth to Patrick a month ago. A strong, healthy boy, oh, his da was so pleased.' Then she lost her sparkle, like a candle snuffed out. 'A few days later, he was working with the ovens. We don't know how it happened but there was a terrible accident and a fire. His burns were... H-he didn't survive.'

The hush in the cottage was broken only by a cluck and a flutter of wings from a restless hen. Orlaith crept on soundless feet to Cormac's side and he laid his arm around her shoulders, wishing they had put her to bed before now.

Tears filled Mary's eyes as she continued, 'His own ma and da would've let me stay with them. Patrick was their grandson too, after all. But I told them I wanted to go home to my own family. They were very kind to me and I do miss them but...I had to come home.'

Patrick whimpered in his grandmother's arms. Mary reached out and Maggie handed him to her.

'Shush, love,' she whispered, and put her wet cheek next to her baby's.

Maggie said, 'I think he's soiled himself...'

Mary wiped her face with the back of her hand. 'I'd better take care of him.'

'No, dearie, I can do it.' Maggie's tone was compassionate. She seemed ready to forgive Mary all of her transgressions; perhaps she felt her daughter had suffered enough without being burdened with accusations from her family as well. 'You're after a long journey. Go up to the loft and get some rest. I'll bring him up to you once I've tended to him.'

Mary gave the baby back to her mother. Maggie cupped her chin.

'You'll feel a bit better in the morning,' she said.

Cormac's gaze followed his sister as she climbed the ladder to the loft. The change that had been wrought upon her during her time away was even greater than that which had come upon Bridget. She had grown into a young woman, but she seemed to have faded in some way. Her manner had lost the bright vivacity he remembered from their childhood and she looked haggard, as though her contact with the wider world had taken its toll on her. Only her fair hair remained the same, retaining the rich colour that just she and he, out of all their siblings, had inherited from their father.

The baby gave another soft cry. He had tufts of dark hair and quite different features from his mother; he must take after his father too. Cormac glanced at Maggie. She already had the glow of a doting grandmother about her as she asked Orlaith to search the dresser for a cloth.

Even though Mary had suffered a tragic misfortune, he hoped her return might bring some long-lost happiness to their mother.

Chapter 12

Though she was fully dressed and ready to go down to breakfast, Bridget lingered at her dressing table to pore over the wooden bird once again. Still so impressed by the quality of the workmanship, she traced each meticulous contour, picturing the hands and blade that had brought it to life.

A knock at the door startled her and she instinctively hid the bird behind her jewellery box. Why had she done that? It was a gift from her fiancé; she should not feel guilty to be caught looking at it. She placed it out in full view again as she called, 'Come in.'

Her visitor turned out to be Ellen, bearing a glass of an indeterminate brown concoction on a tray. The lady's maid's freckles had bloomed in the summer weather and they splashed across her nose and both cheeks in liberal quantities. Nose wrinkling, she held the tray at some distance from her body as she entered the bedchamber.

Bridget was pleased to see her, dubious burden notwithstanding. Ellen was lady's maid to her mother, not herself, but they retained a personal connection which stemmed from Bridget's early years in Dublin. Ellen had been the only other person in the city who had known Cormac and with whom Bridget could lament his absence, and she had provided solace as much as the limitations of her station had allowed.

Her discretion in such matters was her most admirable trait, given her constant proximity to Bridget's mother. She had travelled with them from Oakleigh as a housemaid but Lady Courcey had set much store by her abilities and groomed her for the higher position of lady's maid, despite her youth, dismissing Ellen's predecessor ('That French *imbécile...*') once she had attained the suitable skill set for the role. When she had been promoted, Bridget had found it difficult to address her by the more correct title of 'Ryan' and both had been happy for her to continue on a first name basis.

Instead of her usual composure, Ellen looked rather embarrassed as she said, 'Her ladyship instructed me to bring this to you, miss.'

She placed the tray gingerly on the dressing table. Bridget squinted at the glass and took a cautious sniff. The stench of vinegar was overwhelming.

'What is it supposed to be?'

'A tonic, miss. To encourage a satisfactory waistline.'

Bridget twisted her lips. 'On my mother's recommendation, you say?'

Ellen gave an apologetic nod. 'She's considering the upcoming wedding.'

'Hmm. Can I not just have my stays tightened?'

'I'm certain she's expecting that as well.'

Bridget made no move to pick it up. 'Maggie McGovern thinks I'm too thin. I saw her eyeing me critically when she thought I wasn't looking.'

With the greatest tact towards her mistress's evident opinion on the subject, Ellen said, 'Maggie McGovern has raised four daughters to fine physical health so I can't fault her general judgement.' She brightened. 'Did you hear her eldest has returned?'

'Mary? She's come home?'

'Just the night before last. It's welcome news. She's been gone from Oakleigh even longer than I, but we were very close as small girls.'

Ellen related how Mary had shown up, so unexpectedly, as a widow and a mother. Bridget pitied Mary for the loss of her husband but was glad for Cormac that, after the deaths of two members of his family, his sister had come back to make them somewhat whole again. She gave the wooden bird a surreptitious caress and then returned her reluctant attention to the mud-coloured liquid before her.

'Could I pour it into the chamber pot?'

'The housemaid who discovered it would think you were dying.'

'And I suppose tipping it into a flowerpot would lead to the plant's actual demise. Perhaps you could ensure its delivery to the scullery? It smells potent enough to be a cleaning agent rather than a refreshing beverage. I believe I shall require you to intercept any future endeavours of this nature.'

Ellen's mouth twitched. 'As you wish, miss.'

Lady Courcey and Garrett were already seated when Bridget went down to breakfast but Lord Walcott had not yet appeared. She went straight to the platters on the sideboard and made a point of stacking her plate a good deal higher than her appetite necessitated.

If her mother noticed, she chose not to comment. Instead, she said, 'I have had a delightful idea, Bridget.'

'Indeed, what is it?' she asked warily as she took her place at the table. She had made up her mind to discourage any more long rides across the estate. Brewer was on the mend but she had no desire to run the risk he might fall ill again.

'As you know, Mr Lambourne's birthday is approaching in August. He was thinking of going back to the city for the occasion but I suggested he stay here and tempt his acquaintances down to Oakleigh for a week or two instead. You could invite some ladies as well. What do you think of that?'

'That sounds lovely,' said Bridget, pleased at the thought of seeing her friends again.

'There is no need to go to any trouble,' Garrett said modestly. 'I am content for it to be a quiet event.'

'Nonsense.' Lady Courcey waved his protestations away. 'You deserve a birthday celebration and I will be the one to host it for you. It is the least I can do, considering you have given me the greatest gift of all in making my daughter so happy.'

Garrett beamed at Bridget; her returning smile was somewhat less bright.

'It may also prove to be an impetus for my lingering brother to remove himself to his own estate at last,' Lady Courcey added dryly.

***

Cormac had located a sunny spot outside the stable doors and was sitting on a stool while he mended some stitching on a bridle when a shadow fell over him and a gruff cough announced the presence of Fintan Kelly.

He jumped to his feet and said, 'Mr Kelly, how can I help you?' but the answer was obvious as the old gardener held out his spade, its wooden handle broken into two jagged pieces. Knowing that Fintan looked after his tools with as much devotion as his gardens, Cormac recognised it as the same weapon which had connected with his rump all those years ago. He accepted it cautiously and examined the splintered shaft, wondering what – or who – had been on the receiving end of it this time.

Fintan seemed to read his mind. 'Years of service has cracked it, is all. I didn't whack it off that boy's head, though I had a mind to. Found him defacing the statue of Venus with clumps of mud.' He didn't go into any further detail but his complexion reddened in rage at the memory. 'I've sent him to Mr Buttimer this time 'cause the goddamn brat won't listen to me. He'll lose his post if he's not careful but he doesn't give a fig for my warning. All he says is he'll make money some other way.'

A look of shame crossed the gardener's lined face. Then he drew himself up and gave a brusque nod towards the broken spade.

'Get that back to me quick, boy,' he said and stalked away.

'Cormac!'

He glanced about and saw Mrs Kavanagh framed in the doorway to the kitchens.

'Leave that, lad, and go around to the front entrance. I've been told they want an extra pair of hands.'

'What for?' he asked, recalling the last time he had been sent in that direction.

'Lord Walcott's leaving. They need some help with his luggage.' Her tone was subdued but she made an effort to bark, 'Hurry on now!' in her old authoritative manner. She could not wallow in her family's misfortunes forever, after all.

She returned to her kitchens while Cormac, abandoning both the spade and the bridle by his stool, made his way around to the front of the big house, where a carriage and a cart stood side by side. Two footmen and a couple of the other stable hands, including Liam, were hoisting some large trunks onto the cart.

'Looks like there's more luggage here than came home with the two ladies,' Cormac said under his breath as he joined them.

Liam, purple in the face from strain, didn't reply as he tried to lift a trunk. Cormac gave him a hand in heaving it onto the cart and then they went back to the steps where several more trunks waited.

Lord Walcott was standing with Lady Courcey at the top of the steps, overseeing the operation. Cormac noted that it was Mrs Walsh, rather than Mr Buttimer, who waited in respectful attendance upon them and presumed that the butler was still giving Malachy Kelly an earful.

'Take care with that,' Lord Walcott called to the two footmen who were struggling with an enormous chest between them. 'It contains the belongings of my precious ones.'

The precious ones in question were worrying his ankles, giving piercing barks of discontentment. Cormac imagined that being shut up in a carriage with those ill-tempered creatures for hours could not be anything but torturous.

Lord Walcott, unmindful of his dogs' yapping, turned to Lady Courcey with an exaggerated expression of melancholy. 'I shall be sorry to say farewell to this place. I have thoroughly enjoyed my time here as lord of the manor.'

'And we shall be most sorry to see you go,' his sister replied, although she seemed to be bearing their imminent separation with a distinct lack of sorrow.

Lord Walcott sighed. 'Nevertheless, we soldier on as pressing needs dictate we must. Affairs at Lockhurst Park demand my immediate attention so I shall travel on to England after only a brief sojourn in Dublin. And from your perspective it is of course advantageous to have more space for future guests.' He looked over his shoulder into the dimness of the hall. 'Is Bridget coming to bid me farewell?'

'I have sent Ryan for her. She should be here in a moment.'

Cormac helped Liam haul the last trunk onto the cart and then he made a quick escape around the side of the house. As he turned the corner, he heard the voices of Bridget and her attentive fiancé floating out the doorway.

***

Following Lord Walcott's departure from Oakleigh, the planning for Garrett's birthday celebrations could begin in earnest. Thanks to her mother's tuition earlier in the summer, Bridget was able to conduct the preparations adeptly and the next two weeks passed in a flurry of activity. She spoke to Mr Buttimer about engaging musicians for a night of entertainment in the ballroom, to Mrs Kavanagh about a menu for the birthday feast, and to Mrs Walsh about accommodations for all the guests. Invitations were issued to ten acquaintances in all, five gentlemen and five ladies. The most important of these to Bridget was Miss Madeleine Wallace, the dearest friend she had made during her time in Dublin. Madeleine's older, married sister would also come, along with Miss Isabel Gardiner – a lively girl of limited means but ample wit – and the twin Hyland sisters who had been presented as debutantes at Dublin Castle on the same evening as Bridget. Some of the company would be travelling from their own country residences but none of these would be superior to Oakleigh and she could not wait to greet them all and show off her grand manor.

Two mornings before the guests were due to arrive, Bridget was seated with Garrett in the drawing room, discussing potential daytime activities which would amuse their visitors during their stay. They were alone and, as a consequence, he had positioned himself quite a bit nearer to her on the sofa than could be deemed proper.

'I do believe everyone would take pleasure in a jaunt across the estate,' she commented.

'Indeed,' he said, shifting even closer, his hazel eyes glowing with ardour.

'We could have picnics and play bowls on the lawn.' Her voice had become rather breathy. She was aware of the whole length of his body a hair's breadth away from her own and, even as she made a half-hearted attempt to retreat to a more respectable distance, thoughts of a particular nature raced through her mind: the vague rumours she had heard of what she might expect on her wedding night. With him in such proximity, her imagination was running amok.

'I hope the weather will be obliging...' Her words trailed off as he reached for her hand and stroked it. When she turned her head, their lips were only inches apart. They met with the lightest of touches. Eyes fluttering closed, she felt his hand move to her torso, resting just below her breast. It was an impertinent gesture and she should not allow it but for the first time since he had come to Oakleigh she was feeling as she had in Dublin, wholly captivated by his charm. She trembled as his fingers skimmed upwards over her bodice...

There was a timid knock on the drawing room door and they jerked away from each other. The door swung open to reveal Cormac's sister, Bronagh, clutching a tray with a teapot, two cups and a plate of biscuits. The girl could not possibly have seen anything but in a way Bridget felt that being observed by Bronagh was almost the same as having Cormac's gaze on her. She wilted at the very idea of him coming upon a scene such as that.

She waved Bronagh forwards and the girl set the tea tray down on a small table by her knee, eyes averted as she glanced around the room. Bridget supposed she was dazzled by Garrett, just like all the other maids. Only yesterday she had witnessed a housemaid bump into him by accident as she left his bedchamber with his bed sheets bundled in her arms; the girl had expelled a loud squeak, then had started to cry in mortification and fled.

'Thank you, Bronagh,' Bridget said, having come to accept these reactions as normal around her fetching fiancé.

Bronagh gave her a fleeting look and an awkward curtsey and hurried from the room.

'Do you know all the servants by name?' asked Garrett. 'That is quite an accomplishment.'

She pondered the fact that she considered Cormac's sisters to be practically her own. Though she did not like to keep secrets from Garrett, her instinct told her that to declare this sense of affiliation with a lower class family would not be received well.

'No, not all of them,' she said.

He did not seem to much care about her answer; he was already reaching for her hand again. She, however, had recalled her sense of propriety and leaned away to pour the tea.

Chapter 13

Cormac ducked under the vine-draped arch which marked the entrance to Oakleigh's gardens and followed the path in search of Fintan Kelly. After he had returned Fintan's spade to him with a brand new handle, the gardener, in a rare mood to offer praise, had declared the work of such good quality that he had instructed Cormac to reinforce some of his other implements weakened by long years of heavy use. Thus he now carried a rake and a hoe, each with fresh wooden shafts, over his shoulder as he looked around impatiently for the old man. It was nearing evening time and he still had numerous stable duties to complete before his working day would be done.

The gardens consisted of a broad expanse of lawn in the centre, bordered all around by a walkway lined with flower beds and tall hedges on both sides. Periodic gaps in the hedges allowed access to the central grassy area and every now and then the walkway widened to accommodate a piece of sculpture or a bench. He had almost reached the end of one side of the gardens when he heard voices drifting around the corner ahead of him.

'...so long as you think 'tis safe,' a girl was saying.

'I swear 'tis,' a boy responded. 'It should happen tonight. I'll meet you at the kitchens?'

'I'll be there.'

He rounded the corner and came upon a sculpture on a wide plinth: the statue of Venus, her polished, white body free of mud. On the edge of the plinth sat Malachy Kelly and Bronagh. The boy had one hand on her leg while the other was coiled in a length of her dark hair which had escaped from beneath her maid's cap. She jumped up at the sight of Cormac but Malachy stayed where he was, a lazy grin playing about his mouth.

Cormac glared at them. 'What the hell are ye doing?'

'This isn't what you think—' Bronagh began, her cheeks red with heat, but he cut her off.

'Get yourself back to the kitchens,' he snapped. 'They'll be preparing the dinner already. Mrs Kavanagh will throw a fit if you're not to hand.'

She flung a mulish look at him and a swift glance at Malachy and then she darted away down the garden path. Cormac turned to the boy, allowing the rake and hoe to drop to waist height in a threatening gesture.

'Stay away from my sister,' he said. 'Don't come near her again.'

Malachy gave a careless shrug. 'Whatever you say. I'm not that keen on her anyway.'

He rose from the plinth, thrust his hands in his pockets, and strolled away in the opposite direction to Bronagh.

Cormac watched him go, not trusting him for a second. What had he heard him say? 'It should happen tonight.' It wasn't hard to guess what was on Malachy's mind. His blood boiled – Bronagh was only twelve.

Deciding that he had not given his sister sufficient warning, he strode after her, still clutching Fintan's implements. When he reached the kitchens, he found Mrs Kavanagh in a foul mood and Bronagh nowhere in sight.

'Where is she?' he demanded of Margaret.

'She came in just now and said she'd gotten horribly sick outside.' Margaret's expression was anxious. 'She's so unwell she's had to go straight up to bed. Mrs Kavanagh's furious but it can't be helped.'

'I want to go up and see her,' he said, alarmed that Bronagh could lie so convincingly.

'You'll do no such thing, lad,' Mrs Kavanagh barked from across the kitchen. 'You've your own work to be getting on with. Margaret can look in on her in a while. Out of here now with those tools. We've a dinner to put together and we're down a pair of hands.'

She started shouting orders to the kitchen maids who scurried to do her bidding. Helpless, Cormac retreated from the kitchens, worried that the cook had prevented him from giving his sister the most important cautioning advice she had ever needed.

Later that night, he lay in the stable loft, sleep far beyond his reach. An image of Malachy's insolent face floated before his closed eyelids; he trusted the boy to heed his warning as much as he trusted him to do an honest day's work. Could his and Bronagh's arrangement still be going ahead? Cormac couldn't let such a thing befall his sister.

After dithering a while longer, he rose from the straw. If their rendezvous was happening, it would have to be after all the other kitchen servants had retired for bed, and the blackest part of the night would suit Malachy and his ungallant intentions. Intuition told him that now was the moment to go and investigate. He hoped to God there would be nothing to find.

He slipped down the ladder from the loft without disturbing his fellow stable hands and picked his way carefully across the lower level of the stables in the pitch dark. He knew the dimensions of the building with his eyes shut but there was no telling which careless chap might have left a sack of grain abandoned on the earthen floor. It would do no good to trip and make a noise – if Malachy was skulking about, he wanted to catch the boy, not give him a chance to run away.

Out in the cobbled courtyard, a sliver of moonlight guided him to the door of the kitchens. His stomach sank; a flickering glow glimmered through the gap at the bottom where all should have been darkness at this late hour. He squirmed as he imagined finding Bronagh and the head gardener's grandson locked in an embrace. He could already feel his face flaming with the embarrassment it would cause. But better that than to allow his sister's virtue to be compromised.

Bracing himself, he lifted the latch and pushed the door open. He was relieved to discover Bronagh sitting alone at the bench, a candle beside her on the kitchen table. It seemed she was still waiting for her companion to appear. Maybe he had succeeded in scaring Malachy off after all?

She had been staring miserably down at her lap but looked up in fright at the sound of the door opening. It occurred to him that this was an odd reaction, considering the impending tryst. Her eyes widened upon recognising him and she leapt to her feet.

'What're you doing here?' she hissed.

'I came to stop this,' he said, closing the door behind him. 'I won't allow you to be so thick-headed.'

Her eyes flashed. 'Go away. You don't tell me what to do.'

'Yes, I do,' he said. 'I'm the only man in your family. If Da were here, this is what he'd do to protect his daughter.'

She looked aghast. 'You have to leave now.' With a grunt, she tried to shove him back to the door.

He refused to budge. 'When's Malachy coming?'

She just shook her head and pushed harder, but she was no match for his strength.

He grasped her shoulders. 'Bronagh, think about what you're doing. He'll ruin you.'

Shrugging out of his grip, she said, 'You don't know what you're talking about.'

His laugh was harsh. 'D'you believe he loves you? His intentions aren't honourable. He'll take what he wants and then thrust you aside without a care for what becomes of you. Haven't you thought about the consequences? You'd lose your position here. Your reputation would be destroyed and who'd marry you then? For Christ's sake, *think*!'

She wrapped her arms around herself as if she were cold. 'That'll only happen if he gets caught. And he won't.'

'If *he* gets caught? There are two of ye in this situation. And make no mistake, he'll hang you out to dry if it comes to it, saying you lured him in and suchlike.'

'No, it was his idea!' she protested. 'Him and the others!'

His mouth went dry. 'The others? What d'you mean?'

She tucked her lips in, pressed tight like she would never speak again.

Cormac narrowed his eyes. 'When's Malachy supposed to be getting here?'

She said nothing.

He seized her shoulders again and shook her hard. 'Tell me what's going on! What've you done?'

She gaped at him in shock; he had never been so rough with her before. 'It'll be fine,' she said. 'We'll get away with it.'

'Get away with what? What's happening tonight?' His breath stuck in his throat. 'Is Malachy already here?'

She hesitated and then nodded.

'*Where?*'

After a long silence, she said, 'They were going to start in the drawing room...'

He let go of her as though she were a burning coal and she flopped down on the bench.

'He's stealing from the big house,' Cormac said, stunned. 'And you're helping him?'

All of her bravado leaked away as her chin lowered and wobbled. 'I am,' she whispered.

He sat on the bench and put an arm around her. 'Why on earth would you get mixed up in such a harebrained scheme?' he chided gently.

'Malachy needs the money.' She gulped. 'He says if he makes enough he'll be able to marry me in two years. He wants to leave Carlow and take me to America.'

So beneath the tough exterior she was just another young, infatuated girl with ambitious dreams.

'You've got to tell me everything,' said Cormac. 'What arrangement did the two of ye make for tonight?'

'I was to come downstairs at midnight and unlock the kitchen door to let him in. I've to lock it again after he leaves. Tomorrow some things might be noticed missing but there'll be no telling where they've gone and no proof of who took them.'

Cormac shook his head; only dim-witted Malachy could have come up with a plan of such little finesse.

'How'd you get the key?' he asked. 'Did you steal it from Mrs Walsh's set?'

'No!' She looked affronted; he almost laughed at the irony of it. 'It hangs on a hook by the door.'

'Has Malachy ever set foot in the house before? How'd he know where to go?'

'I told him where all the rooms were. This morning I convinced one of the housemaids she was needed elsewhere and delivered the tea things to the drawing room myself so I could look 'round and see what could be taken.' Shame made her cheeks glow red.

'And he brought others with him?'

'Two.' Her lip curled in distaste. 'I didn't know they were coming.'

'Bronagh,' he said, endeavouring to be patient, though a desperate urgency fired through his veins. 'They're going to get caught.'

She peered up at him fearfully. 'Don't say that.'

''Tis the truth. Malachy's too greedy and won't know when to stop. He'll start with the drawing room and then the library and then he'll see no harm in searching upstairs and he and his friends'll make noise and be discovered. I've got to stop him.'

'No, you can't! He'll be raging!'

'I don't give a damn how he'll feel. I'm not letting him steal from Oakleigh.' Apart from the detrimental effect it would have on his sister's position if the thieves were found out, it was a thundering disrespect to the finest property in the country.

'I won't let you leave this kitchen,' she said, a little of her earlier fire returning.

He stood and strode to the door that led above stairs. She jumped up and dashed past him, trying to block his way.

'Cormac, please!'

'For the love of God, think sensibly!' he exploded. 'If Malachy gets caught, who d'you think he's going to blame for giving him access to the house? And he won't even be lying! You're in serious trouble and the only way to save you is to get him and his cronies out of the house right now.'

A shadow of uncertainty crossed her face and he pressed on, 'If you do have a fancy for him, then this is in his best interests too. You don't want to see him locked up, d'you? Or worse?'

That hit home. After a momentary sagging of her shoulders, she straightened up. 'Then I'm coming with you.'

'No, you're not.'

'He won't listen to you but I might be able to convince him!'

There was no time to debate with her any further; they had delayed long enough.

'Fine. Make sure you're quiet.'

She hopped out of his way and he pulled open the door, hurrying for the kitchen stairs. She had said the thieves were going to start in the drawing room so that was where he would begin his own search, although he didn't think they would still be there if their plan was to make swift work of the place.

He realised he had been giving Malachy too much credit for intelligence when he and Bronagh emerged into the entrance hall, saw the drawing room door ajar, and heard loud whispers coming from within.

Shaking his head in disbelief, he marched across the hall, Bronagh hastening to keep up behind him. Though he was unafraid of Malachy and his boys, he eased the drawing room door open with wariness to survey the room inside.

A grimy lantern rested on the mantelpiece and by its meagre light he could make out the scene before him. He spotted Malachy's greasy hair first, falling across his face as he bent over in front of the fireplace to cram something into a deep sack. Two other youngsters whom he did not recognise were huddled by Bridget's grand piano, laying out their spoils across the long back of the instrument. From what he could see, silver had been their goal, and they were counting out an impressive array of candlesticks, spoons and frames, ready to fill their own sacks.

He pushed the door open as wide as it could go and it produced a faint squeak at its uttermost extension. The thieves looked around in alarm but Malachy visibly relaxed once he saw Cormac standing there.

'Relax, lads,' he said. 'We're not in any danger.'

His companions didn't look convinced. Malachy straightened and flashed a wicked grin when Bronagh appeared by Cormac's side.

'This fellow's the brother of our little accomplice tonight. He's not going to tell on us or he'll get his baby sister into all kinds of trouble.'

Cormac clenched his jaw. Malachy was, of course, right. His only hope was to persuade the boys to see sense and leave before someone else discovered them.

'Put the sacks down and walk away,' he said, his voice even. 'Just get out now, while ye still can.'

Malachy laughed, not even attempting to keep quiet. In a brash gesture, he swept a silver-framed mirror from the wall behind him and placed it in his sack. It made a chinking noise as it settled against the other stolen goods.

'I'm warning you,' said Cormac, 'this won't end well if ye stay. At the very least, you'll be shaming your grandfather who's served the Courceys for decades. At worst, you could be facing a convict ship or a noose.'

'There's nothing you can say to stop me,' Malachy said, unconcerned. 'But you should tell your sister to go back to the kitchens. She's still got a job to do.'

Bronagh stiffened and Cormac clutched her hand to give her support.

'Malachy, please change your mind,' she said, her voice not betraying the quiver he felt in her fingers. 'There must be another way to make money than selling things belonging to Oakleigh.'

'For sure, but this is by far the easiest,' Malachy tossed back and his companions chuckled.

'You tell the hussy,' one said, while the other raised his own sack and began packing it with the silver items on top of the piano.

Cormac was by no means going to stand around and allow his sister to be called a hussy. He darted forwards, seizing the shirt of the first lad while wrenching the sack out of the other's hand.

'Take back what you said,' he growled, 'and then all of ye walk out of here and never set foot on this property again.'

The boy screwed up his face as though waiting for a punch to be delivered. Cormac felt more than happy to oblige but, as he let go of the lad's shirt to pull back his fist, a censorious voice stopped him in his tracks.

'None of you move or I will shoot you dead.'

He whirled to see Mr Buttimer standing in the doorway, clad in a nightshirt and nightcap. The sight of the stodgy butler in such casual attire would have been amusing had it not been for the two grim footmen who flanked him and the pistol he held raised before him. One of the footmen, Denis, had seized Bronagh's arm and she struggled helplessly in his grip.

Cormac watched as Mr Buttimer's face altered upon recognising him. Any hope that the butler might see the situation as it truly was, with Cormac trying to stop the theft instead of being involved in it, disappeared as the man's expression went from disbelief to disgust.

His gaze alighted on Malachy next, who was swearing under his breath. This time Mr Buttimer's surprise was not so great, though his revulsion intensified even further.

'Caught in the most despicable act,' he said through gritted teeth. 'You shall all receive justice for this.'

Chapter 14

Bridget stirred as a firm hand shook her.

'Miss, you have to get up.'

When she dragged her eyes open, she realised that the shutters were closed and not even a fragment of daylight penetrated the bedchamber. Was it still night then?

'Ellen,' she slurred. 'What time is it?'

Setting a candlestick on the bedside table, Ellen said once again, 'You have to get up, miss.'

This time Bridget caught her urgent tone. She sat up, the bedcovers falling from her shoulders. 'What's wrong? What has happened?'

Shadows playing across her face, Ellen said, 'There's been a burglary in the house. Her ladyship wants you by her side as soon as you're dressed.'

'Oh, my goodness! Has Garrett been wakened too?'

'No, miss, he's still asleep in his chamber. Her ladyship desired this to be a family matter only.'

She would say no more and Bridget understood that she would only get further details from her mother. She hastened out of bed; Ellen assisted her in dressing and then led her to the study.

Despite the very late – or very early – hour, Lady Courcey was in full attire with not a pleat of fabric nor a hair pin out of place. She sat in a wingback chair, hands folded in her lap. Inexplicably, Bridget could read a note of excitement in her mother's countenance.

'Mother, will you tell me what has happened?'

Lady Courcey did not answer, instead indicating that Bridget should take the chair beside her own. With the two ladies facing the room at large, Bridget had the impression of waiting to be attended by royal courtiers.

'Ryan, you may send in Buttimer now,' said Lady Courcey.

The lady's maid departed and the butler entered, his face as grave as though someone had died. He moved to stand in the centre of the room. He too was dressed, though the last two buttons of his vest were improperly fastened.

'Buttimer,' said Lady Courcey, 'you have given me the briefest account of the events which have taken place in this house tonight. I now wish you to provide me and my daughter with a thorough description of the particulars of this most contemptible occurrence.'

'Indeed, my lady,' said Mr Buttimer, bowing. 'As I said to you a short while ago, when I was forced to have your slumber disturbed with this shocking news, by which I myself am so appalled, considering some of the offenders are your ladyship's servants and therefore in principle under my command, a lapse in authority for which I do so humbly beg your pardon, though it must be admitted that the male culprits are outdoor staff and hence not in my direct line of responsibility, and the girl, being a scullery maid, ought in truth to be held to Mrs Kavanagh's account—'

'Yes, yes, go on.'

The butler cleared his throat with a sanctimonious cough. 'To give you a full report, my lady, Mrs Walsh and I had completed our nightly duties as we always do before retiring to bed—' He looked stricken. 'That is to say, before retiring to our *separate* beds for I would never—'

'I understand, Buttimer.'

'Ahem, quite. Our duties upstairs fulfilled, we went upon the assumption that Mrs Kavanagh had done likewise downstairs, as that is her area of dominion, a fact which she has stated to me on several occasions, for she does not wish me to excessively supervise her responsibilities down in the kitchens, though she said it in rather more indelicate terms than that...' At an arched eyebrow from his mistress, he propelled ahead, 'The manor went to sleep, family and servants alike, as usual. But I was roused during the night by' – he reddened – 'a matter of a personal nature, and being thus alert I thought I heard a distant noise in the lower part of the house. Stepping out into the corridor, I heard it again. Voices. I could tell at once that they were not people who had any right to be in the manor at that hour.'

Bridget had been listening to the butler's long-winded and pompous account with amusement but she felt her mirth dissipate at his last words. Intruders inside the house and its inhabitants asleep upstairs? She shuddered at the idea.

'I was swift to wake my footmen, two strong lads with sensible heads on their shoulders. I knew they could be relied upon to act with courage should the situation turn violent. Though I had no intention of using it unless strictly necessary, I brought with me the pistol which his lordship—God rest his soul—bestowed upon me when I gained my position here as butler in order to best protect the household in times of need, which duty I do hope I filled tonight to the best of my—'

'You did. Continue.'

'I led the footmen downstairs, feeling it only right that as head of the staff I ought to lead our advance upon the intruders. I was wary for an ambush from any side but at length

I ascertained that the voices were coming from one location, the drawing room. I signalled to the footmen that we should approach with care.'

Not for the first time, Bridget wondered whether Mr Buttimer was a war veteran of some kind – could he have had some involvement in the rebellion thirty years ago, defending the 2nd Baron from angry rebels?

'It sounded like the trespassers were having an argument, which meant we were able to reach the drawing room without detection. Our presence being a surprise, I was able to neutralise a retaliation from them with the threat of a shot from my pistol. They carried no weapons to speak of and desisted with vocal protestations but no physical violence. I ordered my footmen to detain them down in the kitchens and wasted no time in alerting Mrs Walsh who got Miss Ryan to waken your ladyship so the deplorable incident could be brought to your attention.'

He bowed again at the conclusion of his report but Lady Courcey did not deem him finished yet.

'What were they trying to steal?'

'The silver, no doubt with the unpardonable intention of selling it on.'

'Remind me, how many intruders did you count?'

'Five, my lady. Four lads and one girl.'

'And how many did you recognise?'

Bridget saw him shift with discomfort and, strangely, glance in her own direction.

'Three.'

'Thank you. You shall now get your footmen to escort these criminals into my presence to answer for their actions.'

'At once, my lady.'

After the butler had departed from the study, Lady Courcey said, 'This is an unimaginable state of affairs.' Her tone was sombre and yet there was still that animated glint in her eye; she seemed to be quite enjoying herself. 'The perpetrators of this crime must be suitably punished, do you not agree?'

Recalling the vision of strangers rooting through the manor house a floor below them, Bridget did not hesitate to reply, 'Yes, they must.'

Her response appeared to give Lady Courcey immense satisfaction.

Mystified, Bridget said, 'Ought we not to have Mr Enright present though?' Part of the agent's role was to serve as the resident magistrate on behalf of the Courcey title; his attendance seemed pertinent to the proceedings.

'It would take too long to send for him at this hour. He may administer my judgement in an official capacity at a later stage but I wish to dictate it without delay.'

Mr Buttimer soon returned with the information that the offenders were outside the study, ready to be brought in when it pleased her ladyship to receive them. She waved a hand and they filed in, escorted by one of the footmen. Bridget's gaze slid over the boys she did not recognise and instantly latched on to the face of the last person she would ever have expected to see here.

She could not prevent her audible gasp, though her hand flew to her mouth to stifle it. Cormac met her eyes, his expression strained but not ashamed. He straightened his shoulders and took his place in the line next to...was that his *sister*? She was more successful at smothering her shock this time, though she was no less astonished. What justifiable reason could have brought Cormac and Bronagh into contact with this band of burglars?

With the presentation of the criminals, she had no further reason to wonder why Lady Courcey was relishing this incident so much. Of course she would be too impatient to wait for the proper course of justice when here was an opportunity to crush

Bridget's longstanding connection with Cormac once and for all. For had Bridget not only just agreed that the thieves had to be punished? That meant imprisonment at the very least, if not... Her heart thudded in her chest. There had to be a rational explanation for this. There *had* to be.

She looked at the rest of the boys in the line. They were lads of maybe fourteen or fifteen, no older. One of them seemed familiar and she thought she might have seen him working in the gardens once or twice, but the others were strangers to her. All three had a disagreeable air about them, with grubby clothes and shifty expressions, and she was positive they were the true instigators of tonight's crime. But convincing her mother of this would be an enormous task.

Mr Buttimer stepped forwards. 'My lady, the identities of the offenders have been established. This boy here is Malachy Kelly, grandson of Fintan Kelly who has tended Oakleigh's gardens these forty years. The pair next to him are his supposed friends, Seamus Sheedy and Billy Maher. Malachy has been working as a gardener on the manor grounds since April of this year but the other two are not known to us on the staff. I would venture to say that Fintan will be outraged by his grandson's actions and have sent for him to come to the house as soon as possible to attest to that.'

Malachy looked unperturbed by his grandfather's imminent arrival.

Mr Buttimer continued, 'The last two are Cormac and Bronagh McGovern, brother and sister, in your employment as a stable hand and a scullery maid. Their father is deceased and they begged for their mother not to be informed of tonight's events. Cormac says he can speak for them both.'

Cormac inclined his head to corroborate the butler's statement. Bridget stared at him, willing him to communicate to her what was really going on but his attention was fixed upon

Lady Courcey as she had just risen from her seat. For the first time, Bridget wished she was already the baroness. She had no power here but that of persuasion. And Lady Courcey was out for blood.

Her gaze raked along the line. Seamus and Billy were the most frightened and shrank before her. Malachy looked resentful while Bronagh's chin jutted out in defiance. Cormac seemed the calmest of them all.

She addressed them in cutting tones. 'Do any of you deny that you were in the drawing room of this house tonight?'

They all shook their heads.

'Do any of you deny that an act of theft was taking place in the same drawing room?'

They shook their heads again but Cormac's eyes narrowed and Bridget could see why. Lady Courcey was phrasing her questions so that all five could be condemned together, without individual voices.

'You therefore acknowledge involvement and culpability in this crime. I have already sent for the constabulary to remove you from the premises. For those of you who have been in my employment, I regard this as the most profound betrayal of trust and a terrible reflection upon your positions as servants in my household.'

Cormac's voice rang out. 'Can't we present a defence, your ladyship?'

Bridget admired his nerve and peeked sideways at her mother to gauge her reaction. The lady's mouth tightened but she seemed to still feel she had the upper hand for she indulged him by saying, 'I can see no evidence to the contrary of what I have just pronounced. Do you have facts to offer which can prove otherwise?'

'I do, m'lady.' He paused. 'Though I'm reluctant to tell them as they may be seen to place my sister in a bad light.'

Bridget threw him a sharp look. Did he have a way of absolving himself from this fiasco while implicating his sister still further? That did not sound at all like his nature, and yet if even one of them could get out of this without a sentence of imprisonment, death or transportation, then perhaps that could be considered a success...

'Indeed?' sneered Lady Courcey. 'Proceed.'

Cormac took a breath. When he spoke again, his words were slow and deliberate and it was clear he was making a conscious effort to sound more formal in his manner of speech. 'My sister is only twelve, your ladyship, and impressionable. She is far too young to be having romantic notions but Malachy Kelly turned her head with empty promises. She agreed to meet him tonight because, in her innocent mind, she believed he wanted to talk and get to know her better. This is where I acknowledge my sister's foolishness at not having the sense to recognise the risk she was taking. While I cannot say for certain what would have happened, if anything of a scandalous nature had occurred between them the blame would have had to be laid upon Malachy, him being three years older and taking advantage of a gullible girl with sentimental feelings.'

Bridget was watching Bronagh when the maid's eyes flicked towards her brother and then focused back on the floor. This version of the story was new to her. A quick scan of the room assured Bridget that no one else had noticed the furtive glance. Malachy looked furious but Cormac's words continued without a break, hindering his protestations.

'For my part, I deem it fortunate that this was not what Malachy had intended because I could not stand such a thing befalling my own sister. However, the alternative was no better. He and his friends were waiting in the courtyard when she unlocked the kitchen door. They pushed past her and disappeared into the house, despite her efforts to stop them. I am sure you will forgive a twelve-year-old girl's powerlessness in preventing three lads older and bigger than her from doing exactly what they wanted.'

Lady Courcey did not react to this remark.

'When she saw the sacks in their hands, she could tell they were up to no good. She knew she should inform someone but feared how it would look for her, considering she had unlocked the door through which they had gained access to the house. So she went to a person she could trust.' He shrugged and went on, 'I was asleep in the stable loft. She woke me up and told me what had happened. I too wanted to avoid wrongful blame being placed upon her so I sought to resolve the situation by myself. I followed the boys into the house and was trying to convince them to leave when Mr Buttimer and his footmen found us. I understand how it may have appeared but neither my sister nor I had any involvement in the theft because we bear too great a respect for the rich history of Oakleigh and a deep pride in being able to serve here.'

Malachy seized his opportunity as soon as Cormac stopped speaking. With a snort, he said, 'That's all drivel. The two of them are up to their necks in this too, I swear it.' His face lit up with dawning inspiration. 'In fact, it was the other way 'round. *We* were trying to stop *them* from stealing.'

This assertion lacked so much credibility that Bridget was confident even her mother could not fail to see it. Nevertheless, the lady pursed her lips in deliberation before addressing Cormac again.

'It seems we have one person's word against the other. In the interest of erring on the side of caution, and bearing in mind that your presence in the drawing room cannot be denied, you and your sister will still have to go with the constables.'

'Ask Mr Buttimer,' Cormac said loudly. 'He will tell you who to believe.'

It was a bold thing to prevail upon the butler like that but, to Bridget's surprise, Lady Courcey turned towards Mr Buttimer, seeking his opinion. He too looked taken aback but puffed out his chest.

'My lady, you know I am a man of profound morals and can only ever speak the truth. I am therefore compelled to confess that Malachy Kelly has not proved himself to be the most reliable or honest person in the course of his employment as a gardener at Oakleigh. He has received several warnings about his behaviour, and his grandfather has even been obliged to refer him to me for castigation. Cormac McGovern, on the other hand...' The butler glanced down the line to where Cormac stood. 'I have never been able to fault his hard-working attitude or his loyalty to this estate. John Corbett, the stable master, speaks very highly of him. As for his sister, I cannot claim to know her so we may need to consult Mrs Kavanagh for a true assessment of her character.'

The look on Bronagh's face told Bridget that the cook's testimony would be liable to harm her case instead of help it.

'No need,' she interjected. 'I can vouch for her myself. I have encountered Bronagh on a number of occasions this summer and can say that in all instances she has been a cheerful and charming girl. The idea that she might be involved in this is preposterous.'

Both Cormac and Bronagh maintained bland expressions at this fanciful description. At that moment, there was a discreet knock on the door and the second footman, Denis, entered.

'Fintan Kelly's here, sir,' he told Mr Buttimer.

After a nod from Lady Courcey, the butler said, 'Bring him in.'

The aged gardener stalked into the study, no trace of infirmity in the way he held himself erect. When he laid eyes upon his grandson, his jowls quivered in anger. He swept his cap from his head and faced Lady Courcey.

'M'lady, I can't apologise enough for my grandson's outrageous behaviour.'

This startled her. 'Do you not wish to verify the validity of the accusations against him before accepting them as fact?'

He clicked his tongue. 'I'm not one bit surprised to hear them and can readily believe he's been acting the fool. He's a shame to my family and to Oakleigh and a sound punishment is all he deserves.'

Malachy's jaw dropped upon hearing his grandfather defame him in such a manner. It was plain that up until this point he had expected his connection to the old man to acquit him from any harsh sentence.

'Granda,' he began in indignation, but a glower from Fintan silenced him.

'Do with him what you will, m'lady,' he said. 'And please accept my humblest apologies for the sins of a boy who's no longer a grandson of mine.'

With that, he jammed his cap back on his head and stamped out of the room again.

Confronted with the severity of the old gardener's contempt, everyone perceived that, in a debate of truth between Malachy and Cormac, the odds were overwhelmingly in Cormac's favour. Lady Courcey looked as livid as Fintan Kelly as she realised what she must do.

'The girl and her brother are free to go,' she muttered. 'But,' she said with a vindictive gleam in her eyes, 'they shall each be docked a week's wages for having become embroiled in such an appalling incident. In fact, the girl shall be docked two weeks on account of her loose behaviour, be it innocent or no. I will not have servants engaging in clandestine meetings at midnight on my estate, even if it is just to "talk".' Her tone implied just how much she believed that element of the story.

In light of where they could have been heading when they departed from the room, Cormac and Bronagh seemed disinclined to make any objection to this.

'As for these others...'

Lady Courcey turned her ruthless gaze on the three lads. Billy's chin trembled but Seamus was scowling at Malachy, who appeared to be in a state of utter disbelief.

'Attempted theft of such valuable property is a most serious crime. Had the silver been removed from the premises, a penalty no less than hanging would have been appropriate. Given that the goods are still present and intact, I shall be merciful and consider transportation instead.'

Bronagh swayed as though she might faint at the thought of her would-be sweetheart being banished all the way to Australia.

Bridget hastened to speak up. 'And that would be a just punishment for hardened criminals beyond saving,' she said, nodding vigorously at her mother. 'Although I suppose we must be fair and take into account the young age of these boys and the fact that this is their first offence. A term of imprisonment may well be the more proportionate sentence.'

Lady Courcey gave her a calculating look. After a pause, she said, 'An extremely long term of imprisonment then.'

Some of the tension in the room eased as the threat of transportation receded.

Just then, another knock on the door and a clinking of keys heralded the appearance of an anxious Mrs Walsh. 'My lady, the constables are here.'

To Bridget's consternation, Constables Quirke and Tierney strode into the study. She sent up a silent prayer that they would not allude to their encounter with her at The Pikeman in front of her mother – that revelation was the last thing needed tonight. But they were preoccupied with the matter at hand; Constable Tierney was bouncing with excitement, while Constable Quirke looked like he wished for nothing more than his bed.

'Your ladyship,' he said, 'who do you wish us to take into custody?'

Lady Courcey swept a hand out to indicate the felons, her gesture coming to a reluctant stop just before the McGovern siblings. Bridget read the disappointment on Constable Tierney's features – his judgement of Cormac that day in Ballydarry was not to be borne out after all.

'Take them away,' the lady commanded. 'I shall ensure my will in this affair is conveyed to my representative in the court proceedings.'

She jerked her head to communicate her dismissal of all present. The constables herded out Malachy and his friends, all three dumbfounded at the way events had unravelled, and Mr Buttimer flapped at the others to follow suit.

Bridget stared at Cormac as he left the study. Just before he passed through the doorway, he cast a glance in her direction. His expression was one of deepest gratitude.

When the door had shut on the last retreating back, Lady Courcey turned to her daughter.

'I hope you will not learn the hard way the consequences of such leniency,' she said with a rather ominous insinuation. Before Bridget could respond, she went on, 'If he has woken, Mr Lambourne will want to know what the commotion was all about. You shall not feel the need to tell him any more than the barest details of what has transpired. And I will tell Buttimer not to let this spread among the servants.'

The lady's message was clear: the fewer people who knew about the incident, the better. On the surface, it did no good to gossip about such grave matters. But furthermore, the attempted theft had exposed a real danger to her property and even her person, had the thieves made it upstairs and been of a more cunning or murderous variety than Malachy and his cohorts. She didn't want anyone else to be made aware of that vulnerability.

'I understand,' said Bridget, and she reached out tentatively to touch her mother's arm.

Lady Courcey gave a cold shrug and turned away.

***

The enormity of the risk Bronagh had taken only seemed to dawn upon her once they left Lady Courcey's forbidding presence. Her knees buckled in the hallway outside the study and Cormac had to support her all the way down to the kitchens.

Although sunrise was near, it was not yet time for the servants to begin their working day so the kitchens were empty. The constables steered their charges towards the back door but Malachy twisted in the older constable's grasp and stretched out a beseeching hand to Bronagh. She fell into his arms and he touched her cheek in a tender gesture quite unlike anything Cormac had ever seen in his behaviour. He wanted to smack the boy's palm away but permitted them this final moment – they would never have another. Malachy leaned in close and whispered something in Bronagh's ear. Then the constable jerked him away and he, Seamus and Billy lurched out the back door.

When they had disappeared, Bronagh let out an anguished sob and, abandoning the tough exterior she always worked so hard to maintain, wept on Cormac's shoulder with the desolation of a young girl whose world had ended.

'I'm so sorry,' she choked. 'I n-never meant to c-cause such trouble.'

'I know,' he said, stroking her back. 'Don't worry anymore about it. You're out of harm's way now.'

Her tears gradually diminished to intermittent snuffles. After one last hiccup, she wiped her eyes, thrust out her chin, and vanished through the door that led to the servants' stairs. It would be a long climb to her bed at the top of the house, her footsteps heavy with a misery she would bear alone. She would be too proud to divulge this incident to anyone, even Margaret. With a rush of compassion for his stubborn sister, Cormac headed back to the stables, where he would also keep his silence.

Now it was mid-afternoon and he was grooming Bonny in her stall after a bout of exercise in the paddock. He suppressed a jaw-breaking yawn; he was weighed down by fatigue, thanks to lack of sleep and the strain of the previous night's events. At least no one was keeping an eye on him beyond the half door. He didn't envy Bronagh who was enduring an exhausting day under the watchful gaze of Mrs Kavanagh. However, that was a great deal preferable to being escorted by a constable to a sentencing in a courthouse. While her heart was bruised, her reputation and position were secure.

As were his own, but it had been a close call. It had required some quick thinking on his part, not to mention a helpful contribution from Bridget which she had been in no way obligated to provide.

A light rap on the half door made him look up. As though his thoughts had summoned her there, Bridget stood beyond it.

'May I come in?' she said, as if she were at the door of his home.

He waved his arm in a flourish. 'Any visitor's welcome in my grand dwelling.'

She gave a small smile but it was quick to evaporate. She glanced over her shoulder before slipping through the half door and he wondered if Mr Lambourne or Lady Courcey lurked in close proximity. He doubted whether he had the energy to face either of them right now.

'I'm alone,' she said. 'I told them I wished to investigate stable space for our guests' horses.'

He nodded. He knew about the impending birthday celebrations; the whole staff was in a state of frenzy preparing for them.

She approached Bonny and rubbed the mare's forehead affectionately. Then she turned to him and said in a low voice, 'I want to talk to you about last night.'

He picked up a brush and busied himself with Bonny's white coat. 'I can't say enough how sorry I am it happened.'

'You do not need to apologise. I know very well you had no involvement. Your sister though...' Her teeth caught the tip of her tongue. 'Did she have something to do with it?'

Sighing, he said, 'She did, the daft girl.'

Bridget's brow creased. 'Then perhaps I should not have defended her.'

'Please don't regret it. She's been foolish but she knows now what she did was very wrong. The shame'll stay with her a long time, 'specially when our family feels the pinch of the cut wages.'

'I do wish my mother had not resorted to that measure. Still, perhaps there will be compensation some other way.' There was a secretive air about her as she said this but she did not elaborate, instead saying, 'You are sure we can trust her?'

'I'm sure. That Malachy Kelly was a rotten influence. With him gone, she'll never do anything like that again.'

'I hope that is true. I would hate to think I had compromised the security of the manor.'

'You haven't,' he assured her. 'And I'm very grateful for your kind words on her behalf, although calling her a cheerful and charming girl might've been pushing it a bit. She's so sullen sometimes, I want to wring her neck. But she's a good girl at heart. She just has some growing up to do yet.'

'Well, she has a decent older brother to help her out there,' Bridget said, smiling. 'One who exhibits a fine grasp of formal language for a stable hand, I have to say. You acquitted yourself admirably in front of my mother.'

He felt his cheeks go red. 'Arrah, I couldn't have spent so many years 'round you and not pick up a fancy word here or there. But I can't say 'tis a habit that'll catch on. Apart from the fact that my family would be quick to tell me I was having notions about myself, it takes too much effort to pronounce everything right.'

She let out a soft laugh. 'I suppose that is true. Speaking of your family, Ellen told me it has been augmented by the recent return of your sister from Dublin. I am so glad for you that Mary has come home.'

'Thanks. My mother's been in better spirits since she's come back.'

'I am very pleased to hear it,' said Bridget.

He chose not to mention that while his mother seemed happier, his sister did not. In truth, he was worried about her. She flitted about the cottage like a ghost and hardly stirred herself to take care of her own child, save to nurse him. After the first night, she refused to speak of her husband or her time in Dublin. He had urged her to go visit Ellen, since they had been such close friends as young girls, but she had greeted the suggestion with a lethargic shrug. He hoped she would soon settle and become content with her lot in life, altered though it was from what she had expected it to be.

In the silence that followed, the only sound was the brush flicking along Bonny's coat. Bridget's lips parted like she was going to say something else. He looked down, focusing very hard on removing the dirt with short strokes.

When he looked up again, she was shutting the half door behind her.

Chapter 15

The guests began to arrive the following day. Bridget found that her enthusiasm for the imminent festivities had been tempered by the grave events surrounding the burglary but, when the first carriage rolled up the avenue, she resolved to put all sombre thoughts from her mind. The incident had passed and it was now her duty to be a delightful hostess.

She and Garrett went outside to welcome their visitors, reaching the bottom of the front steps as the carriage drew up and a footman jumped down to open the door. Madeleine Wallace emerged, auburn ringlets bouncing around her face, and gave a squeal of excitement when she saw Bridget.

'Oh, you are a dear angel for inviting us!' she exclaimed. 'I shall be forever indebted to you for brightening the dullest summer of my life!'

Her sister, Catherine, alighted next from the carriage, assisted by her husband, Mr Howard Spencer, a limping gentleman twenty years her senior. Theirs had been a match arranged by her parents and, judging by her grimace as she sidled out of his grasp, it was not an especially happy one. Bridget experienced a dart of gratitude towards her mother that she had refrained from inflicting such a fate upon her.

They had scarcely returned to the house when the next carriage pulled up, this one carrying Garrett's companions, the

Ashford brothers and their cousin, Mr Matthew Parnell. A third carriage, bearing Miss Isabel Gardiner and the Misses Hyland, arrived later in the afternoon, by which time there was quite the merry atmosphere all around. A long-time London acquaintance of Garrett's, Lord Newby, happened to be visiting Dublin for the summer and he also travelled down to Oakleigh, though he was the last to make an appearance, not arriving until the next morning.

It had been years since Oakleigh Manor had been so full of life. Every bedchamber was occupied, every stall in the stables contained a whinnying horse, every seat was taken at mealtimes, and every corner of the house overflowed with laughter and chatter from morning to night. For the servants of the household, such a large company signified extra toil in washing, cleaning and cooking, so Bridget had ensured in advance that Mrs Walsh enlisted several local girls to help cope with the enormous workload.

Garrett's twenty-sixth birthday occurred two days after the guests arrived and the entire group celebrated the day with entertaining pursuits. In the morning and afternoon, they held a number of bowls tournaments, starting with individual contenders, then pairs of gentlemen and ladies, and lastly male and female couples. The Hyland twins proved to be an unstoppable force but Garrett and Bridget won the couples tournament to the cheers of all assembled.

In the evening, a sumptuous dinner was to be followed by a night of dancing in the ballroom. Before she went down, Bridget sent for Ellen and asked her to be discreet in bringing Garrett to her bedchamber.

'It is nothing untoward,' she promised upon seeing Ellen's shocked face. 'You may leave the door ajar and listen to reassure yourself.'

Still looking doubtful, Ellen withdrew to obey her instruction and Garrett came in soon after, glancing around in curiosity.

'I don't quite know what to make of such a summons,' he said, winking at her.

She blushed. 'I'm aware this is not quite proper, but I wanted to give you your birthday present in private.'

She held out a small item wrapped in a navy satin cloth. He took it from her and removed the cloth to reveal a striking pocket watch with a gold chain attached. There were some scratches on the casing but the metal shone with long years of assiduous care.

He gaped at it, astounded. 'It is exquisite, my darling. Where on earth did you get it?'

'It belonged to my father. It was the only thing of his that my mother allowed me to keep. I want you to have it.'

He closed his hand over it in reverence. 'This means so much to me. Thank you.'

'I wish you the happiest of birthdays,' she murmured, voice thick with emotion, and they embraced.

As he held her, her feeling of contentment was disturbed by the prospect of London but she pushed it away, determined that the evening would be one of perfect bliss.

They descended the broad mahogany staircase together and led their guests into the dining room for a lavish feast, which was presented with great formality and grandeur. Much later, they continued the party into the ballroom, where a group of musicians struck up a lively waltz as they entered. Garrett guided Bridget onto the floor and then, after waiting for the leading couple to dance a few bars on their own, other pairs began to join in. Mr Spencer declined to partake on account of his limp but his wife accepted Lord Newby's offer to dance with alacrity. Bridget observed that Mr Parnell partnered an enchanted Madeleine three dances in a row and wondered if she was witnessing a match in the making right here in her ballroom. The younger Ashford brother, meanwhile, defied convention and twirled around by himself, waving his arms in the air and calling for more wine. The atmosphere was carefree and festive, and Bridget did her best to convince herself that nothing could make her happier in this moment.

***

Cormac rubbed his eyes as he closed the door of the last stall. The stables had never been so full and his working day had never been so long than since the fine folk from the city had come to stay. It was well after dark and he was looking forward to nothing more than his bed of straw in the stable loft but, just as he started to climb the ladder, he heard his name being called and turned to see Liam's lanky form silhouetted inside the stable doors.

'Don't you want to come to the kitchens? Mrs Kavanagh might be generous with the leftovers tonight, seeing as she put on a spread for about a hundred.'

He considered the suggestion, decided his bed could wait a little longer if a chance to sample Mrs Kavanagh's delicious desserts was in the offing, and jumped back down from the ladder. He and Liam left the stables, crossed the courtyard and entered the kitchens, where he got the immediate sense of the aftermath of a storm. All around the room, red-faced maids slumped in exhaustion on benches, the hearth and even the floor, looking as though they had simply collapsed where they stood. Half-empty dishes lay discarded on the kitchen table, including the remains of some giant fowl in a bed of vegetables which must have been the magnificent centrepiece of the birthday dinner. Most mouth-watering of all, he spied a few leftover slices of two tarts and a cake down at the further end of the table. Mrs Kavanagh herself sat in front of them, arms folded over her enormous bosom as she surveyed the carnage with immense satisfaction.

'All went off without a hitch,' she announced to Cormac and Liam. 'Mr Lambourne sent back a message of his particular appreciation of the raspberry tart.'

'No surprise there. Everyone knows your tarts have no equal,' said Cormac, though he didn't think the cook required much buttering up tonight. He approached the table. 'Raspberry, you said?'

'Help yourselves, lads, help yourselves!' she said, beaming, and they did not hesitate.

Margaret and Bronagh, huddled in the corner by a stack of freshly scoured pots, laughed at their enthusiasm, though Bronagh's laugh was rather shaky. The previous night, she and Cormac had gone home to confess their absent wages to their mother. He had advised Bronagh to invent a story about a breakage in the kitchens while he himself had claimed the necessity to set aside some money to replenish the supply of nails in his father's tool chest; the last thing their mother needed was to learn of the near disgrace that had come upon her two children. Even though Maggie had tried to hide her dismay, Bronagh had perceived it and her remorse had been palpable. She would feel raw about both that and the loss of Malachy for a long while yet, but at least the ache would ease with time and it gladdened Cormac to see her making an effort to be cheerful tonight.

He was on his fourth bite of tart when the inner kitchen door opened and Ellen entered. She too looked fatigued, though not quite as much as the kitchen staff did.

'Lady Courcey has just retired to her bedchamber,' she told Mrs Kavanagh. 'The young people are still dancing but her ladyship says our duties above stairs are finished for tonight.'

'Thank heavens for that.' The cook heaved herself up with a grimace. 'Now I can go and rest my weary bones.'

She departed from the room with a pointed remark about expecting a spotless kitchen the next morning, to which the maids responded with grudging acquiescence. Once she was gone, Ellen sat in her place and helped herself to some of the raspberry tart too. The atmosphere remained relaxed, in spite of her position above the other servants. She displayed none of the airs and graces her French predecessor was rumoured to have had in abundance, nor was she like the supercilious lady's maids who had accompanied their mistresses to Oakleigh for the birthday celebrations but did not deign to socialise in the kitchens. Her approachable manner gave Margaret the courage to slide onto the bench next to her, an eager look on her face.

'Tell us, Miss Ryan, what was it like? I want to know every detail!'

Ellen smiled and began to recount all the things the lowly maids below stairs were not permitted to see, the fashionable gowns and dazzling jewellery and elegant hairstyles. '...and one of the young ladies was wearing a dress the colour of autumn leaves. I heard her tell Miss Muldowney she had purchased it in London.'

'London!' Margaret said, entranced. 'Ah, how I'd love to see it.'

'Miss Muldowney herself had a beautiful comb of pearls in her hair. Everyone commented on how striking she looked.'

'And what about the gentlemen?' Margaret pressed, her eyes starry with romance. She had always been the most fanciful of Cormac's sisters, captivated by stories of chivalrous knights and rescued maidens and everlasting love.

'Needless to say, Mr Lambourne was the handsomest man in the room,' said Ellen. 'I was there attending to her ladyship when he and Miss Muldowney commenced the first dance together. He danced so well, she was in raptures in his arms!'

Cormac pushed away the last few pieces of tart as he recalled that he could not dance at all.

'And the musicians?' It was plain that Margaret wished to paint a vivid picture in her mind of the whole occasion.

'Oh, they're very talented. In fact, if we go outside we might be able to hear them. Lady Courcey had Denis open the ballroom windows for air before she retired for the night.'

Margaret hopped up at once, all tiredness forgotten. She dragged a half-hearted Bronagh to her feet and then turned to Cormac. 'You coming?'

'Of course he is,' said Ellen, 'and so is Liam.'

Liam, who had gone a little red with all the talk of dresses and dancing gentlemen, now turned the deepest shade of beetroot.

'I don't—' he stuttered.

'You'll come if Cormac comes, won't you?' she said and glanced at Cormac with her eyebrows raised.

He understood her meaning and rose reluctantly. 'Fine, we're coming.'

Margaret clapped her hands and was first out the back door. Bronagh gave a shrug that said she was open to any form of torment to procrastinate the rest of the washing up and went after her. Cormac, Liam, Ellen and some of the other more curious maids followed.

Out in the courtyard, faint strains of music wafted to them, becoming stronger once they went around the side of the house. Moving along until they could see the open ballroom windows but were out of sight themselves, they stood and listened to the swelling music and the buzz of animated conversation of those dancing to it.

Margaret's face lifted towards the stirring sounds. 'I want to dance to it,' she said dreamily.

'Then let's,' said Ellen straight away. 'Cormac will dance with you and I can dance with Liam.'

Cormac had to smother a chuckle at his friend's petrified expression. It might be said that a lady's maid could do a lot better than a stable hand but the greater truth was that Ellen could do a lot worse than quiet, dependable Liam. She took a firm hold of his hands and Cormac followed suit with his sister. The other maids joined in too, giggling.

He stood on Margaret's feet three times and almost tripped her up before she said she might try Bronagh as a partner instead.

'I'm sorry,' he said. 'I've never been able to dance.'

''Tis only that you've never learned.' She patted him on the arm. 'If you practised it, you'd get better.'

He could not envisage any future where he would be required to practise dancing but he just gave her a good-natured kiss on the cheek and allowed Bronagh to step in. Leaning against the wall of the house, he watched the others dance – Liam looked to be holding his own surprisingly well, judging by Ellen's radiant smiles. Cormac pictured Bridget twirling in her fiancé's sure grasp with the same sparkle in her eyes. The raspberry tart rested like a heavy ball in his gut and he wished he had gone straight up to the stable loft after all.

There was a lull in the music and the servants, laughing and breathless, ended their dance with bows and curtseys.

***

The sky outside was beginning to lighten when the revellers in the ballroom chose to retire. Climbing the staircase to bed, everyone congratulated Garrett once more on his birthday and applauded Bridget for hosting a superb party. She beamed at her guests through her exhaustion and made her way to her bedchamber. She had barely eased the pearl comb out of her hair, however, when she heard a knock and opened the door to find Garrett on the threshold. He put his finger to his lips, slid inside, and closed the door behind him.

'What—' she started in surprise, but he cut her off with a tight embrace and a passionate kiss on her mouth. She giggled but pushed him away. 'No, we mustn't.'

'Oh, but we must,' he said and kissed her again.

This time he was rougher, pressing her back against the nearest bedpost. She struggled to break free of his grip and slipped sideways onto the bed, her curls tumbling around her shoulders. He leaned over her and attempted a seductive smile.

'Come to me, my darling,' he slurred.

'No!' She slithered under his reaching arm and darted to the opposite end of the room. 'You are intoxicated. Please leave.'

He staggered on the sheepskin rug. 'But we're going to be married soon. Why not enjoy our wedding night a little earlier than planned?'

Appalled at the suggestion, she spluttered, 'Absolutely not! Leave me this instant.' She pointed to the door to emphasise her order.

He shot her a disgruntled look, swivelled on his heel in a vain attempt at dignity, and stumbled out. She expelled a ragged breath and stared at the door, which he had left ajar. What a way to ruin the end of what ought to have been a perfect evening.

The little sleep she attained was broken and unsatisfactory; every time she began to drift off, she felt the hard wood of the bedpost digging into her back and smelled the alcohol on his breath. She supposed she was at fault for having placed Garrett on such a high pedestal, but this was a disheartening way for him to fall.

When she left her bedchamber later that morning, he stood outside it wearing an expression of utter contrition.

'Darling,' he said as soon as she appeared, 'how can I ever make sufficient apology for my conduct last night? I'm ashamed beyond belief. You must think me a thuggish lout but I swear I did not mean to offend you and I am so very sorry for it. Can you find it in your heart to forgive me?'

She gave him a disapproving glare. 'I shan't pretend that I wasn't shocked at the way you behaved. Please do not ever repeat it.'

'Never,' he vowed, grasping one of her hands. 'Truly, I cannot say what came over me. I don't think I have ever had that much to drink in my life, let alone in one night.' He winced. 'And I have the pain in my head to prove it.'

She smiled against her will. 'It serves you right.'

He grinned and then became serious. 'I promise never to upset you like that again,' he said and brought her hand up to press it to his cheek.

'Very well,' she conceded, and they went down to breakfast reconciled.

Chapter 16

Over the next week or two, the August weather became punctuated by heavy rainstorms which burst into existence with sudden force and then slunk away as though they had never happened. Bridget, Garrett and their company were obliged to stay indoors and entertain themselves by playing cards and billiards while they waited for the storms to pass. Once the conditions turned fine again, they engaged in outdoor activities, the guests determined to make the most of their sojourn at Oakleigh, which all agreed to be an exceptional country estate.

On one such fair-weather day, the gentlemen seized the opportunity to fish on the banks of the Sruhawn, while the ladies opted to take a stroll down the tree-lined avenue. As they emerged from the front door of the manor, Bridget saw that the blue sky was populated with thick, white clouds which billowed and roiled, never keeping the same shape for long. It reminded her of a game she had played with Cormac when they were children: they used to lie side by side at the very bottom of the abandoned limestone quarry, faces pointed up to the sky, and pick out various shapes in the clouds before they swirled into something unrecognisable. Her greatest triumph had been a cloud which had coiled itself into a letter 'B', although Cormac had disagreed, saying it looked more like a turnip with holes in it.

Nostalgia tugging at her, she followed the other ladies down the front steps and onto the avenue, the fine gravel crunching softly beneath their shoes. A fresh breeze blew about them and she drew her shawl tighter around her shoulders as she listened to her companions lament the changeable conditions.

'It is a shame we have not yet been able to enjoy a picnic,' said Madeleine's sister, Catherine, her expression nonetheless cheerful, as it always was in the absence of her aging, limping husband. 'It would be disgraceful if we came all this way and never had a meal out of doors.'

'Yes, but there is no telling what this weather will do next,' Miss Isabel Gardiner said, squinting skywards. 'Judging by this bright day, I could declare that we ought to go ahead with our picnic right away but, knowing my propensity for misfortune, it would pour down on us before we had the blankets laid out.'

The others laughed.

'What we need,' said Madeleine, 'is a country person. I've heard they have an excellent understanding of weather patterns. I'm sure they could forecast it for us with no difficulty.'

She peered around, ringlets swinging. Just as Bridget was on the verge of making a quip about Madeleine expecting a country person to spring out of the ground at her command, her friend announced, 'There's one, shall we ask him?'

Turning, Bridget saw Cormac making his way around the corner of the manor house. He carried a tool chest in one hand and a few lengths of timber over his shoulder and appeared to be heading for the avenue, just like the ladies. Her insides somersaulted at the sight of him.

'Excuse me,' Madeleine called out.

He approached them, keeping a secure hold on the timber. The breeze lifted his fair hair, tousling it across his forehead.

'Can I help you, miss?' He addressed Madeleine, as she had been the one to hail him.

'Yes, can you tell us if you think it will rain today? We are debating whether to have a picnic but do not want it ruined by the weather.'

He shook his head. 'Today's not the day for a picnic, miss. Looks to me like it'll rain in about ten minutes. D'ye see that blacker cloud over there?'

They swivelled as one to where he pointed and saw that there was indeed a darker cloud blooming among its white companions.

Isabel said, 'Oh, dear.'

'My advice would be to stay near the house today. Save the picnic for a brighter afternoon.'

He started to move on past them. Isabel, however, eyed him up and down in appreciation and, to Bridget's intense annoyance, said coyly, 'But will you not get wet yourself if you keep going? You did say it will rain soon.'

He gave the briefest glance towards Bridget as he turned back to them but she could not tell whether he had picked up on the brazen nature of Isabel's remark. He just said, 'That's a risk I'll have to take, miss. There's a fence down near the entrance needs mending and it's got to be done today, rain or shine.'

Isabel pouted prettily at him but did not say anything else. He made to go again, passing Bridget as he did so. Without warning, he caught her eye, murmured, 'I see a bear,' and winked before striding on down the avenue.

She felt a grin spread across her face. He too had remembered the game. She gazed upwards and glimpsed the bear, its paw raised as though waving, just before the head floated away from the body and the cloud became another misshapen form.

'What did he say to you?' asked Catherine.

'Oh, he wished us a pleasant walk,' said Bridget, the internal parts of her body still pitching about madly.

Meanwhile, Madeleine was saying in a scandalised voice, 'And you, Miss Gardiner! Flirting with a servant, whatever will you do next?'

Isabel tittered, a rather irritating sound to Bridget's ears. 'You could all see he has good looks. It was just some harmless fun!'

Thinking Isabel was a more vacuous girl than she had taken her for, Bridget cut in, 'Let's walk on, shall we?'

Less than a quarter of an hour later, they were hurrying back to the house for shelter as the black cloud opened above them, just as Cormac had predicted.

The following day, however, the afternoon was sunny and warm with seemingly little chance of rain, so the group decided to have their picnic at last in the manor gardens. They sat on blankets laid out on the grass, munched on delicious refreshments prepared for them in the kitchens, and played a rematch of bowls, the men quietly intent on beating the formidable pairing of the Misses Hyland.

Within an hour or two, Bridget found she was developing a bad headache. When the exuberant laughter and heated debates over scoring became too much for her, she took Garrett aside and told him she might go indoors.

'Are you quite well, my darling?' he asked.

'I'll be fine. I just want to lie down for a short time until the headache passes and then I shall come back out.'

'If you are sure—oh, good shot, Newby! Knocked her right out of the way.'

Accepting that his attention would always be divided while sports were at play, she gave him a resigned smile and went into the house. She lay down on her bed, hoping a brief nap might cure the headache, but after a few minutes the pain worsened so she thought perhaps a stroll in the fresh air would do her more good. Not wanting to disturb the kitchen staff, doubtless already in the throes of dinner preparations, she slipped out the front door and walked around the side of the house to get to the cobbled courtyard. She glanced about for Cormac but he was nowhere to be seen. Trying to ignore her disappointment, she passed by the stables and the paddock and opened the gate into the Gorteen.

***

Cormac tossed the mouldering rail onto the growing pile at his feet. He was down near the entrance to the avenue again, making further repairs to the boundary fence which divided the manor grounds from the rutted lane beyond. Closer scrutiny yesterday on what had appeared to be a couple of posts fallen into decay had revealed a whole section of fence turned rotten and a bigger task than he had anticipated. He had been obliged to enlist a second pair of hands to help and Liam had joined him to rebuild it. They laboured in companionable silence until he found he was too curious to keep quiet.

'So,' he said casually, as they lifted a new length of timber into place. 'Ellen Ryan?'

He thought Liam would only manage an incoherent stutter but, with no trace of a blush, the lad said, 'Miss Ryan puts the lady into lady's maid.'

Impressed by this unexpected eloquence, Cormac picked up his father's hammer and drove a long nail into the wood. 'D'you think you'll ask for her hand one day?'

'Might not get the chance. Where her ladyship goes, Miss Ryan's got to go too, and Dublin might as well be America for all the good it'll do me.' Liam shrugged. 'Besides, I've a ways to go before I'm worthy of her. I can't offer marriage 'til I've a bit of money saved and a decent home to take her to as well.'

Liam was scarcely a year younger than him but Cormac felt as though the boy had just matured into a man in front of his eyes. As he opened his mouth to wish him heartfelt luck in his endeavour, he realised he could no longer sense the heat of the sun on his back and looked up to see the sky darkening with ominous clouds. A stiff wind plucked at his sweat-dampened shirt and, without so much as a spit of warning, heavy raindrops began to pelt down.

''Tis going to be a monster of a storm,' he called over the instantaneous noise, and they gathered up the implements from his father's tool chest and ran for cover. As they reached the top of the avenue, they spotted the picnickers abandoning their bowls match and hastening indoors.

Their first duty upon returning to the stables was to settle the horses, which had become skittish at the onset of the turbulent weather. Then, in a rare instance of idleness, they stood at the double doors with John Corbett and some of the other men and simply stared out in awe at the torrential downpour. It pounded against the windows of the big house and struck the cobblestones with enough force to drown out the horses' fretful whinnying. Large puddles swelled across the courtyard, spreading like a spilled inkpot on a sheet of paper. Beyond the orchard wall, the tops of the apple trees flailed about and Cormac pictured the fruit making its premature descent to the ground. Even as he watched, the light diminished to the mere visibility of dusk, the storm clouds looming low and black.

All of a sudden, a rectangular glow materialised in the gloom as the back door of the kitchens swung open and none other than Mr Lambourne dashed out into the rain. His valet, Brewer, followed on his heels, hunched against the deluge as though exposure to it would bring about certain death. They splashed across the cobbles and sprinted into the stables, causing the congregated men to jump back from the doorway to make way for them.

'Have you seen Miss Muldowney?' Mr Lambourne exclaimed. 'Is she here?'

Cormac grew alarmed at once. 'Isn't she in the house?' he demanded in return, adding quickly, 'Sir.'

'We've searched all the rooms but cannot find her, and the servants have not seen her for hours. Could it be possible that she has taken refuge in one of the outbuildings?'

'She's not here in the stables,' said John, 'but maybe she's in one of the barns or the orchard.' He signalled to the two stable hands nearest to the double doors. 'Go check them out, chaps, and be quick about it.'

They ducked out into the pouring rain. Cormac itched to follow them.

'Did she take her horse?' John asked the remaining men.

Having only just calmed the mare in her stall, Cormac said, 'No, Bonny's still here.'

'That means she's on foot then, wherever she is.'

Mr Lambourne ran his hands through his damp hair, looking frantic. 'She must have gone out before the storm began. She could be anywhere, and caught in *this*!'

John stayed calm. 'She might yet be discovered on the grounds, sir. And, if not, we'll send out a party to search for her right away. We'll find her, don't you worry.'

Cormac shifted from foot to foot, impatient for the return of the two stable hands. At last, they came running through the doorway, rainwater streaming from their clothes.

'No sign of her, sir!' one of them gasped to Mr Lambourne.

John was swift to take charge, sending Brewer back indoors to seek the aid of every male servant who knew how to ride. Mr Lambourne did not hesitate to authorise the use of any horses belonging to the guests, declaring that they would be only too happy to offer what assistance they could. John nodded his gratitude and turned back to the men.

'Listen up! We'll go out in pairs. Ye two, make for Ballydarry, she may have taken refuge in one of the dwellings there. The rest of ye, spread out in every direction, towards the Sruhawn, the woods, the hayfields. Check any likely place where she could've found shelter. She mightn't see nor hear ye coming so be thorough. And keep alert for thunder and lightning. If it starts, take cover or ye'll be in danger yourselves. Saddle up now, fast as ye can, and let's bring her home safe!'

There was a flurry of movement as the men hastened to the stalls but Cormac ran up to the stable master. 'The quarry, John!'

'The quarry?' he repeated, mystified. 'What reason would she have to go that far, and on foot no less?'

Desperation and conviction rose in Cormac in equal measure. ''Tis a possibility. We shouldn't rule it out!'

Arguing the matter would only cause further delay.

'Fine so, you and Liam head for the quarry. Hurry now!'

By the time he led his horse out of its stall – a fine specimen belonging to Lord Newby – the footmen and guests' valets were flocking into the stables. Mr Lambourne called for Commander to be saddled too but John put out a restraining hand.

''Tis best you stay behind, sir,' he said, 'so you can be here when we get her back to you.'

Mr Lambourne's shoulders drooped and he stood aside to let Cormac tear past, Liam right behind him on his own mount.

The clatter of hooves as they rode out of the courtyard was lost in the din of the storm. Out in the open, the full force of it truly registered and Cormac gasped as the rain battered on his head and back. Thankfully, Lord Newby's horse didn't shy at being plunged into such tempestuous conditions and

Cormac pushed forwards across the Gorteen, not checking to see whether Liam kept up with him or not.

The limestone quarry lay beyond a thin belt of woodland to the south of Oakleigh, in the shadow of the Blackstairs Mountains. When it had been deserted during their childhood, it had afforded them an ideal location for a variety of hide-and-seek games. After Bridget had left the estate, he had sometimes visited it by himself and hidden in one of her favourite spots, recalling the echo of her laughter around the stony pit that had always given her away, but once Lord Walcott ordered work to restart there it became a hive of activity again and he was no longer able to extract that little bit of comfort. He hadn't been back in years and there was no reason why she would return there herself. It was a mere bear waving in the sky which drove him towards it now but he cleaved to that hunch with all his might.

A flash of brightness on the horizon made him flinch in his saddle. Several seconds later, a loud crack rumbled all around them. He glanced back at Liam who urged his horse up beside him to shout, 'Shouldn't we—?'

'You can. I'm not.'

It was reckless but he didn't care. He did mind the fact that Liam followed him without further objection, but that couldn't be helped.

They raced across field after field until they reached the shelter of the woods, by which point they were soaked through, their sodden clothes sticking to their skin. Caution compelled them to slow their pace under the trees as the animals could trip over an unseen root if they were not careful. Impatient, Cormac guided his horse along as fast as he dared.

The canopy of foliage deadened the noise of the storm to an extent, enabling Liam to call from behind him, 'Are you sure about where we're going?'

Cormac only nodded in reply, his whole being concentrated on the way ahead. He cast perfunctory glances to left and right and did not protest when Liam shouted for Miss Muldowney at regular intervals, but his instinct told him she had not taken cover in these trees.

On the other side of the strip of woodland, they were able to increase their pace again. Wind and rain whipped into his face but he disregarded it. He strained to see any sign of the quarry; he knew it was somewhere nearby, though the murk veiled even the lofty mountains from view.

Then a blaze of lightning lit up the way and revealed the boundary of the pit not twenty feet in front of him. Only for the timely flare of light, he would have pitched unseeing over the edge. As it was, he had to halt his horse with a sharp jerk of the reins, skidding on the muddy ground. The animal neighed in fright and he gave it a reassuring pat on its neck before dismounting, his joints stiff with the wet and cold. Liam pulled his horse to a stop next to him and did likewise.

They both scanned the quarry but it was too dark to make out anything other than vague mounds of stone far down in the bottom of the hole. The workers had abandoned the site in their own rush for shelter and it appeared quite as forsaken as when he and Bridget used to play there.

'Can you see her?' he yelled above the raging wind.

Liam chewed his lip as his gaze roved over the pit plunging down before them. Another flash illuminated the scene.

'What's that over there?' he bellowed, pointing.

But Cormac had seen it too. As the light died, he glimpsed something fluttering among the inert boulders. Was it a piece of fabric, the hem of a dress maybe?

He thrust his reins into Liam's hands. 'Keep him steady while I go down there.'

He approached the edge of the quarry and began to pick his way down into it. The rock was slick from the heavy rainfall and he more or less slipped towards the bottom, unmindful of his torn clothes and grazed skin, until he got to the place where he imagined he had seen some movement. Casting around, he thought for a heart-stopping moment that he had been mistaken, that there was nothing here and they were no closer to finding her, but then he distinguished a bare arm stretched out on the ground. He darted forwards. She lay crumpled behind a large boulder, her sleeve ripped and flapping in the wind. Relief flooded through him but it dissipated when he saw her closed eyelids and slack mouth. Was she unconscious? Or worse?

'Bridget!' he cried in panic, dropping to his knees beside her.

She did not respond. He touched the side of her head. His fingers came back dark and sticky before the rain washed them clean again. Terrified, he bent down close to her parted lips. There was a beat of ringing silence, during which he could no longer seem to hear the storm, as though the thunder and wind were suspended by the same dreaded anticipation that filled him, and then he felt the lightest quiver of breath on his skin. She was alive.

The gale resumed in his ears as he lifted her into his arms and turned to make the treacherous ascent back up the wet slope. Struggling up the incline, he was grateful when Liam appeared beside him and together they managed to get her to the top of the pit. Liam had tied the horses to a bush and the two animals stood waiting, eyes rolling. Cormac handed Bridget's limp form to Liam, leapt up onto his horse, and took her back, settling her with care in front of him.

'You go on ahead!' he called down as Liam untied the horses. 'I'll be slower now with two of us. You go on and tell them we're coming.'

Liam nodded, jumped onto his own horse, and swung around to gallop back the way they had come. Cormac followed, trying not to jostle Bridget unduly. She was like a wounded bird in his grasp, frail and motionless. Her hair and clothes were saturated and her skin was freezing to the touch. The blood he had found came from a grim-looking gash at her temple. Petrified for her life, he clung to that delicate, barely perceptible rise and fall of her chest that told him she was still breathing. He held her close to try to pass some of his own body warmth on to her, a somewhat futile gesture for he was almost as cold as she was and wracked by violent shivers.

'Hold on, Bridget,' he whispered, willing her to obey his plea.

She made an effort to rouse herself. 'Cormac?' Her voice was feeble.

'Shush.' He put his lips to her ear. 'Don't worry, we're not far from home.'

His horse picked its way through the narrow strip of woods and then they were riding back across the fields, keeping to the lines of hedges as much as possible to avoid being out in the open. He wasn't sure but he thought the storm might be moving away towards the east. The thunder and lightning had diminished and the wind too had lessened to an extent, though the rain still pelted down. He was just thinking they had to be nearing the big house when the giant's claw loomed out of the gloom. Only a few fields to go. Offering up a prayer of thanks, he pressed his horse forwards on one final spurt.

'Just a bit further, *a ghrá*,' he murmured to Bridget, tightening his arm around her waist.

He rode into the courtyard to find it almost empty of people, the rest of the men still out searching, but Mr Lambourne stood waiting in the rain beside Liam, his arms outstretched to take his fiancée. Exhausted, Cormac surrendered her to him and the gentleman whisked her inside the house at once. He nearly fell as he tried to get down from the horse himself but Liam was there to help.

'There are some spare clothes in the stables,' he told Cormac. 'Mrs Kavanagh said to get changed and come into the kitchens. I met John so he's gone out to spread the word that we've found Miss Muldowney.'

Cormac soon sat on a stool in front of the kitchen hearth in dry clothing, although his hair was still plastered to his head and his hands and feet were numb. He had a blanket wrapped around his shoulders and he huddled towards the fire, urging his chilled bones to heat up. The cook patted him on the back as she handed him a bowl of steaming soup.

'Well done, lad,' she said for the twentieth time. 'Bless you for bringing the young lady home safe.'

Margaret and Bronagh, all work forgotten, clustered near their brother and discussed the state of Bridget, whom they had glimpsed as she was carried through the kitchens upstairs.

'She was pale as death,' Bronagh said in a rather detached manner. 'That wound looked nasty too.'

'Will she recover?' Margaret's tone was hushed.

Bronagh lowered her voice too so that Mrs Kavanagh, who was passing some soup to Liam at the kitchen table, would not hear. 'Depends. I remember when she and Cormac used to go larking about in all weather. Back then, she had the constitution of a horse and no fear of her. But now...'

'What's different now?' asked Margaret, and Cormac grimaced at the many possible answers to that question.

'Haven't you seen her since she's come back? She's a proper lady now, gotten used to easy living. She's so frail a strong wind could blow her over. In fact, it wouldn't surprise me if that's what happened to her today.'

Just then, the back door opened and several more men trooped inside, dripping water. Mrs Kavanagh clicked her fingers at Cormac's sisters and they scuttled away to help her distribute soup, while he slid his stool to the side of the hearth to make room for the others.

He hated to admit it but he had to agree with Bronagh. Seven years of a soft life in the city had transformed a robust, healthy girl into a far more fragile young lady. He feared Bridget would not get through this ordeal without great difficulty.

CHAPTER 17

Cormac was right. Tidings spread around the estate the next day that Miss Muldowney was confined to bed, gravely ill with a fever, and her fiancé would not stir from her bedside. Their guests, shocked by the terrible event and loath to intrude, departed from Oakleigh the same afternoon with best wishes for her speedy recovery. The servants, both indoor and outdoor, conversed in whispers about the young lady's poorly state and how there was a strong possibility she might not survive. Cormac felt sick whenever he overheard these covert exchanges and started going home to his family's cottage every night to avoid them, but even there it was an incessant topic of discussion.

'The craythur,' his mother took to saying over and over again. 'How awful. The poor craythur.'

On the third evening, he came home with the news that the physician had bled Bridget with no visible results, and Maggie could not seem to let this go.

'It made no difference? Didn't her fever drop even a little bit? Didn't they notice any change in her temperature at all?'

'I've no idea!' he burst out, weary of the constant questions. 'That was all Ellen Ryan could tell me. I don't know anything except she's still ill and hasn't woken up or said a word.'

He rubbed his forehead in frustration. Bridget's failure to improve was tormenting him. He kept asking himself if there was something more he could have done when he found her to prevent her condition from deteriorating so much. Everyone commended him for having returned her as safely as he did, but he waved away the praise, uncomfortable with the attention and dispirited by the lack of encouraging tidings.

When he dropped his hand, he caught his sister Mary observing him.

'What?' he said, irritated.

'Nothing,' she replied quietly.

After five days he could bear it no longer. He dawdled in the courtyard near the kitchen door after breakfast, knowing that Mrs Walsh came down to the kitchens at the same time every morning to discuss the dinner menu with Mrs Kavanagh, and darted inside as soon as the harassed housekeeper appeared.

'What is it, Cormac?' she snapped.

Dispersing with any preamble, he said, 'I want to see Bridget.'

She looked incredulous. 'That's Miss Muldowney to you. And don't be foolish. You're a servant, her ladyship would never allow it.'

'Then ask Mr Lambourne. He'll allow it.' He supposed he should feel guilty for taking advantage of the man's good nature but in this case he was beyond caring.

She frowned. 'Why do you want to see her? What purpose will it serve?'

'I don't know,' he said honestly. 'I just need to, even if 'tis only for a minute or two.'

She exchanged a glance with Mrs Kavanagh, who muttered, 'It's a brazen request but he did save the girl's life. Remember how close those two were when they were children.'

After considering this, the housekeeper gave a grudging shrug. 'I shall make an enquiry. Come back here at noon and you will find out then.'

'Thank you, Mrs Walsh.' It was as much as he could hope for.

He slipped out of the kitchens. The weather was warm and dry, as it had been every day since the ferocious storm, and the sun winked down in mockery of the dark mood that pervaded the grounds. He glowered up at it before disappearing into the shadows of the stables.

He returned to the kitchens just before noon and helped his sisters peel potatoes until Mrs Walsh arrived. When she swept in, he looked up in anticipation.

'You're to come up now,' she said, her mouth taut with disapproval. 'Her ladyship was against the proposal but the gentleman said he could not refuse. He feels obliged to you on account of you saving his fiancée's life.'

Cormac had counted on this. He nodded, laid down his knife, and followed her to the servants' stairs. She led him up through the bowels of the house to the second floor where they emerged onto a long corridor of closed doors. These were not the usual sleeping quarters for the family; a guest bedchamber must have been set aside for Bridget's sick room.

Mrs Walsh stopped outside one of the doors and knocked softly. A voice answered from within and they entered.

The room was dark; the shutters had been closed over the windows and the only light came from flickering candles on the dresser and a bedside table. By their weak glow, he saw Bridget lying in the bed, a diminutive form on the broad plane of the mattress, shivering in troubled sleep. Her skin was flushed and damp strands of hair clung to the sides of her face. There was one bandage wrapped about her head and another tied around her forearm which lay outside the bedcovers – the first bound the injury she had sustained at the quarry and the second was evidence of the physician's bloodletting.

Mr Lambourne sat beside the bed, clasping her hand. Lady Courcey stood behind him by a shuttered window. She looked displeased – no doubt recalling the last time she and Cormac had come face to face – and made no move to even acknowledge his presence, but Mr Lambourne rose as he came into the room.

'It's Cormac, isn't it?' To his surprise, the gentleman reached out and shook his hand. 'I haven't had the opportunity to thank you for bringing Miss Muldowney back to me. I am very grateful to you. As you can see, she's not well right now but when she is better she will thank you too.'

'You're welcome, sir,' said Cormac, his voice a little hoarse. 'Has there—has there been any improvement in the young lady?'

'None.'

Mr Lambourne waved Cormac forwards. He stepped to the opposite side of the bed from Lady Courcey and stared down at Bridget. Now that he was this near to her, he could see that the rumours around the estate had not been based on falsehoods or even exaggeration. She looked like she was on her death bed. Sweat coated her forehead, she was gaunt from lack of food, and her breathing came shallow and raspy. His heart sank. Could any girl survive an illness like this?

He casually rested his hand on the flower-patterned bedcover, next to where her own lay, clammy and motionless. Gazing at her closed eyelids, he imagined the dark brown eyes beneath and silently begged her to beat the fever. Fight this, he urged her. You have to get better. Please wake up.

She stirred in her delirium and mumbled something incoherent. He grimaced in despair, losing hope that she would ever recover. Was it a matter of days, or even hours, before she lost her weak grip on life? Now he knew why he had wanted to see her – it might be the last time he saw her alive. His chest constricted painfully with regret for all the things that had been left unspoken between them.

After several more long moments, during which he drank in every aspect of her, committing each detail to his memory, he looked up at Mr Lambourne and Lady Courcey.

'I think I should go now,' he said, his voice low.

'Yes, you should,' the lady agreed in clipped tones.

He surreptitiously let his hand touch Bridget's as he removed it from the bedcover. Lady Courcey shifted but passed no remark.

As he followed the housekeeper out of the room, he glanced at Mr Lambourne. The gentleman was wearing a pensive expression and did not acknowledge his departure.

Cormac went home that evening to find Mary wandering in front of the cottage with a preoccupied air. The hens pecked near her feet but she shooed them away crossly. When he approached, she looked up with a nervous glance.

'Come on, let's go for a walk,' she said, eschewing any kind of greeting.

Smothering his perplexity at her strange manner, he followed her around to the patch of woods behind the cottage, an area which had provided the McGovern siblings with excellent opportunities for amusement as they had grown up. She led him in among the trees; it was cool and dusky, and unseen owls hooted as they commenced their nightly forage for mice.

'Any more news on Bridget?' she asked without a great deal of concern.

He hesitated. 'She's still the same. I...I went to visit her today.'

Her eyes widened. 'They let you see her?'

'Her fiancé agreed to it 'cause I was the one who found her and brought her home.'

She pursed her lips as though she did not think much of the fiancé's judgement. 'And how was she?'

'Very sick,' he said, still tormented by the vision of Bridget's wasted form. 'She was delirious, she didn't know I was there. And my being there didn't please her mother.' He sighed. 'Maybe it wasn't the wisest idea to go.'

She snorted as she pushed a protruding branch out of her way. 'Of course it wasn't! I can't believe you did it.'

'I was worried about her, I needed to see how she was. Anyone else would've done the same.'

'Anyone with an ounce of common sense would've stayed away. You're just a servant. You'd no right to be there.'

It was true but he set his jaw, refusing to agree out loud.

After a beat, she said softly, 'Are you in love with her?'

He walked ahead of her without reply.

She gave a short laugh behind him. 'I knew it, I could tell. Listen,' she called, her tone growing urgent, 'don't get involved. Just keep away from her. Trust me, 'tis the best thing you can do.'

He stopped and turned to stare at her. 'What makes you such an expert on the subject?'

Anxiety creased her forehead and then she clenched her fists with resolve. ''Cause I was once in the same position you're in now. I reached beyond my station and received my just punishment for doing so.'

Bewildered, he said, 'What d'you mean?'

'I mean I've never been married. Patrick's an illegitimate child.' And she looked at him with blue eyes as clear as his own.

He was not as shocked as he should have been. The perfect husband, his tragic death – had he suspected all along? 'Why'd you lie to us?'

''Cause I was so ashamed of myself.'

He waited.

She plucked a leaf from a twig above her head and twirled it between her fingers. 'D'you know where Auntie used to live?' she asked cryptically.

'What's that got to do with—I just know her address, from writing to you. Kildare, wasn't it?'

'Yes, in a small village like Ballydarry. It wasn't much to speak of, but the road through it was used by the local gentry.'

She gazed past him with a faraway look in her eyes.

'One day, I was returning from the apothecary's house with Auntie's medicine when I saw him riding up the road. He noticed me too and I swear time stopped. We didn't say anything but kept staring at each other 'til he passed me by. Oh, it was a magical moment! I dallied at Auntie's gate to look back and caught him looking back too. I think I might've fallen in love with him right there.'

She smiled, an expression of joy which made her seem youthful again.

'He started to ride past more often and I always watched for him from the house. In a life dull as mine, it was the only piece of enjoyment I had. Every time he glanced 'round, I wondered was he hoping to spot me. About a week later, I was hanging out the washing in the garden when I heard a voice at the gate. It was him! He said he'd come 'specially to see me, that he couldn't stop thinking about me. I was terrified Auntie would see him through the window—she was a very proper lady, our Auntie—and I told him he had to leave. He asked if I would go for a walk with him that night instead. He was so nice, I couldn't help myself. I said I would, once I'd put Auntie to bed.'

Cormac could not decide if he was more appalled by his sister's lack of inhibition or the blackguard's exploitation of it.

'A walk?' he said, his tone laden with accusation.

Her eyes hardened. 'He was a perfect gentleman in every regard. He took me to a river walk on a remote part of his estate—the most picturesque place I'd ever been, with the moonlight shining on the water—and we talked for hours. Before we left, he kissed me in a way that made me feel like God had put us on this earth for no one but each other. We visited the same spot several more times over the following month or two. He said he felt privileged to share a place of such beauty with a face of such beauty. Oh, he was so gallant and romantic, what girl wouldn't have fallen for him...?'

She trailed away, lost in blissful recollection.

'So what happened?' Cormac prodded.

Her face fell. 'He left to take up residence in Dublin. He didn't want to go but he had to. I was heartbroken. I thought I'd seen his charming smile for the last time.' She dropped the leaf to the ground. 'And then Auntie died. I knew it was my only chance to find him 'cause if I went home, I'd never get away again. So I went to the city to search for him. I stole what little money Auntie had kept hidden under her mattress. It wasn't a lot but it got me to Dublin.'

'And did you find him there?'

'I did, eventually. I was overjoyed! He was so happy to see me too and came to visit me often in my room. You can judge me all you want but our passion had become too great. Patrick was conceived at that time. I didn't tell him at first 'cause I wanted to keep it for the right moment.' She took a long breath. 'And then he stopped coming to see me, without a word of warning. The next I heard of him was he'd gone to England. I couldn't understand it. He said he loved me, that I mattered to him, and yet I didn't matter enough to be told he was leaving the country.'

Cormac shook his head. Had she been so blind that she could not see he had been using her?

'But he came back last month, only a few days after Patrick was born. I hung about near his house, waited 'til he left by himself, and then went up to him and showed him his son.'

Her voice had gone husky, but she did not cry. 'He was like a different person. He said he didn't want to see me, didn't want to see either of us again. And he just walked away.'

Cormac's frustration at his sister's short-sightedness was tempered by his compassion for the pain she had endured; she had suffered atrocious treatment from this man. He drew her into a hug and she laid her head on his shoulder.

'That was when I decided to come home. There was nothing left for me in the city. It was rotten there most of the time anyway, smelly and noisy. I *was* working in a baker's but it wasn't like how I described it to yous. They were terribly mean to me. They worked me to the bone and all I got was a dingy room and one meal a day. When they found out I was with child, they kept me on but treated me even worse. I was prepared to suffer it all for him though. I loved him. I still do.'

This time, frustration won out over compassion. 'How can you be so loyal to him? He hurt you, he abandoned you and your son!'

She pulled out of his embrace. 'He made me feel alive.'

In the face of such wilfulness, he stifled any further recriminations; she would never hear them. Instead, he said, 'Why'd you tell me all of this?'

''Cause I don't want you to make the same mistake I did. I believed the son of a rich lord could be happy with a poor girl like me but I was wrong. The upper classes value money and land and social status above everything else.'

He folded his arms. 'Bridget's not like that.'

'Really?' she said with raised eyebrows. 'And who's she engaged to, a stable hand or a wealthy gentleman?'

'She's with him 'cause she loves him,' he mumbled.

'Then forget her right now. If you go on wishing and hoping, you're just going to get hurt like me. Nothing can come of it, only misery and heartbreak.'

'I'm not wishing or hoping for anything except for her to get better.'

'Even that's caring too much. But I won't advise you any further. I've said my piece. And I know you'll keep my secret,' she added, her voice laced with the merest hint of a threat.

She was right, he would. There was no point in burdening their mother with such a tale of compromised morals. Let her hold onto the poignant love story Mary had spun; she would be happier with that.

They returned to the cottage in silence. When they were almost there, a thought occurred to him. 'If you've never been married, where'd you get that ring?'

Her gaze dropped to the wedding band on her left hand. 'I stole it. From a dead woman I found lying in the gutter.' She looked at him. 'You see the desperate things my foolish love made me do? Don't let yourself sink to such a wretched state.'

He hung back as she entered the cottage, her foot swinging out at a hen which came too near. She had warned him against the risks of losing one's heart to the wrong person, but her caution rang hollow.

Because everything in her demeanour had said she would do it all again for one more moonlit walk by the river.

CHAPTER 18

As her mind came back to consciousness, she became aware of an acute ache in her temple. Her head felt as heavy as lead; it was fortunate she was lying down because she would not have been able to raise it even an inch. There was a pain in her arm too but that was more remote and easier to ignore.

Where was she? Her eyes seemed glued shut but indistinct sounds came to her – voices murmuring nearby.

'...how long more can she last?'

'...difficult to say, sir...very weak...if she does not wake up soon...'

They were talking about her. She tried to speak but her mouth did not seem capable of forming the words.

A third voice, curt and unforgiving. '...almost a week since she fell ill...your efforts have been entirely ineffective...'

'My sincere apologies, my lady...not easy to treat a fever...'

She was so tired and hot. Sleep tugged at her again but she was just too warm. If only someone would take these suffocating blankets off her. She strove to move them herself but her arms were dead weights.

'Did you see that? I thought her hand twitched.'

'It may have just been a shiver from the fever, sir.'

'No, this was different. More deliberate. Look at her eyes!'

She struggled to open them, to see who was there, to prove she was indeed awake. With a tremendous effort, she cracked her eyelids apart.

And when she saw his face, she knew, even through her exhaustion, that his was not the face she had wanted to see.

At first, she could only stay awake for short periods, just long enough to swallow some gruel. Although the fever had burned itself out, it had left her weakened and disorientated. Still, when she slept it was now a more restful slumber and, as her health improved, her speech became lucid again and she was able to recount what had happened on the day of the rainstorm.

'I had that headache, if you recall,' she told Garrett, after taking a mouthful of water from the glass on the bedside table. Her tongue felt woolly from lack of use. 'Lying down did not relieve it so I thought a walk in the fresh air would do me more good. That did indeed help, which encouraged me to keep going. I had a vague notion that I would like to visit the quarry but I started to turn back when I noticed the weather had changed. I was already too late though. The storm came so quickly.' She rubbed at the bandage on her head as her temple prickled in pain. 'I lost my bearings. The landscape looked so different in the gloom and the rain. I must have circled back towards the quarry and lost my footing at the edge. I remember very little after I fell down the slope. I think I came to once or twice but only for brief moments. The next thing I was aware of was waking up here.'

'What I cannot comprehend is why you would have had any inclination to go to the quarry in the first place,' said Garrett.

'I used to play there as a child, that is all,' she murmured.

But he was not prepared to let it go. 'Who did you play with?'

'Just a friend of mine.'

'Was it that fellow Cormac?' he said, with far more perception than she would have liked. 'The one who found you and brought you back?' When she did not answer, he asked frankly, 'What is your connection with him?'

'We were good friends growing up,' she said, unable to avoid his direct questioning any longer. 'There is no more to it than that.'

'Good friends with a stable hand?'

'He wasn't a stable hand when we were children.'

'And now?' he pushed. 'Are you still friends now?'

'No,' she said, with regret in her heart. 'Not now that he is a worker on the estate.'

He did not look convinced. 'He came to visit you when you were sick.'

Her pulse quickened. 'He did?'

'It was quite unorthodox to allow him in here but I thought I would be generous to him as he had saved your life.' Garrett arched an eyebrow. 'He looked devastated when he saw you. Not quite the reaction of a friend who is no longer a friend.'

She tried to appear indifferent. 'I don't know what you expect me to say. We spent our childhood together. Of course he is going to feel concern for my welfare, even as adults. But there is nothing beyond that. He knows his place.'

With a doubtful shrug, Garrett asked her if she would like some more water, and the conversation moved on to whether she might soon have an appetite for something more than gruel.

When he left her sick room in the evening to dine downstairs with Lady Courcey, she finally had time to reflect on that thorny exchange. Suspicion had been raised in his mind on the nature of her relationship with Cormac. She had made light of its significance but Cormac's coming to visit her was so atypical of a servant's acceptable conduct that it had been bound to provoke scrutiny.

Was it possible that Garrett had grounds to be distrustful? Cormac's actions may have shown he cared more for Bridget than he should, but his feelings were irrelevant so long as Bridget did not reciprocate them. Did she?

At the start of the summer, she had been certain of her love for Garrett – his charming ways had led her to believe no one could make her happier. However, seeing Cormac again had brought that certainty into question. Seven years away had dulled her memory of how special he had been to her, and it was only when she had returned that the strength of that feeling had come flooding back. She had spent much of the summer denying the fact but her recent mishap at the quarry had compelled her to face it at last.

It stemmed from a hazy recollection of her journey back to the manor. She had stirred from unconsciousness to find herself on horseback, encased in Cormac's arms. She had been frozen, drenched and dazed, but she had sensed his sturdy chest at her back, she had felt his lips at her ear, she had heard his words of comfort, and she had been comforted. There ought to have been more fear but she had felt so protected in his grasp.

It had reminded her of their childhood, of his solid presence throughout the distressing experience of losing her father – his swiftness to catch her when she sagged to the ground, too weak to face the reality that her dear papa was dead; his own insistence upon going to the funeral, despite the fact that his class, his religion and her mother forbade it; his expression of such burning compassion that her heart felt too full for words. The sincerity of his friendship had instilled a sheer conviction in her: she would always be safe and well with him because he would do anything for her. How had she allowed herself to forget that?

These thoughts were confusing, not to mention draining. She could feel what little energy she had sapping away even as she lay unmoving in the bed. She began to doze off, her musings scattered and unresolved. In the last moment before oblivion took over, his murmured words drifted to her again. He had probably believed her to be insensible of her surroundings but she had caught what he had said. '*A ghrá*', he had called her.

'My love'.

When she awoke the next morning, she was still alone; her mother and fiancé no longer felt it necessary to keep a constant vigil by her bedside now that it had become clear she would recover. Lady Courcey in particular, after an initial wave of maternal relief, was swift to restore her aloof demeanour, seeming almost self-conscious at having expressed undisciplined emotion. While Bridget felt hurt at this neglect, it provided her with the opportunity to send for the one person whom she was sure could answer her burning questions.

Ellen responded promptly to her summons and entered the chamber with a beaming smile. 'Miss, it cheers my heart to see you awake. You had us all so worried.'

'I am sorry to have been the cause of such distress,' said Bridget, easing herself into a sitting position, 'but thanks be to God the worst is past now. Do come and sit.'

Ellen perched on the edge of Garrett's chair. 'What can I do for you, miss?'

Bridget leaned towards her. 'I have only received vague accounts of the events that took place on the day of the storm. I'm aware that Cormac found me but I know nothing else. Can you enlighten me? Do you know what happened?'

'I do,' Ellen admitted, colouring a little as she added, 'Liam Kirwan, one of the other stable hands, told me afterwards.'

'Then tell me, and do not leave anything out.'

Still rather red, Ellen said, 'Well, when Mr Lambourne raised the alarm after the storm began, Cormac was the one who thought of looking for you at the quarry. Liam said he had a hard time keeping up with him across the fields. Cormac was intent on finding you if he had to go to the ends of the earth to do it.'

Bridget felt something inside her flutter at this. Assuming a calm exterior, she said, 'Go on.'

Ellen became more at ease as she continued her tale. 'It was foolhardy to keep riding once the lightning started, but I suppose if they hadn't it would have been much longer before you were found.' She described their headlong dash to the quarry and Cormac's reckless descent down the rocky slope. 'I saw his shirt afterwards because he brought it to his sister to be mended. It had been so ripped to shreds that Margaret just tore up the rest of it for rags.' She leaned forwards, eyes wide and animated, as she recounted the rest of Bridget's rescue. '...and after Cormac handed you over to Mr Lambourne, he nearly fell trying to get off his horse, he was so cold and exhausted. Mrs Kavanagh gave him hot soup and the best spot in front of the fire. It's hard to please that woman but Cormac could do no wrong in her eyes that day. We were all so grateful to him for bringing you back safe.'

Bridget was speechless. Cormac had gone far beyond the duty of a servant to locate her in the storm – he had risked life and limb in his efforts to do so. It was the most selfless thing anyone had ever done for her.

'I wonder how he guessed you might be at the quarry. That was very lucky.' Ellen attempted to maintain a neutral expression but it was evident that this was not the first time that question had been broached in the household.

Lacking the guile to invent an evasive answer on the spot, Bridget could only speak the truth. 'I suppose he just knows me very well,' she said, feeling she had not comprehended how much so until now. It had been their fleeting reminiscence about cloud formations that had pushed her on towards the quarry that day – she had yearned to revisit that place of youthful joy and innocence and, contrary to the version of events she had given Garrett, had grown determined to get there, even when the storm had begun to brew. She may well have died at the bottom of that hole, had it not been for Cormac's extraordinary intuition.

She did not deem her unguarded remark to be perilous in Ellen's presence but she still hurried on, 'Garrett said that Cormac came to visit me while I was sick, is that true?'

'Yes, I overheard Mrs Walsh telling Mr Buttimer how Cormac as good as demanded to see you. He'd been asking me at every opportunity how you were and I had no news to give him so I suppose he decided to find out for himself. Mrs Walsh said he got quite a shock when he saw how poorly you were. I met him that afternoon and he was miserable. I think he feared the worst was going to happen.'

'But he knows I am recovering now?'

'He does, miss. You should have seen his face when he heard you had woken. He lit up brighter than the sun and moon put together.'

Bridget lay back on her pillows, a warm glow spreading through her whole body. 'Thank you for telling me, Ellen.'

Chapter 19

Garrett's sigh escaped his lips, unobtrusive but undeniable. He endeavoured to cover it up with a cough as he cast a look of boredom to the sick room's ceiling. Even though Bridget had been disappointed by his increasing absences, she now found his restless company unwelcome. He fidgeted in his chair until her aggravation became too much to suppress.

'Is something the matter?' she snapped. 'Do you need to be elsewhere?'

'No, no, of course not.' He glanced around the dim room. 'I suppose I am a little weary of our surroundings. No doubt you too find it dreary. Never mind, it will not be very long before you are better and can leave this room altogether.'

'If the gloominess bothers you, you can open the shutters.'

'Mr Abbott advised us to keep them shut for now. Your eyes have become unused to the daylight, and we are to expose them only by degrees.'

'My eyes will be fine. Open the shutters, and the windows too. Let some fresh air in.'

With a huff, he stood to pull open the wooden shutters and unfasten the windows. Sunlight streamed into the room, engulfing the meagre light of the candles. The brightness did sting her eyes but she said nothing; more soothing was the refreshing breeze that wafted in. Garrett went to the dresser and the bedside table, blew out all the candles, and then sat back down again. The transformation of the room had a mellowing effect on them both – they smiled at each other, abashed.

'I'm sorry if I have been short with you,' she said, offering her hand in a gesture of peace.

He took it and kissed her knuckles. 'I am sorry too. I should be more supportive. You have been through a terrible ordeal.'

'Let us talk about something else, something positive. Have the apples ripened in the orchard yet?'

'I have no idea,' he said, amused, 'but there cannot be anything more positive to anticipate than our upcoming nuptials. That has to be the most exciting event in any girl's life!'

Her responding smile was tight. 'Of course.'

'Now that the summer is drawing to a close, we shall be returning to Dublin very soon and then you can begin making your preparations for the most wonderful wedding in living memory.' He patted her hand. 'The other girls are going to be so jealous of you, even more so when they see you heading off to the glamorous city of London.'

Her attempt at pleasantry promptly disappeared. 'London again,' she complained. 'Must you keep bringing that up?'

He frowned. 'Yes, I must. We have many arrangements to make with regard to moving your possessions, choosing our servants, and so on. We cannot delay much longer.'

'But I told you I do not want to go to London.'

'And I told you it was not your decision to make.'

'Are you going to force me?' she said, shocked. 'When I become your wife, will my opinion cease to matter?'

He folded his arms. 'This is childish behaviour. Stop pretending that you do not understand how society works. A woman must obey her husband in every respect, you know this very well. Your obstinacy will get you nowhere and I won't tolerate much more of it.'

Eyes smarting, she turned away from him. 'I think I need to sleep now.'

'Yes, perhaps you will wake with a more sensible attitude towards marriage,' he said waspishly, and he left the room without another word.

She stared at the wall, sleep the furthest thing from her mind. Was that really her fiancé who had just left her side? Such nastiness was incongruent with the man she had promised to marry back in March. Did that charismatic, attentive gentleman even exist? Or was it all a facade – had he merely dazzled her the way she had seen him dazzle the maids time and again?

With a sinking heart, she could see that he was unyielding about taking her to London. He had brushed aside her refusal to go with such indifference that it was clear her view on the subject was of no consequence. He saw her as his inferior; her wishes were to take second place to his own. She was only a woman, after all.

Was every woman consigned to this fate when she married, dismissed as easily as a child or a dog? No, she resolved at once. When she was growing up, she had been witness to a happy marriage based on a foundation of mutual support and compromise, not in her own home but in Cormac's. Jack and Maggie McGovern had built a home and raised a family together, sharing the pertaining burdens and joys. Was it therefore a question of social class? If she were poor, would she be treated more equally by her spouse? Such a theory spoke volumes about the shortcomings of the upper classes to which she belonged.

Sighing, she rolled onto her back and gazed up at the decorative cornices that bordered the ceiling. For the first time, she felt stifled at the thought of her future. No decision would be in her control; Garrett would command her in every way. Did she trust him to choose what was best for both of them? Perhaps he believed this move to London would make her content. There was no denying that she would rise higher in society and participate in a far more dynamic social calendar than she had ever known in Dublin. Maybe she would find herself indebted to him for bringing her to such a vibrant city.

Doubtful and disheartened, she fell into an uneasy slumber. When she awoke an hour or two later, an idea that had been hovering in the recesses of her mind came right to the forefront. It was as though she had marshalled her thoughts in her sleep and now she knew just what she needed in the midst of all her confusion.

Her mother came to her with the news that the physician was going to call in the evening to check on her improvement. She was about to leave the room again when Bridget called her back.

'Can you stay for a moment, please?' she said.

Lady Courcey opted to stand at the foot of the bed rather than take a seat beside it. 'What is it?'

Seeing that she was not in the mood for idle chitchat, Bridget mustered her courage and went straight to the point. 'I would like to invite Cormac to visit me here.'

'Certainly not,' said the lady straight away.

This was the reaction Bridget had been expecting and she was already armed with her response. 'I know you think it is inappropriate but you have been kind enough to allow him to come once before. At the time, I was unconscious and unable to express my gratitude for his good deed. I would like the opportunity to thank him in person for saving my life.'

Lady Courcey sniffed. 'It is unnecessary.'

'On the contrary, I feel that it is very necessary. You have raised me from childhood to always conduct myself to the height of good manners. It would be a grave mark of disrespect not to personally convey my thanks to the individual who rescued me from the clutches of death.'

'You are being overdramatic,' said Lady Courcey with the faintest touch of a sneer.

'You nearly lost your only daughter to a terrible fever mere days ago. That is not an exaggeration. I could have perished in the quarry but Cormac delivered me to safety in time. We should both be grateful to him and he should be made aware of it.'

Lady Courcey looked sour. 'Have you mentioned this request to Mr Lambourne?'

'No, but I am confident he will agree with me,' Bridget said with more conviction than she felt.

'We shall go along with what he thinks,' Lady Courcey declared. It was plain that she expected Garrett to side with herself rather than with his fiancée.

To the surprise of both mother and daughter, however, Garrett consented to the meeting. Pleased to have avoided another argument with him, Bridget cast a look of triumph at her mother and, after one last effort on the lady's part to dissuade her, Cormac was summoned.

Before his arrival, Bridget ensured that she was propped up on plump pillows, that her hair was brushed and pinned back from her face, and that a bouquet of flowers had been placed in a vase upon the dresser. The cumbersome bandage around her head had been replaced with a more discreet dressing now that the wound was nearly healed. She did not like to think of the dreadful state she had been in when Cormac had seen her last and meant to make herself fully presentable this time. Lady Courcey and Garrett positioned themselves by her bedside, one taciturn and the other contemplative. Their aloofness detracted from an otherwise pleasant atmosphere.

There was a knock on the door and Mrs Walsh entered, followed by Cormac. Bridget felt her insides flutter as they had done when Ellen had related the story of his bravery in the storm. His fair hair was windswept but he tried to flatten it down as he came into the room. His blue eyes flicked to the corner where Lady Courcey and Garrett stood, registering their cool demeanour. Then his gaze transferred to Bridget and his expression lifted with relief and gladness.

She tried to conceal her own pleasure at the sight of him as she said, 'Good evening, Cormac.'

'Good evening, Miss Muldowney.'

'I appreciate you coming to see me. I hope it was not an inconvenient time to step away from your work.'

'No, miss, I was exercising one of the horses but another fellow is looking after him now.'

'That's good.' She took a breath to steady her nerves. 'You must know why you are here. I want to thank you from the bottom of my heart for saving me on the day of the storm. But for you, I may not have survived to be sitting up in this bed right now.'

'I only brought you home,' he said with humility. 'It was the physician who made you better.'

'If you had not found me, the physician would have had no one to tend to.'

He gave her a respectful nod. 'However it happened, we're all very glad you're on the mend. Everyone in the stables and kitchens told me to give you their best. And my mother sends her regards as well.'

'That is very kind of them all. Please make sure to pass on my thanks for their concern.'

Cormac shifted uncomfortably; glancing to her side, she saw Garrett fixing him with a look of intense interest. His gaze was neither friendly nor unfriendly but he was absorbing every aspect of their exchange. Perhaps his reason for consenting to this meeting had been to get the chance to observe them together.

'Mother? Garrett?' she said. 'Could you leave us for a minute or two?'

'You have thanked him,' said Lady Courcey. 'There can be nothing more to say.'

Bridget turned to her fiancé. 'Please? Just for a few moments.'

His attention switched to her and she kept her expression as innocent as possible as he searched her face.

'Very well,' he said, 'but not for long. Mr Abbott prescribed constant rest. Prolonged visits are not advisable.'

'I shall bear that in mind.'

Garrett, Lady Courcey and Mrs Walsh left the room with several backward glances. As soon as the door was shut, Bridget patted the bedcover.

'Come sit.'

He looked a little shy as he moved forwards and sat on the edge of the bed beside her.

'Thank you again for what you did. The storm was far worse than I expected it to be. I did not realise the danger I was in.'

He gave her a lopsided smile. 'You've never been good at predicting the weather.'

She chuckled. 'True. I am so grateful to you. I shall be forever in your debt.'

'Please forget about it. I'm just glad you're safe and getting well.'

'I'll never forget it.' She hesitated for the merest second before plunging on, her desire to confide in him too great to resist. 'It was an act of gallantry where otherwise I have been exposed to the most uncivil behaviour.'

He was immediately alert. 'What's wrong?'

She dropped her gaze to the bedcover. 'It's Garrett.'

'What about him?' He sounded almost too keen to hear that Garrett had committed a transgression of some kind.

'He is making me move to London.'

There was a beat of silence and she looked up to see that he was as taken aback as she had been when she had first found out.

'*London*?'

She nodded.

'But why? Your home's here.'

'That is what I keep telling him but he does not want to listen. I believed I could convince him at least to remain in Dublin, if not in the countryside, but he is adamant that we shall go to London. The decision has been made.' She sighed. 'I do not want to go. I love Ireland and I love Oakleigh. I cannot bear the thought of going so far away.'

He swallowed but said nothing. The wall still existed between them as heiress and servant, preventing him from articulating his feelings.

And yet she wanted to hear what he was thinking. She yearned for him to open up to her with the familiarity they had once shared. The flutter inside her insisted upon it.

She grasped one of his hands. It was rough from years of toil on the estate. He stared down at her fingers wrapped around his.

'Do you want me to go?' she whispered.

Liberated, he raised his eyes to meet hers. 'Of course not. I never want you to go.'

It was all she needed to hear. Without further contemplation, she leaned forwards and pressed her mouth upon his. Taken by surprise, he did not react for a second but then all of a sudden he was kissing her back and she could tell that he had been longing for this just as she realised how much she had been longing for it too. They had always had a special connection and now she sensed it flowing between them through their lips and tongues and clasped hands. The kiss should have been clumsy but it wasn't. It felt as though they had been this intimate for years.

When they broke away, they had only a moment to stare breathlessly at each other before they heard the creak of floorboards outside the door. This time, his reaction was instantaneous; he was on his feet and standing at the end of the bed before the door had fully opened. Anyone walking in would believe that he had not moved even a foot closer while he and Bridget had been alone.

It was Garrett. Lady Courcey, Mrs Walsh and a bearded man holding a black case stood in the doorway behind him.

'Darling,' said Garrett, 'Mr Abbott has just arrived to see you. He wishes to assess your condition and advise us on how best to proceed in facilitating your convalescence. He also emphasises that you must not have any more visitors until you are quite recovered,' he added meaningfully.

Bridget nodded at her fiancé and then looked back at Cormac. 'Thank you once again for coming and for your actions on the day of the storm. Do please pass on my thanks to Liam too, seeing as you have just communicated to me that he played no small part in the incident.'

'You're welcome, miss, and I'll be sure to do that. Keep getting better. We all hope to see you up and about the place again soon.'

Then he was gone and the physician was by her side, ready to subject her to his numerous tests.

CHAPTER 20

'And that's the last of it,' the farmer's wife announced as Cormac tucked the final parcel into the nearest pannier of the pack horse.

'Thank you, Mrs McKinty,' Margaret said, passing a basket to Bronagh with care.

Mrs Kavanagh had ordered the two sisters to collect an array of produce from McKinty Farm and, as it was too much for them to carry, Cormac had accompanied them with a horse that could bear the bulk of the goods. Now laden with baskets of eggs, blocks of cheese and various cuts of meat, they left the farmyard with an affectionate farewell from Mrs McKinty, who was inclined to reminisce on the numerous times Cormac and Bridget had inveigled titbits from her when they were young.

On a dry day, such a task was a pleasure rather than a chore and the girls were in good spirits as the three of them walked along a leafy lane dappled in autumn sunlight, although a cool wind gusted about them. Cormac let their chatter wash over him without paying much attention, his thoughts deeply occupied elsewhere.

Bridget had kissed him. She had held his hand and kissed him with fervour. He could not say what it might mean in the long run, but it did signify one thing: she was having misgivings about Mr Lambourne. Her act of infidelity and her unwillingness to go to London both showed that she was no longer satisfied with the man she had chosen to marry. All summer, Cormac had stood by and endured her engagement because he believed it was what she wanted. Now he knew differently.

Mrs Walsh's words darted through his head.

'Be careful, lad,' the housekeeper had murmured to him after he had left Bridget's sick room. 'You're treading on dangerous ground.'

At the time, he had dismissed the warning – what did Mrs Walsh know about anything? But now, after the passage of several days, his mind had plummeted back to reality. He had not seen Bridget since their kiss and his initial elation had become tempered by doubt and second-guessing over what she was feeling and what she might do next. If she was still confined to her sick room, she had no means of seeking him out, but the torment of waiting and not knowing was making mere days feel like months.

A woman appeared around a bend in front of them, a thin shawl draped negligently at her elbows. He recognised Mary's distinctive locks of fair hair and waved. It occurred to him that she was precisely the person he could talk to about Bridget. She might not be sympathetic but she comprehended the circumstances and would perhaps offer some female insight.

When she approached, the peevish line of her mouth communicated that she wasn't pleased to see them – she probably deemed them an unwelcome intrusion on her solitude. His mother had confided in him, not without concern, that Mary had taken to going for long walks since she had returned home. She craved her own company over anyone else's, even her son's. She had always been somewhat temperamental in nature but she seemed even moodier now. Still, who could blame her, considering all that she had suffered?

They stopped in the lane, Cormac tugging on the horse's lead rope to bring it to a halt.

'Where are yous coming from?' Mary asked. A flurry of the breeze caused the end of her shawl to trail in the dirt but she didn't seem to notice.

'McKinty Farm,' said Margaret, and Bronagh uncovered her basket to display tidy rows of brown eggs. 'Where are you going?'

Mary shrugged. 'Nowhere in particular.'

Bronagh scowled. She had been only ten when she had been sent to work at the big house – now, two and a half years later, she and Margaret were still toiling away while their older sister had returned to live a life of little responsibility.

'Why aren't you at home helping Ma?' she said, her inflection coloured by more than a trace of bitterness. 'Didn't you learn how to clean house and make bread while you were away? With another pair of hands, she'd get through her work a lot quicker.'

'Ah, I'd only be in Ma's way,' said Mary. She made no mention of the son she had left in her mother's care.

Cormac sensed Bronagh's aggravation and intervened. 'I'm going to come home this evening,' he said to Mary. 'Can I talk to you about something important then?'

She looked indifferent. 'Fine so.'

'We'd best be getting back to the kitchens,' Bronagh said, adding pointedly, 'There's always so much to be done.'

Mary gave another listless shrug, tugged at her shawl, and walked away from them without so much as a farewell. Cormac and the other two girls were about to move on when they heard the clopping of hoof beats and a rider came into sight, trotting up the lane towards Mary. Discerning the figure's black hair and proud bearing, Cormac experienced a lurch of guilt and then anger. He had kissed this man's fiancée but Mr Lambourne wanted to take Bridget away from Oakleigh for good. At last, he had a genuine reason to dislike him.

Mr Lambourne passed Mary first; she started as he rode by, as though shaken from her brooding thoughts. Instead of stopping to hail Cormac and the girls, he nodded curtly and hurried on, vanishing around the next bend in a cloud of dust. Cormac stared after him with an uneasy feeling; did the gentleman suspect that there had been inappropriate conduct between himself and Bridget?

Margaret let out a wistful sigh. 'Isn't Miss Muldowney just the luckiest? Ellen Ryan said she couldn't have made a better match.'

A knot formed in the pit of Cormac's stomach. He glanced behind him, but Mary had already disappeared from view around the turn in the lane. It would have to wait until later.

He encouraged the horse onwards with a click of his tongue, and the three of them resumed their walk back to the big house.

***

Bridget rested in a chair by the window in her sick room with a blanket draped over her knees. September had stolen in while she had been convalescing and she could sense the change of season in the air that came through the small gap in the window. The summer heat was gone and a brisk breeze whispered of cooler days to come.

Her head throbbed with an ache that had nothing to do with her wound. She had kissed Cormac. It had been an impulse she could no longer contain, but what did it mean now she had gone through with it? She could not deny that there was an overwhelming part of her that very much wanted to kiss him again. But another part reminded her emphatically that she was betrothed to a different man. It was appealing to imagine it not being so but absurd to believe it could ever be otherwise.

A sense of foreboding sat heavily upon her. She had the impression that she was balancing a house of cards before her. What would it take for them all to come tumbling down?

A precise rap on the door interrupted her thoughts.

'Come in,' she called and the footman Denis entered, everything from the buttons on his livery to the buckles of his shoes polished to a high shine.

'Are you ready, miss?'

Mr Abbott had, to her relief, granted his consent at last for her to return to her own bedchamber, and so she had enlisted Denis to assist her down the stairs. Lady Courcey was to be occupied until luncheon in another meeting with Mr Enright, Garrett had absconded with Commander for the morning, and she did not have the patience to wait for an occasion more convenient to them.

Putting aside her blanket, she rose to her feet and took Denis's arm. She was very glad to escape this oppressive room that had been the manor's infirmary for over two weeks. Nonetheless, she cast a fleeting glimpse behind her as she left, taking one final look at the spot where she and Cormac had shared their kiss.

Even though she only had to descend a single flight, she could feel her energy depleting step by step; by the time she gained the lower landing, her breath was coming short and her legs trembled.

'Nearly there, miss,' said Denis and she leaned on him gratefully.

As they took the last few steps towards the door of her bedchamber, a man's raised voice came from the entrance hall below.

'...just not acceptable, Brewer!'

The valet's reply was inaudible but proved to be dissatisfying to Garrett, who gave a growl of irritation. 'I expect you to maintain the highest standards at all times. Such slipshod attention to detail is intolerable.'

This was followed by heavy footsteps on the staircase. Denis attempted to urge Bridget on but she stopped him with a light pressure on his arm.

'Just one moment,' she murmured, curiosity winning out over fatigue.

Garrett strode onto the landing, looking like he had taken the stairs two or three at a time. He checked at the sight of her and the strangest expression flashed across his face – was it resentment? He offered her a perfunctory bow, then turned on his heel and marched down the corridor towards his own bedchamber.

By this stage, Brewer had gained the top of the stairs too. He carried a pair of his master's gloves, one of which had a small rip on the cuff. Had something so insignificant provoked Garrett's displeasure?

'Good day, Miss Muldowney,' Brewer muttered and, giving her a polite nod, followed his master.

Frowning, Bridget allowed Denis to lead her on to her room.

***

Cormac entered the cottage at twilight to find his mother and youngest sister in a giggling heap on the hearth. One of the hens squawked from the rafter above, the end of a spool of yarn caught around its legs and the rest of it dangling like a pendulum. Orlaith jumped up to grab it, missed, and started laughing again.

'Silly Henrietta, come down!'

'Hush, you'll wake the baby,' Maggie said, trying to curb her own amusement, but Patrick slumbered in a basket in the corner, oblivious to the commotion. She smiled at Cormac as he kissed her cheek. 'Good to see you, my dearie. How's Bridget these days, do you know?'

'Getting stronger, I hear,' he said evasively, looking around. 'Where's Mary?'

'Isn't she with you?' She gazed over his shoulder as though she expected Mary to come through the door after him.

'No. Why would you think that?'

'She went for a walk earlier. When she came home, she told me she was hoping to start work at the big house and wanted to get your advice about any available positions. It cheered me no end to hear her talking about her future at last. Didn't she find you?'

'I met her on her walk but never saw her after that. I was working in the stables for the rest of the day though, so she'd have found me if she'd asked anyone where I was.' His brow furrowed. 'And she hasn't been back here since?'

'No,' said Maggie, beginning to look anxious. 'She's never out this late but I assumed she was fine 'cause she was with you. Where d'you think she could be?'

'I don't know. If she's in a better mood, maybe she decided to go see Ellen Ryan? But she'd have to wait 'til Ellen finished attending her ladyship, and that could be any time.'

Maggie relaxed. 'Arrah, that might be it. We'll wait so. But I'll be giving her a talking to when she gets back for worrying her mother. Are you hungry?'

'When am I not?' he said with a grin.

'Well, you can wash that muck off your hands first. I lived with your father long enough to know exactly what you've been shovelling today.'

Orlaith stopped snatching at the swinging spool of yarn. 'I'll go get the bucket,' she said and skipped out the door, returning a moment later with her two arms wrapped around the half-full bucket of water. She offered it to her big brother with an adoring gaze. 'The rope's missing.'

'Thanks, chicken. Is it?' he said, but he was thinking about the conversation he'd planned to have with Mary. Did he dare broach it with his mother instead? He scrubbed his hands together in the water. 'Ma...?'

She was standing beneath Henrietta again, hands on her hips and an appraising gleam in her eye. 'What?' she asked without turning to him.

He lost his nerve. 'Ah, could Mary have gotten lost in the woods?'

Maggie dismissed the suggestion with a flap of her hand. 'She knows those woods better than anyone. Before she went away to live with your aunt, she and Patrick used to run wild in them.' She paused. 'She might've twisted her ankle, or took a tumble. I hadn't thought of that.'

He wiped his hands dry on a rag from the dresser. 'D'you want me to go look for her?'

She bit her lip. 'Maybe you should.'

'I'll go right now so.' He gave her a reassuring smile. 'I bet I'll find her wandering towards home with no notion of how late 'tis.'

But when he headed back outside into the deepening dusk, his own apprehension mounted; not even Mary at her most distracted could fail to notice how dark it had become. He jogged up the lane first, hoping to meet her returning from the big house, cheerful after a nice chat with her old friend.

He stopped dead when he reached the brick-lined well at the side of the lane. 'The rope's missing,' Orlaith had said.

A shiver of dread slithered up his spine.

With a sharp intake of breath, he spun about, retraced his steps to the cottage, and strode into the woods behind it. The very worst idea imaginable bloomed in his mind but he pushed it aside. She had fallen somewhere, that was what had happened. He would stumble upon her huddled at the base of a tree and clutching her injured leg, and she would wipe her cheeks and cover up her fright with an accusatory remark about how long it had taken him to find her.

He picked up his pace until he was sprinting. Please God, he prayed, let her be safe. He shouted her name, calling out to her again and again. He crashed through the undergrowth, casting around for any sign that she had been there. The woods were not very large but she could be anywhere in them. Or she might not even be in them at all. He could hunt for hours and never come across her.

Darkness fell fully but still he ran and yelled, yearning for her to call back. Even though he had been just shy of eight years old when she had left, he had many vivid memories of their childhood together: finding an injured bird and nursing it back to health; waiting for their father to come home from the stables and competing over who would hug him first; playing hide-and-seek among these same trees he was hurtling through now. She had begged not to be sent away to care for their ailing aunt and now he wished with every fibre of his being that she had been able to stay and avoid all the heartache she had experienced since.

His breathing grew laboured and he developed a searing stitch in his side but, though he slowed down, he continued to stumble on, swiping his sweaty hair out of his eyes. After a while, he could not tell whether he was still going forwards or circling back on himself. He too knew these woods well, but somehow the trees looked unfamiliar and ominous, looming from the shadows to scratch his skin and tear his shirt.

At last, long after alarm had turned to blind panic had turned to exhaustion had turned to numbness, he slipped and fell hard on the ground. Ignoring the stab of pain that shot up through his knee, he searched around, his fingers grasping on what had halted his momentum; it felt like a thin piece of cloth. Holding it up in the dark, he could make out the vague shape and thought it might be a shawl. A hand of ice gripped his heart and he leapt to his feet in fear.

He stared about, straining to see through the gloom, and perceived a dark shadow among the trees ahead. He rushed forwards but skidded to a stop as soon as the shape became clear.

It was his beloved Mary, suspended from a tree branch, a rope stretched tight around her bare neck.

His anguished cry reverberated through the silent woods. He ran to his sister, pulled his knife from his pocket, and hacked at the offending rope until it snapped, but he was far too late.

He held her cold body close. As he rocked her and cried out to her vacant, blue-lipped face, something she had said to him rang in his head. 'You see the desperate things my foolish love made me do?'

She had nurtured a tragic view of love – had it played a part in her committing the most desperate act of all?

CHAPTER 21

Venturing downstairs for breakfast for the first time in more than a fortnight, Bridget found Garrett brooding alone at the table, an unfinished plate of kippers before him. He jumped to his feet at her appearance.

'Good morning, my darling,' he said with a beaming smile. 'Your presence is a true sign that you are on the mend, and very satisfying to see.'

She mustered a half-hearted smile in return and, when he leaned in for a kiss, hastily offered him her cheek. He stood back, disappointed, but she pretended not to notice as she sat opposite him, relieved to take a rest, although her legs were not quite as shaky as the previous day. At the same time, there was a soft tap on the door and Ellen entered, carrying a tray with a glass of some sort of green-coloured infusion. A sweet, minty scent wafted in with her.

'Another tonic for you, miss,' she said, her voice thick. 'Her ladyship was quite insistent. It is the physician's recipe and supposed to restore your strength.'

She kept her head down as she set the tray on the table but Bridget could see that her eyes were red and puffy.

Her brow creased. 'Ellen? What is the matter?'

'There's nothing the matter, miss.' She dropped into a curtsey, avoiding Bridget's eye. 'Would you like to take your tonic now or after breakfast?'

'Never mind the tonic. I can see you are upset. Tell me what is wrong.'

Garrett folded his arms, evidently bored by her interest in the woes of a lady's maid.

Tears seeped out of Ellen's eyes. 'Oh, it's too terrible to speak of.'

Bridget was now quite alarmed. 'What do you mean? What on earth has happened?'

'I don't know if I should even tell you,' said Ellen, glancing sideways at Garrett. 'But you'll be bound to find out sooner or later.' She gulped back a sob. 'It's shocking news. The poor family. Poor Cormac.'

Bridget's breath caught in her throat. 'Cormac?' Garrett looked at her sharply, but in that uncertain moment she did not care. 'What tragedy?'

'His sister, Mary. She's...dead. She hanged herself.'

Bridget gasped in horror. Garrett made an involuntary movement but said nothing.

'I don't believe it,' she said in a strangled voice. 'What would drive her to do such a thing?'

Ellen was crying freely now. 'I cannot even imagine. When I went down to the kitchens this morning to ask Mrs Kavanagh to prepare the tonic, she told me Margaret and Bronagh had been called home in the middle of the night. A little later, Liam came in with the news that Cormac had found Mary hanging from a tree in the woods.' She faltered. 'H-he brought her home in his arms and their mother fainted when he carried her into the cottage. That unfortunate woman, her husband and now two of her children dead in less than three years. It's dreadful.'

Bridget began to weep too. Her heart went out to Cormac; to discover his own sister dead, how horrifying. What a devastating tragedy for his entire family. Poor, poor Maggie. And little Orlaith, only five years old, she wouldn't even be able to understand what was going on. She would just know that they had lost someone dear to them and could never get her back.

Across the table, Garrett's face was impassive and he displayed no sign of compassion for the luckless family. How could he be so cold? He met her reproachful stare with empty eyes.

'I am sorry, my darling,' he said. 'I do not know who this girl was but it is a tragic loss for her family. Perhaps I should leave you for a while so you can compose yourself.'

And he rose and departed from the room without a backward glance.

***

The fire had burned low. Cormac dropped a sod of turf onto it, then leaned his forearm against the hearth wall and stared at the glowing embers. It had to be two or three in the morning but he was wide awake. His vigil would last through to the dawn.

Muted sobs drifted down from the loft above. He was not the only one still wakeful but he had sent his sisters to bed over an hour ago; there was no need for them to stay up with the remains too.

He winced. It was such a detached word. It meant nothing more than bones and flesh. It didn't signify breath or heartbeat, passion or irritability, daughter, mother or sister. Everything that had made her who she was, flawed as she was, had vanished.

He turned and gazed at her body, laid out on the table in preparation for burial. In the subdued firelight, her fair hair shimmered about her face like a halo. A dainty kerchief had been tied around her neck to hide the tell-tale marks of her violent end. A spray of pansies lay entwined in her hands.

Her body rested at peace but what of her soul? Father Macken had refused to come. Mary had committed a mortal sin, precluding any guarantee of salvation for her. Fearing she would writhe in eternal purgatory, Maggie had prayed over her for hours. She continued to do so now in the shadows on the far side of the table, lips moving silently, and would carry on until Mary was removed from the cottage. The immoral nature of her passing stipulated a burial at night but Cormac would not consent to that. He didn't want to hurry her into the ground – she ought to be waked properly, for his mother's sake more than anything.

He stepped up to the table and tenderly tucked a lock of hair behind his sister's ear. Why had she done it? How could she have believed there was no way to go on? He shut his eyes, remembering her confession in the woods. She had been in pain, and only he had known how much. Could he have foreseen this? Could he somehow have prevented it?

He bent to kiss her forehead and murmured, 'Please forgive me.'

The fire crackled as the turf flamed up. On the other side of the table, his mother began to keen.

Needless to say, there was no gathering of mourners; Ellen Ryan had been the only person to come to convey her condolences earlier in the evening. But John, Liam and, somewhat surprisingly, Fintan Kelly turned up the next morning to help Cormac bear his sister to the site of her interment. She had to be buried in unconsecrated ground beyond the walls of the church's graveyard, denying her a resting place next to her father and brother. It was an ignominious departure from this life but she had chosen it for herself.

Fintan declined to come back to the cottage afterwards but Liam hung around awkwardly in one corner while John kept a consoling grip on Maggie's hand by the now-empty hearth. The cottage seemed even more like a tomb when it no longer housed a corpse. Orlaith's hens had been shunted outside and, without their familiar scratching and clucking, the silence was oppressive. All eyes stared at the table, now a bare slab apart from a single pansy which had slipped from its posy. Margaret cradled the baby and rocked him as he stirred in his sleep, unaware that his mother had been buried in the earth.

All Cormac wanted was to get away from the morose faces and dismal atmosphere. He had done his duty as the man of the family; he had held himself together as long as was necessary. Now he sensed the fractures forming in his self-control, felt the despair beginning to smother him as his emotions crowded in.

He could not bear it anymore. He mumbled an excuse to Bronagh, who was standing nearest to him, and ran from the cottage.

It was good to be out in the fresh air – he could breathe again. He strode forwards without any destination in mind; he just wanted to keep moving. His knee still hurt from when he had fallen on it in the woods but he pushed through the pain, inconsequential as it was to all the rest. The lane and fields were quiet except for the merry twittering of birds in the hedgerows. He focused on the cheerful birdsong – anything to forget the thud of soil falling into a freshly dug grave.

The big house came into view on the horizon and he realised that his feet had automatically brought him along the route he followed to get to work. When he saw the imposing building rising in the distance, he knew what it was he yearned for. The only person he wanted to be with on this horrible day.

But it was risky. He had already provoked suspicion by making two visits to her bedside. Mrs Walsh had warned him to be careful so it had become more evident, at least to her, that there was the possibility of some kind of indiscretion. He would have to sneak in and take care that no one saw him.

He passed the paddock, mercifully empty, and reached the stables, where he took cover down the side of the building; he had no inclination to face his fellow stable hands today. Hugging the corner, he peered across the courtyard to the back door of the kitchens. He hesitated. How was he to get to her? The first obstacle was Mrs Kavanagh – she wouldn't be likely to let him pass through the kitchens unimpeded, personal misfortune or no. Then there was Bridget's location. Would she still be in her sick room or had she left it? Moreover, what were the odds that, if he did manage to find her, she would be alone?

Just as he had made the reckless decision to chance his luck and hope for the best, the kitchen door opened and Ellen emerged. Relieved, he gave a low whistle and she looked around in curiosity. When she saw him lurking by the edge of the stables, her eyes widened and she scurried over to him. He pulled her by the elbow into the building's shadow.

'I didn't expect—' she stuttered. 'I came out to look for Liam. I wanted to meet him when he returned from—oh, Cormac, I can only say again how sorry I am about—'

'Thanks,' he interrupted. 'I need to see her. Will you help me?'

She paused. Indecision, sympathy and fear mingled on her face before she said, 'Yes. Wait for a sign from me.'

She went back across the courtyard and re-entered the kitchens. A few minutes later, she reappeared at the doorway and motioned for him to hurry. He darted across the cobbles and was over the threshold in seconds.

'Mrs Kavanagh's in the pantry but she won't be there for long. Miss Muldowney's strength is returning so you'll find her in the drawing room. She's alone. Lady Courcey's in the study writing letters and Mr Lambourne's gone out riding. I don't know how much time you have but I wouldn't stay long if I were you.'

'Thank you, you're an angel,' he said and she coloured.

He crossed to the inner kitchen door and made his way up the narrow stairs into the back of the entrance hall. Stealing over to the drawing room, he eased open the door and crept inside, echoing the steps of the silver thieves that summer.

Bridget lay on a sofa near the piano, propped up by cushions and cocooned in a blanket. A closed book sat on a low table by her elbow; she was staring into space. Her head turned when the door opened and shock registered on her features, instantly followed by sorrow and compassion.

'Cormac,' she breathed.

'Ellen let me in...' He felt he should explain why he had shown up in such an illicit manner, but he supposed that might be obvious, considering the circumstances.

He went over and knelt by the sofa. She touched his cheek. That was all it took for the dam inside him to burst and overflow with anger and regret. She laid his head in her lap and stroked his hair, while he cried for his lost sister.

At length, the outburst of emotion subsided and he grew quiet.

'I wish I could have been there for you,' she whispered. 'I wanted to come but my mother refused to let me out of the house.'

Raising his head, he wiped his face on his sleeve and attempted a weak smile. 'I'm not surprised. I wouldn't have let you come either. You almost died of a fever recently, if you recall.'

She smiled back. 'Since when could something like that ever stop me?'

'Since you grew up and became a lady.'

Her face fell. While her question had been a throwaway remark, his answer had been quite serious. He lifted her palm to his lips and kissed it to show he had not meant to be unkind.

She put her other hand behind his neck and pulled him closer. This was a very different kiss from the last. That one had been spontaneous, urgent, impossible to suppress, but this was tender, delicate, lingering. They drew it out as long as they could, savouring the tastes, the sensations. He breathed in, losing himself in her captivating lilac scent.

The sound of voices out in the hall split them apart.

'Yes, my lady,' they heard Ellen say loudly. 'I'll be sure to do that for you at once.'

'There is no need to shout,' came Lady Courcey's disapproving response. She was almost outside the drawing room door.

Bridget looked at Cormac in panic. His gaze swept the room, taking in the critical lack of hiding places among its decorative pieces of furniture. The door began to open. The only thing he could do was dart behind the sofa and crouch down while Bridget fumbled for her book, just as Lady Courcey entered the room with a very nervous Ellen in her wake.

'Where are you going?' he heard the lady say in annoyance. 'I just asked you to call for the tea.'

'R-right away, my lady.'

The door shut with an ominous snap. Footsteps advanced, changing quality as they passed from floorboard to rug, and then a chair creaked as it took Lady Courcey's weight. Cormac's heart sank.

'How are you feeling?'

'Much better,' Bridget mumbled. 'In fact, I believe I am well enough to go for a walk. Shall we take a turn around the gardens?'

Lady Courcey sniffed. 'Do not be absurd, you are still too weak for that. You cannot venture out of doors until you are fully recovered. Although, if you are feeling that much improved, perhaps we could talk about what we plan to do after your convalescence is over. We ought to remove to the city as soon as possible.'

'Oh. May we not stay here a few months longer?'

'No. Our intention was always to leave at the end of the summer and you know very well that it would be impractical to even attempt to organise the wedding while living in the country. We shall need to make frequent visits to the dressmakers and florists, as well as manage the issuing of invitations and a hundred other things. It would be ludicrous to expect to arrange all of that from here.'

Cormac cringed. This was the last thing he wanted to hear right now. Bridget must have thought the same for she asked, 'Have you heard from Uncle Stuart?' in a patent effort to steer the conversation in a different direction.

'Yes, I was just writing my reply to him. He complains that he is suffering from gout, small wonder. He has postponed his return to England, intending to reside in Dublin until after the wedding. Now, we must consider your appearance. You shall, of course, wear your grandmother's pearls...'

As Lady Courcey went on, Cormac grew more and more uncomfortable. Too fearful to shift his weight and unable to close his ears, he hunched down behind the sofa and listened to her talk about the very event that would separate Bridget from him forever.

Two pairs of steps came into the drawing room the next time the door opened – a tinkle of china indicated a housemaid, while an anxious clearing of the throat communicated Ellen's presence. Over the sound of the tea tray being placed on a table,

Ellen said, 'My lady, Mrs Walsh wishes to speak with you on some housekeeping matters.'

'Tell Mrs Walsh I am having tea with my daughter and I shall discuss these matters with her later.'

The two pairs of steps retreated from the room.

Lady Courcey remained for another excruciating hour, the best part of which she spent talking about the upcoming wedding. By the time she rose to leave, Cormac was ready to explode with tension, his body aching and his mind reeling.

'At least this illness has given you a slimmer figure,' was the lady's parting remark. 'You should fit into my wedding dress with very few alterations.'

As soon as the door closed, he let out a low groan and stood clumsily, stretching his stiff legs. Bridget reached out to him.

'I am so sorry—' she began, but he stopped her with a shake of his head and touched her hand to say he understood. Without a word, he headed for the door and, checking first that Lady Courcey was nowhere in sight, made good his escape.

When he entered the kitchens, he found that Mrs Kavanagh had resumed her post, kneading dough on the flour-covered table. An expression of pity filled her face for a brief moment until she realised he had just come from above stairs and her look turned to one of suspicion.

'What have you been doing, lad?' she barked.

He shrugged and did not answer. Ellen was also there, flitting about restlessly; he caught her eye and nodded his thanks. She looked downright relieved as he walked out the door.

Chapter 22

Cormac returned to work the next day, determined that life should go back to normal as soon as possible. He wanted no more commiseration so he marched into the stables with his jaw set and his chin raised, challenging the men to remind him of the calamity that had befallen his family. John was the first to take the hint and simply ordered him to clean out a particular stall. Liam tossed him a pitchfork and the others turned away to their own tasks. Grateful, he strode into the stall and immersed himself in the physical labour, hoping exhaustion would induce temporary forgetfulness.

However, that night he learned that, while his working life might regain some semblance of normality, his family life was broken beyond repair. He went home across the fields after sundown, bone-weary and longing to be already asleep in the loft above the stables but knowing that to stay there would be an act of selfishness when his mother needed him. Only he had not comprehended how much so until he reached the cottage and heard the wailing from inside.

He flung open the door in panic. The fire had died down to ashes but the moonlight was bright enough to reveal the chaotic scene. Pieces of turf lay scattered on the floor in front of the hearth and what looked like an entire pail of milk had been spilled before his feet; it had soaked into the compacted earth and the room smelled sour. Patrick squirmed in his basket in the corner, his little face screwed up as he screamed at the top of his lungs, while Orlaith was on her knees at the bench by the table, weeping and calling out to her mother.

Maggie sat at the table, silent and unmoving, deaf to her daughter's pleas.

Orlaith's head turned when Cormac entered and she emitted a shriek of relief. Jumping up, she ran over to him and cried, 'Oh, help us, please! Patrick's been bawling for hours, I don't know how to make him stop, and I spilled the milk and I let the fire go out and I tried to start it again but I couldn't and Ma won't get up or say anything at all!' And she burst into sobs.

Alarm coursed through him but he didn't let it show as he lifted her into his arms and hugged her. 'Don't be upset, you've managed fine. Ma's just not feeling well right now. I'll take care of things here, no need to worry.'

He put her sitting on the opposite bench from their mother and set about reviving the fire first. His deft hands were able to coax life where Orlaith's inexpert ones could not, and soon the fire began to crackle. He threw the scattered bits of turf onto it and wiped his hands on his clothes before concerning himself with his screaming nephew. Not having had much experience with babies since his own sisters were small, he took quite some time to calm down Patrick, who needed both cleaning and feeding. Thankfully, some milk still remained in the bottom of the pail. It would do for now, although they would have to try to make arrangements for a wet nurse to come from Ballydarry – with luck, there might be a new mother in the village with some sympathy for their plight. After the baby had sucked every last drop from a rag soaked in the milk, Cormac walked around the room rocking him against his chest until he drifted off to sleep and could be laid back into his basket.

Next, he needed to pacify Orlaith who was still crying in distress. He drew her over to the now-welcoming fireside and wiped at her tear-stained cheeks with his thumbs. 'Have you eaten today, chicken?'

She sniffed and shook her head.

Trying very hard not to feel angry towards his mother, he said, 'There's no milk left for stirabout so I'm going to make you some broth but I need to fetch water for it. Will you stay sitting here while I'm gone? I'll be quick as I can.'

She hiccupped and nodded.

He went outside and felt his heart wrench when his gaze landed on the water bucket, its rope conspicuously missing – he had abandoned it in two hacked-apart pieces in the woods and would never return to that spot to retrieve it. Without the rope, the bucket was useless for collecting water from the well, so he searched the edge of the woods until he found a stream and filled the bucket from that instead. He was not gone for many minutes and he made an effort to stay within earshot of the cottage but, even so, when he came back Orlaith's anxious face told him he had been away too long. He gave her a reassuring squeeze and urged her closer to the fire to warm herself up.

After pouring the bucket of water into a pot, he rooted around the cottage for any vegetables with which he could make the broth. While the absence of potatoes reminded him that he had to set aside time soon to begin harvesting the crop, he did find some carrots and turnips in a cloth bag by the dresser – probably obtained in the village by bartering the hens' eggs – and stood at the table to chop them up, ignoring his mother at his elbow. Then he tossed them into the pot of water which he set over the fire and left to boil.

He eyed the damp patch on the earthen floor with distaste; the odour of the spilled milk would linger for a long time but there was little he could do about it now and he supposed the smell of the hens would eventually overwhelm it. So, while he waited for the broth to cook, he sat down by the hearth next to his sister. She climbed into his lap and he wrapped his arms around her.

'Feeling better?'

Her lower lip jutted out. 'What's wrong with Ma?'

He looked over at Maggie who had not stirred since he came home. Her shoulders were slumped and her blank eyes were cast down to the floor.

'She misses Mary very much,' was all he said.

When the broth was ready, Orlaith gulped it down with the same voracity that Patrick had taken his milk. Afterwards, Cormac put her to bed in the loft, soothing her with gentle strokes down her back and murmuring lullabies until she too fell into slumber.

Now it was time to face his mother. He climbed back down the ladder to the ground floor of the cottage and sat on the bench beside her.

'Ma?' he said tentatively.

She gave no indication that she had heard him.

He took her hands and found them icy cold. Rubbing them briskly, he said, 'Ma, please. Can you hear me? Say something.'

She said nothing, her gaze still vacant of expression.

He got up, poured another bowl of broth, and set it on the table before her. 'Please eat,' he entreated.

No response.

In frustration, he turned for the door. He was going to bang it open in the hope that it would shock his mother into wakefulness, but the more likely outcome was that it would wake Patrick and bring on another bout of wailing, so he eased open the top half of the door and leaned out into the night, inhaling deeply to eradicate the stench of sour milk from his nostrils.

He was in turmoil, despite the calm façade he had portrayed for his sister's sake. What should he do? His mother was falling apart in front of him and it was pitiful to witness. Yes, he too felt the heartache of Mary's death, but Maggie seemed to have given up altogether with the loss of her first-born child. Perhaps it was just too much for her to endure, having already lost a husband and a son. However, this left a burden on Cormac's shoulders which he had no desire to bear; he had been the only man in the family for over two and a half years now but he did not wish to become the only responsible adult as well. He wanted his mother to be strong because otherwise the obligation of caring for her, his three remaining sisters and his nephew would have to take priority over everything else...which would mean he would not be free to pursue Bridget. Guiltily, he knew she was the one he yearned to put first.

Sighing, he ducked his head back inside. He sat down again next to his mother and cleared his throat.

'Ma, you need to accept that Mary's gone. She's gone and we can't get her back. You've got to face up to this.'

There was no reaction at first but then she raised her eyes to his and, at last communicative, they were far too easy to read. Torment and remorse tumbled in their grey depths, a bottomless sea of guilt-ridden despair.

'Jack will never forgive me for losing her,' she whispered.

He gaped. 'You think you're to blame?'

He reached out to embrace her but she tried to push him away, her hands batting him with the strength of a moth's wing.

'I deserve no consolation,' she said in a cracked voice.

Wretched, he said, 'What happened to Mary wasn't your fault.' He wanted to add that if anyone was culpable it was him, but that would mean admitting his awareness of Mary's real grief and divulging the truth of her sordid time in Dublin, which Maggie was in no way ready to hear. 'You couldn't have known what she was going to do. There was nothing you could've done to prevent it.'

'I failed her.' The tears gathered but did not fall. 'Little baby girl, her mother failed her.'

'You did *not* fail Mary,' he said, willing her to believe him. 'You're a wonderful mother. She was just too broken to continue on. You didn't know.'

'I should've known,' she said softly, and her gaze returned to the floor.

Terrified that she would sink back into her frozen state of misery, he grabbed her shoulders and shook her to get her to look at him again.

'D'you know what I blame you for?' he said, allowing some of his anger to finally surface. 'I blame you for neglecting these two children today. When I came home, Patrick was roaring and Orlaith was in hysterics. They were starving. How could you abandon them like that?'

'Wh-wh—' she stammered.

'You've lost a child and that's a terrible thing but there are two more here who still depend on you. Patrick needs a mother now, not just a grandmother, to say nothing of a wet nurse which you should've arranged by now. Are you going to forsake him the way Mary did or are you going to love him and look after him?'

She didn't reply but it was not the desolate silence from before; her eyes were trained on his, steady and focused in spite of their wetness.

'Are you going to love him and look after him?' he demanded again.

Her voice was barely audible. 'I am.'

'Good. Then start with looking after yourself. You've got to eat.'

He pushed the untouched bowl of broth towards her but, doubting the strength of her hand, filled the spoon himself and raised it to her mouth. It had to be cold by this stage but she swallowed it without protestation.

Then she burst into tears and this time she did not resist when he reached out his arms.

Chapter 23

Bridget stood in her bedchamber, staring into the long, silver-framed mirror. She was steady on her feet, her back was straight, her eyes were bright, and her skin had lost its ghostly pallor. All in all, she gave the impression of being in sound health.

This was not good.

She hunched her shoulders and allowed her eyelids to droop as if she were very tired. Then she grasped the cane which Mr Abbott had provided and leaned on it heavily. There was not much she could do about the hue of her skin but, though she was no longer quite so pale, neither could she claim to be rosy-cheeked.

The overall effect was someone who had recuperated from an illness but still had some way to go to full recovery. Much better.

As she turned to leave the room, her gaze fell upon the wooden bird perched on her dressing table. She picked it up, caressed its wing tenderly and, on impulse, scurried to the bedside and tucked it beneath her pillow. Then she resumed her poorly demeanour and shuffled out of the bedchamber, almost walking into Ellen who was passing by with a dress draped over her arm. The lady's maid looked startled and guilty.

'Good morning, miss,' she mumbled.

'Good morning,' said Bridget, feeling rather discomfited herself. Ellen had enabled Cormac to come to her in the drawing room on the day of Mary's burial. How much had she deduced about what had happened behind the closed door? Did she regret her actions now, considering how close they had come to getting caught?

Bridget did not regret it. To have that opportunity to comfort Cormac in the depths of his anguish meant more than she could say. Ellen ought to know that what she had done had been a good deed.

She put out her free hand to stop Ellen from moving on down the corridor.

'Thank you for your discretion,' she said. 'Your kindness does not go unappreciated.'

Ellen glanced about but there was no one else within sight.

'I shouldn't have done it,' she said, hardly moving her lips. 'But I just felt so sorry for him. I thought he needed...a friend.'

Bridget nodded sadly. 'Yes, he did.'

Ellen opened her mouth to speak again but then shut it as though she had thought better.

'Is there something else?'

The lady's maid shook her head. 'It's not my place to say.'

'You may speak freely. There is nobody else listening.'

'Just...' She hesitated. 'Be careful, miss.'

And she hurried on towards Lady Courcey's bedchamber.

Bridget stood still, staring after her. She was right, it was not her place to say that, even in her senior position on the staff, but she had been given permission to speak her mind. 'Be careful.' It was a reasonable warning, but what did it insinuate? Be careful not to get involved with Cormac? Or be careful not to get trapped in an unhappy marriage?

Leaving the question unanswered, she turned towards the mahogany staircase. At the top, she looked at the steps and then at her cane and then below to the empty entrance hall. It would be tiresome to hobble all the way down when there was no spectator present to make sympathetic note of her frailty.

Lifting the cane, she started down the stairs with assurance but had only descended half a dozen steps when she heard a door opening onto the hall below. She let the tip of the cane drop back to the polished wooden boards just in time; Garrett emerged from the drawing room and gazed up at her.

She resumed her descent in a more tremulous fashion and he climbed the stairs to provide assistance. He offered her his arm and she slid her own through it. His other hand reached over to rest on hers where she had placed it at the crook of his elbow. Whereas once she would have viewed this as a sweet, protective gesture, now she saw it as a display of possession.

When they got to the bottom, she let out a little moan.

'Are you in pain?' he asked, genuine concern on his face.

She gave him a brave smile. 'I'm fine, but I do still find the stairs exhausting.'

He guided her to the drawing room and into a comfortable chair. 'Shall I call for a maidservant? Is there anything you require?'

'No, thank you. I just need to catch my breath.'

He took the seat next to her. 'I thought you had been exhibiting encouraging signs of improvement.'

'I thought so too. It seems we were both mistaken.'

He said nothing else and neither did she. She remembered a time when talking had come so easily to them and they had shared their opinions on every topic, great and small, but now it felt like there was a distance between them which no amount of conversation could surmount. She could not deny that she was distracted by her feelings for Cormac, but he too seemed in a constant state of preoccupation. Perhaps he was beginning to suspect that he was not the sole possessor of her affections anymore.

If he did, he would be right. She had betrayed him twice now with Cormac and an insistent, excited voice inside her promised that that was not the end of it. She was seated next to her fiancé but it was not his lips she imagined kissing again.

She pretended to let her breathing slow. At length, she said in a casual voice, 'I believe I am keeping you too much confined indoors. It is not possible for me to go out riding yet, but please do not feel that this means you cannot go yourself.'

He sat up straighter and she knew she had hit the mark; he longed to get away from the monotony of a household that revolved around a convalescing patient.

'I have already gone out once or twice,' he confessed.

'Yes, I know.' And on the last occasion, she added silently, Cormac came and I kissed him. 'Would you like to go again?'

***

Cormac was carrying a bag of oats towards Bonny's stall when he perceived the refined voice of Mr Lambourne outside the stable doors, requesting his horse to be saddled. John Corbett himself entered the stables to carry out the task and the gentleman followed him in, the two conversing about the day's weather and how it might affect riding conditions.

Mr Lambourne was relaxed and affable with John, but his demeanour changed when he caught sight of Cormac; though Cormac was careful to keep his own expression innocent, a subtle coldness clouded the other man's manner. John did not appear to notice anything and continued on to attend to Commander, leaving them alone.

'Fine enough day for riding,' said Cormac.

‘Indeed,’ said Mr Lambourne coolly. ‘The wind is rather fresh but Corbett believes the rain will hold off for the time being.’

‘Probably won’t come down heavy ’til this evening.’

‘I expect to be back before then.’

With a respectful nod, Cormac turned to go on towards Bonny’s stall. He had opened the half door when he realised that Mr Lambourne had come up behind him. The gentleman’s dark eyebrows rose as he asked, ‘Is that Miss Muldowney’s mare?’

‘It is,’ said Cormac, wishing he had chosen a different stall. He could not guess how much Mr Lambourne might read into his personal care of Bridget’s horse but he would sooner avoid rousing any further distrust in the gentleman’s mind.

Mr Lambourne’s mouth puckered in deliberation. ‘It is a shame she did not get to enjoy riding her more while we were here. Now that the summer is over and our removal to the city is imminent, the opportunity is all but past.’

Did he expect Cormac to betray his disappointment at this news of Bridget’s impending departure? He was better at concealing his feelings than that.

‘’Tis indeed a shame,’ he said politely and stepped into the stall, allowing the half door to swing shut behind him.

John returned presently with Commander and Mr Lambourne disappeared outside. As Cormac fed a handful of oats to Bonny, he reflected that the gentleman was now absent from Bridget’s side. Could he seize this chance to go in search of her? But he was reluctant to put Ellen in such a tricky position again. And Bridget might well be in the company of Lady Courcey. It was too great a risk to take, much as he longed to see her.

On this occasion, however, Bridget came to him, not ten minutes after Mr Lambourne had ridden off. He was crossing to another stall with the depleting bag of oats when an irregular tapping sound came to his ears. He glanced out through the stable doors and glimpsed her limping across the courtyard with the aid of a cane, which struck the cobbles each time she took a step.

This was the first time he had seen her outdoors since the storm. Pleased though he was to lay eyes on her, he did not think she ought to be exerting herself so much – she still looked too weak to be walking. John, who had emerged from his workspace to investigate the tapping noise, hastened out into the courtyard to offer his support to her. She took his arm with a grateful dip of her head.

'Miss,' Cormac heard him say, 'while 'tis good to see you're getting better, is it wise to be venturing out so soon after your illness?'

'Thank you for your concern,' came her reply, 'but I believe the benefits of being out in the air far outweigh any subsequent tiredness I might experience. It feels like I have not taken a proper breath in weeks. Although this does lead me to my purpose in coming out here. Is your carpenter in the vicinity?'

Cormac started. Oakleigh only had one carpenter. Was she being too obvious? Would John suspect something? He didn't care. He waited for the stable master to call his name and then emerged from the stables. Her eyes lit up but she was quick to rearrange her expression into one of composure.

'Good day, Cormac,' she greeted him.

'Good day, miss. I'm glad you're back on your feet but would I be right in presuming you don't mean to take Bonny out today?'

She laughed. 'Yes, I am not ready to go riding just yet. However, I do long to be out of doors again. It is so stuffy inside the house. Unfortunately, my mother insists that I am only permitted to walk for very short periods until my full strength returns.'

'Sounds like sensible advice to me,' he said, and John nodded in agreement.

'But it is difficult to say when that will be,' she said with a pointed look. 'I thought in the meantime I could make a compromise with my mother and find a means of being outside while still dutifully resting.'

'What d'you propose, miss?' asked John.

'I would like a swing seat made for the oak tree. I think the orchard is the ideal location for my recuperation as I shall be sheltered but still able to get fresh air. Do you think you can do it, Cormac?'

He had never made any object quite so big as a swing seat but he said without hesitation, 'Of course. I'd be delighted to do anything to help your recovery.'

She gave him a sweet smile. 'Perhaps, then, you could accompany me into the orchard so I can show you what I would like?'

He had to stop himself grinning in return. 'Happy to, miss.'

John saw nothing untoward about this arrangement and even advised them to take their time so as not to stretch the limits of Bridget's strength. Cormac didn't feel quite daring enough to offer his arm to her while still in the stable master's presence so he just led the way to the orchard door and held it open for her to pass through.

It was peaceful beneath the apple trees, which were laden down with fruit ripe for picking. He made sure to set a slow pace along the path but she seemed to grow sturdier with every step, soon not relying on her cane much at all.

He was about to remark on this when she said quietly, 'How are you?'

He considered the question, thinking about all the events that had happened over the past few weeks, the incredible highs and the despairing lows. 'In all honesty? I'm a bit ragged 'round the edges.'

'I understand what that is like.' She sighed. 'How is your mother?'

'She isn't well,' he admitted. He had not mentioned Maggie's breakdown to anyone at the stables, not John nor even Liam, but Bridget he could tell. 'If I'm ragged, 'tis nothing compared to how she's feeling. She's fallen apart. She blames herself for what happened to Mary.'

'Oh no, does she? But she must know it is not her fault.'

'She refuses to see it that way. The day after we buried Mary, I came home to find her sitting still as a stone with the children and cottage in disarray 'round her. That frightened me. I managed to rouse her but she's only a shadow of a person now. 'Tis a struggle to convince her to eat although she's stirred herself enough to at least take care of Orlaith and Patrick.'

'Poor, dear Maggie,' said Bridget, dismayed. 'How much more can she endure? This is dreadful.'

''Tis like all her energy and happiness has leaked out of her. I've been going home every night to try raise her spirits but I've asked Margaret and Bronagh to go for the next few nights. I'm hoping it'll cheer her up to have all her girls with her for an evening or two. Her remaining girls,' he corrected himself, shoulders sagging.

She slipped her free hand into his; it was only then that he noticed she was not wearing gloves. Her expression was compassionate and her fingers were soft. He looked down at them.

'And this is where the guilt starts,' he said. ''Cause I know my sister's dead and I know my mother's in terrible pain but all I want to think about is kissing you.'

He made himself look back at her. She was biting the tip of her tongue but her eyes were bright with anticipation.

'I do not think you should feel guilty about wanting to be happy,' she said.

He bent to kiss her, releasing her hand so he could wrap both of his arms around her. She dropped her cane and succumbed willingly to his embrace. The kiss became fierce; there was consolation and desire in her lips and he was hungry for both. Her body bowed under the force of his eagerness. They did not stop for air, kissing long and hard and feverishly. When at last they pulled apart, they were both panting.

'Nice not to be interrupted this time,' he said once he had regained his breath.

She stared up at him, stunned. He sensed that she was not fully supporting herself anymore and kept his grip tight around her back.

'You going to faint?' he asked.

'I think I am quite literally weak at the knees.' Her cheeks were pink. 'I have never been kissed like that before.'

That gave him an enormous measure of satisfaction. Mr Garrett Lambourne may have riches aplenty but his kisses had never left her so weak that she could not stand.

'I'm glad you liked it,' he said, colouring too.

'I more than liked it. It was incomparable to any other. I felt as though you had an appetite only I could sate, like you wanted to—' But she cut herself off there, the pink having converted to a flaming red.

He might have pressed her to finish the sentence but he could make a reasonable deduction and he preferred to save her further embarrassment. She was a lady after all and, regardless of his empty pockets, he ought to act like a gentleman.

So he swept her up into his arms and said, 'I don't think you can make it by yourself to the oak tree. Shall I carry you?'

She nodded and turned her mortified face into his neck, her chestnut curls tickling his jaw. Smiling to himself, he followed the winding path to the centre of the orchard, leaving the cane abandoned on the ground behind them. When they reached the clearing, he hoisted her up into the branches of the oak and deposited her safely in a comfortable fork. By this time, she had recovered enough to look at him again. He grinned up at her, his head lower than hers due to her elevated position.

'So where d'you want me to put this swing seat?'

'Oh, yes. That was just an excuse to see you. But it might be a good idea, don't you think?'

They chattered for a while about the proposed swing seat, debating which branch would be most suitable, how far from the ground the seat ought to be, and how wide, and whether it should have arms, and which wood he might use. In the midst of all that, they kissed, she leaning down and he stretching up, their lips meeting tenderly, passionately, and every intensity in between. It was an idyllic interlude of pure contentment.

But it could not last forever. The seconds slid away and too soon it was time to leave. When she said it, his gaze fell to the large ruby on her left hand.

'What're we doing, Bridget?'

She ran her fingers through his fair hair. 'Don't ask that today. Let us enjoy this feeling without any complications. Save the worry for later.'

He accepted this; why ruin the enchantment of the moment? Lifting her down from the tree, he carried her to the spot where the cane still lay on the path, and together they walked back through the orchard, letting go of each other's hand only when they reached the green door.

Chapter 24

A blustery breeze tugged at Bridget's hair and caused the ends of her shawl to flap about. Garrett tucked the wayward material solicitously around her shoulders, then offered her his arm and gestured towards the vine-draped arch at the gardens' entrance.

Intending to keep up her charade of fragility for as long as possible, she leaned into him for support as they followed the walkway around the gardens. She knew he and her mother both wished to go back to the city now that the summer was at an end, but they would never force her to travel if they feared she would not survive the journey. And right now the very last thing she wanted was to leave the estate.

'Isn't this nice?' said Garrett, motioning to the late-blooming flowers which grew in meticulous patterns on either side of the path.

She murmured her own admiration of the colourful display and they continued on in silence. She supposed she ought to attempt further conversation but she could not stop thinking about Cormac. The kiss they had shared the day before had been a revelation. It had stirred something inside her, a restlessness which could not be alleviated. Every time she summoned the memory of it, she felt a passionate ache deep in her belly. She craved a kiss like that again, and she was deluding herself if she believed the man next to her could ever provide it.

Making an unwelcome intrusion into her thoughts, he announced, 'It is time to return to Dublin.'

She considered carefully before replying, 'We could not expect you to stay for much longer. When you arrived in July, I doubt you had anticipated still being here in September. How soon do you plan to depart?'

He arched an eyebrow at her. 'I meant both of us. The wedding ceremony cannot take place without the bride present.'

'But there is no rush,' she hedged. 'Wouldn't it be splendid to have a spring wedding? Nature would be just coming to life. There would be new growth on the trees and I could use daffodils for my bouquet. It would be so charming.'

'Nature doesn't come into it. We shall be getting married in the city, so it won't matter whether the trees have leaves or not.'

She changed the direction of her argument. 'You know I am still too weak to cope with such a big occasion. Do you want me to faint as I enter the church?'

He made an exasperated noise deep in his throat. 'Of course not. But I do not believe you are as frail as you are making yourself seem. It has been some time since your illness and you ought to be well recovered by now.'

She stopped and glared at him with as much indignation as she could muster. 'Are you saying you think I am pretending?'

He did not flinch under her gaze. 'Yes.'

She attempted a derisive tone. 'Why on earth would I do that?'

'So you can prolong your residence on the estate and continue certain acquaintances,' he answered levelly.

Her lips parted but no words came out. He was more astute than she had given him credit for. Feeling foolish, but unable to think of anything else to say, she whipped her arm out of his grasp and marched away from him.

'You cannot postpone the wedding forever,' he called after her. 'We will be in London by October, I promise you that.'

His assertion echoed in her mind for hours afterwards, to the point where real panic began to take hold, creeping up her throat to suffocate her. How soon before he forced her to leave? A week? A day? Her time at Oakleigh was running out.

So now she gripped her candlestick and opened her bedchamber door with painstaking care. The corridor beyond was dark and silent, the whole household having retired to bed over an hour ago. She abhorred the idea of sneaking through the house at night like a thief but no other option remained to her – Garrett had proved to be disinclined to go out riding during the day and her mother had been desirous of her company in a protracted perusal of the estate's accounts, making it impossible for her to slip away unnoticed. And she was desperate to seek out Cormac; this could not wait.

The hem of her nightdress swished about her ankles as she tiptoed down the mahogany staircase, the candle flame casting her monstrous shadow behind her. She reached the empty kitchens without incident and, taking the key off the hook on the wall, unlocked the back door. It swung on noiseless hinges, smooth from frequent use.

The clear sky was sprinkled with stars and the night-time air was chilly. Gooseflesh rose on her skin as she crossed the courtyard, stubbing the toes of her slippers more than once on the uneven cobbles. The double doors of the stables were shut but, to her relief, not locked.

At the far end of the stables, beyond the stalls, was the ladder which led up to the loft. She climbed it one-handed, careful to avoid catching her foot in her nightdress's hem. She crept up through the hole in the loft floor and peered around. Several stable hands lay in the straw, so fast asleep that the candlelight did not disturb them. At first, she could not see Cormac among them and feared he had gone home for the night, but then she spotted his familiar form sprawled at the other side of the loft.

Leaving the candlestick by the hole, she crawled cautiously past the other men and nudged his arm. He woke in an instant and she put her hand over his mouth to prevent him making a noise. His eyes widened when he perceived her kneeling beside him in her nightdress and slippers. She jerked her head back towards the ladder and he nodded, indicating that he would follow her down.

Once they were below, she whispered, 'I needed to see you. Is there somewhere we can talk?'

After pondering for a moment, he led her out of the stables and over to the furthest hay barn. Inside, she discerned his carpentry workspace in the corner and the progress he had made on her swing seat – several wooden beams lay side by side, sawn with precision to the same length. Yesterday, they had kissed beneath the oak as they discussed the construction of the seat, and she had said they would save the worry for another day. That day had come sooner than she had expected.

He sat on a haystack and she set her candlestick on the barn floor before joining him. The light of the flame flickered over their faces.

'What's the matter?' he said with concern.

'Garrett suspects something,' she said, her voice subdued. 'He thinks I am feigning my weak condition in order to stay longer here with you. Well, he did not specify you in particular, but we both knew who he meant.'

Silence hovered between them.

'And is that what you're doing?'

She swallowed and stared down into her lap. 'Yes, it is. I don't want to leave you.'

There it was, she had said it. Making that declaration filled her with a conviction that was both instantaneous and profound:

she loved this man sitting mere inches from her. Her heart beat madly against her ribs at the realisation.

His body trembled in reaction to her words. 'I'm very glad to hear that.'

He cupped her chin and raised it so that they were making eye contact. She could read a mixture of eagerness and nervousness in his gaze.

'So what does this mean?' he asked.

'I don't know,' she confessed. 'I have no wish to leave but I am being given no choice in the matter. I'm Garrett's intended wife and therefore obligated to obey him. What else can I do?'

He took his hand away and his expression became frank. 'What're your feelings for him?'

Now was the time to examine herself and truthfully answer that question. 'I believed that I was happy with him. When we were in Dublin, he always seemed so thoughtful and romantic. But he has shown me his unpleasant side this summer. He has been short-tempered and unkind, and I do not care for his behaviour when he has drink in him. Most of all, I am dismayed by his indifference to my unwillingness to go to London. He has brushed my opinion aside like it does not matter, even though he knows his decision will make me miserable. There can be no joy in a union so unequal. And when I compare him to you...'

She gazed into his eyes, so blue and sincere.

'You,' she repeated. 'I was gone for over seven years and yet you are still here beside me, as constant as ever. I am ashamed that I ever promised myself to another man when you have always been the most important person to me. I was so blind but—oh, Cormac, it is you whom I love!'

She threw her arms around him and they hugged so tightly that she was left quite breathless. He murmured into her ear, 'I think you already know how I feel.'

She drew back to look at him; his face was shining with joyfulness. How long and how much had he yearned for this moment? A flood of giddy delight swept over her but it receded as she remembered Garrett.

'But I am engaged,' she bemoaned. 'I am trapped.'

'You're not trapped. You haven't married him yet. You can still leave him.'

'It is easier to say that than to go through with it. Engaged practically *is* married as far as my mother and society are concerned. It would be an utter scandal if we separated now.'

'Is the scandal really something that'd bother you? Don't you think it'd be better to endure a small amount of gossip in the short term than to suffer for decades in an unhappy marriage?'

She did not answer. What he said made sense but fear of her mother's fury kept her undecided.

'Mother would throw me out of the house,' she said at last.

He could not refute the statement; Lady Courcey was probably capable of much worse.

'But 'tisn't like you'd have nowhere to go. You'd have me. I'd look after you.'

Her smile was dim. 'She would throw you out too and we would both be homeless.'

'We'd be fine,' he said staunchly. 'Don't be so afraid to imagine it. We could be happy together.'

She allowed herself to picture such a future: steady, straightforward Cormac at her side rather than charming, selfish Garrett. It would be a more basic life, with none of the luxuries she was accustomed to, but it would be a truer one. Kind-hearted and devoted, he would always take care of her, and she would do the same for him.

She gave him another smile, this one much brighter. He grinned and took her hand, squeezing it.

'I love you,' he said, 'more than you can ever know. Will you marry me instead of Garrett?'

Thrilled, she flung her arms around him again and cried, 'Yes!' with her voice muffled in his shoulder.

He laughed and held her close, then tilted her back so that his forehead leaned against hers.

'I've never thought of anyone else but you,' he said.

Their lips met. She opened her mouth to him and his tongue slipped inside. She welcomed it with her own, tender at first, but with a growing urgency. This was what she needed, this was how that ache in her belly could be satisfied. She entwined her fingers in his hair and pulled him nearer, kissing him harder.

His hand came to rest on the curve of her breast. Her tongue faltered but swiftly regained confidence. He tugged down the neckline of her nightdress and she pushed herself further into his palm. She might not fully understand what she was consenting to but she knew this was the only man upon whom she could bestow that consent. And even though they were going to be married – as soon as they could manage it, she resolved – the impulses of their bodies declared the impossibility of waiting until that occasion.

He made an attempt to demur nonetheless. Withdrawing from the kiss with a valiant effort, he said, 'Are you sure? 'Tis—'tis supposed to be painful. For you, I mean.'

A thought struck her and her guts coiled like serpents. 'Do you know—that is, have you—'

'No, I haven't.' He stroked her cheek. 'But the men in the stables talk. I know enough to get us started. And I think maybe instinct might take us the rest of the way.'

Conscious that she should say no, should exercise prudence, should keep him at arm's length, she whispered, 'Lead on.'

He greeted this emancipation with a quivering intake of breath. His intrepid hand trailed down her stomach, over her hip, along her thigh and past her knee until it found the hem of her nightdress. It slid beneath and travelled back the way it had come, the material slithering up with it. Cool air caressed her bare legs but now she didn't feel the cold; rather, her skin burned as he exposed it.

She shifted and he drew the nightdress over her head. Instead of tossing it away, he spread it out on the haystack behind her, while she kicked off her slippers to complete her state of undress. Her nudity ought to have embarrassed her but how could she think that way when he gazed at her with such appreciation? She scrabbled to remove his clothing too, fumbling ineffectually in her haste to uncover him. He stood to hurry the process, providing her with her first full view of a naked man. Every part of her glowed as she pulled him down into an embrace, her breasts thrusting against his chest. He laid her back on the haystack, the soft material of her nightdress protecting her from the spiky ends of the hay.

'God, you're beautiful,' he breathed and pressed his mouth to her skin.

They explored each other thoroughly with hands, lips and tongues, flesh touching flesh in an exquisite collision of sensation. Their inexperience became apparent as they bumped foreheads or scraped teeth but raw passion rendered such knocks comical and inconsequential. They giggled and groaned and gasped and cared for nothing but seeking the satisfaction their bodies craved.

Then, within the bubble of frantic activity, one tiny movement occurred: his hand alighted ever so gently on her knee, a question, an encouragement, a plea. She responded without reservation, easing it away from the other in an action that felt both sinful and exhilarating.

He edged into position and she welcomed him to her. Their gasps mingled together. There was a little pain but not as much as she had expected, and it was superseded by a sense of completion that nearly overwhelmed her. When he moved inside her, her last coherent thought was that no moment in her life had ever been more perfect.

And he was right. Instinct took them the rest of the way.

Overjoyed in their love for one another, they lay in each other's arms until the dawn crept over the horizon and daylight peeked through the cracks in the hay barn's walls. The candle had burned down to nothing but she couldn't recall when it had gone out.

Reluctantly, she sat up. 'I have to go.'

A smudge of blood showed in the folds of her nightdress. He helped her to put it on, every touch and look a tingling reminder of what had passed between them.

'I love you,' he said and kissed her.

'I love you too,' she replied with a happy smile and left the barn.

Chapter 25

Bridget returned to the house, locked the kitchen door, and replaced the key on its hook. She had got back just in time, judging by the distant sounds of movement on the servants' stairs. She stole through the inner kitchen door and upstairs to her bedchamber, feeling deliciously sore and still able to smell Cormac on her skin. Her plan was to climb into bed and snatch a couple of hours of sleep if possible. After she woke, she would consider what to say when she faced Garrett.

What she did not expect was to find him waiting for her when she opened the bedchamber door.

She took in a sharp breath, too shocked to utter a word. He sat on the edge of her bed, wearing neither coat nor waistcoat, his shirt open at the neck. His face was expressionless and, when he spoke, his voice was just as empty.

'Good morning, Bridget. My behaviour to you in the gardens yesterday was inexcusable so I came to your bedchamber last night to apologise. I'm sorry that I missed you.' He rose and came over to her. 'I'll let you sleep. You must be tired.'

He dropped a weightless kiss on her cheek and left the room.

The breath she had been holding came out in a long shudder. Guilt made her insides squirm. Yes, she had meant to inform Garrett that she wished to put an end to their engagement, but there had been no need for him to know that she had just spent the night away from her bed, undoubtedly in the arms of his rival if he had discerned the incriminating smear of blood on her nightdress. Furthermore, the fact that he had visited her chamber so late at night, and in such a state of undress, implied that he had been intending to make another advance like the drunken one he had attempted on the night of his birthday, perhaps in an effort to seal the bond of their betrothal. She had denied him this experience he so desired and bestowed it upon another instead. He ought to be enraged. So for him to take her betrayal with such composure was unimaginable. She felt far worse than if he had shouted or struck her.

But he had other ways of punishing her. When she went down to breakfast, after spending an hour or two in fruitless pursuit of sleep, she found her mother waiting with a grim expression on her face.

'Where were you last night?' Lady Courcey demanded before she even had time to sit down.

She hesitated. 'Nowhere. In my bedchamber.'

'You are lying to me. I have spoken with Mr Lambourne.' Her mother seethed with anger as she crossed the room to her. 'Were you with that McGovern boy?'

She didn't reply.

Lady Courcey gave her a slap which made her eyes water. She gasped and her hand flew to her smarting cheek.

'So I have a whore for a daughter, do I?' the lady said viciously. 'One who is willing to demean herself with the absolute dregs of society?' She regarded Bridget with narrowed eyes. 'I thought seven years would be enough to rid you of your loathsome fixation but when you gave me that list for compensation I knew that it was not. Did you really think I would not notice his family's name? Are you witless? They got nothing. I would never do a thing to encourage that boy. His association with you was already too dangerous. And it disgusts me to learn how right I was.'

The bottom fell out of Bridget's stomach. Her good deed had failed, and Lady Courcey had shown herself to be far more perceptive than she had realised. Had the lady seen that her daughter still held a deep regard for Cormac ever before she had known it herself?

'I am ashamed to call you mine but consider yourself lucky, girl, for your fool of a fiancé is still willing to marry you.'

She raised her chin in defiance. 'I do not want to marry him,' she declared, and received a harder slap than before. She reeled backwards and reached out to the wall behind her for support.

'You *shall* marry him. Do you think I am going to allow you to bring disgrace upon this family's name? We have a reputation to uphold.'

'I don't care about the family name,' she retorted. 'I do not love him so I will not marry him.'

'And what do you suppose will become of you if you do not? Mr Lambourne's fortune and social status will be lost to you forever. You will lose a mother, for I will most certainly disown a daughter who invites such disrepute upon herself. All you'll have left will be a worthless existence with a penniless, homeless boy who can offer you nothing.'

'He's not homeless,' Bridget said, despite the sickening feeling growing in her belly. She knew what was coming.

But the blow was more terrible than she had anticipated.

'My dear girl, use your head,' her mother snapped. 'Do you think for one second I would keep that boy on my land? He and his whole family would be thrown out of their home faster than you could pack your bags. It would be the end of them, for I am certain they would have nowhere else to go.'

'His whole family?' A wave of horror engulfed her. 'You would not do that.'

'I would, and without a moment's compassion for any of them. It is highly improbable that they would be able to find employment elsewhere to support them all, so they would doubtless starve within months. In effect, you would be condemning them to death. You think about that before you go running to that good-for-nothing boy.'

What made Lady Courcey's behaviour so revolting was that she meant every word she said. She would have no compunction about evicting a whole family out of pure malice. The magnitude of her cruelty was despicable.

Bridget thought of Cormac and the exultation they had shared when they had professed their love for each other last night. She could not give that up; it was so much more genuine than the farce her relationship with Garrett had become.

Then she thought of Cormac's mother. Her husband and two of her children dead, and now the possibility that she would be turned out of her home with her remaining four children and her tiny grandson. She would never survive the emotional turmoil. It was too much for one person to bear.

It seemed to come down to whether Bridget would be selfish and choose her own happiness at the expense of an entire family's wellbeing, or be selfless and relinquish her chance of a future with Cormac for the sake of a family who did not deserve a death sentence.

She began to weep hopelessly.

Lady Courcey ignored her distress. 'Here are your options,' she said with the coldness of a mistress delivering instructions to a recalcitrant servant. 'If you choose the boy, you, he and his family will be consigned to a short life of destitution before you all die in a ditch. If you elect to stay with Mr Lambourne, the family may keep their home and positions. However, either way that boy must go. I want him off the estate by nightfall, do you understand me?'

Still crying, Bridget managed a miserable nod of comprehension. Her mother brushed past her and stalked from the room. After a few frozen moments, she leaned against the wall and slid to the floor in despair.

***

When Bridget left him at dawn, Cormac returned unnoticed to the stable loft. Exhaustion made him drop asleep immediately but too soon he awakened to the sound of the other stable hands stirring. He rose from the straw, yawning and feigning the satisfaction of a good night's sleep.

Despite his fatigue, a current of euphoria streamed through his veins. His beloved Bridget had promised to marry him. She had held him in the most intimate embrace and loved him with a brave and innocent joy that had caused him to adore her all the more. There could be no one in the world as elated as he was right now.

But a lot of things were about to change. Sad though he would be to leave, they could not stay at Oakleigh; Lady Courcey would never abide it. It was going to be hard enough for her to swallow Bridget's cancelled engagement and her choice of a lower class man – and an Irishman, no less – as her husband. It would be best to remove themselves from the animosity that would arise from all that.

They ought to take steps to depart as soon as possible. The most challenging of these would have to fall to Bridget – she was quite possibly at this moment in the throes of a very difficult conversation with her fiancé and mother. After she had concluded that gruelling task, she could gather what few possessions she wished to take with her; the rest of her life would have to be left behind. He did not have many belongings himself, apart from his father's tool chest. His most essential duty would be to explain to his mother that he and Bridget were going away and that they would send for her, Patrick and his sisters once they were settled in a new place. She wouldn't like to be parted from him but he could assure her it wouldn't be for long. There was no need to tell her precisely what had occurred between him and Bridget the night before; he could write and notify her of their marriage once the union had been made official. He bit his lip – who would read the letter for her? He would have to check with Margaret if she had been learning her letters. If not, Maggie might bring the letter to Mrs Kavanagh.

Also of high priority was obtaining a character reference for himself. He would have to find work quickly to support himself, Bridget and, in time, his family, and, while her genteel background might bolster his chances, a character would be the surest course.

To that end, he approached John Corbett at the earliest opportunity that morning, locating him in Bonny's stall where he was examining one of the mare's hooves.

'I think this lady's ready for a visit to the farrier's,' he said, with a glance around at Cormac. 'Might get you to take her tomorrow.'

He cleared his throat. 'John, can I have a word?'

The stable master set the hoof back down and straightened up. 'Fire away.'

'I was wondering if you'd give me a character.'

John looked dumbfounded. 'You're not leaving us, lad?'

'I am, actually. I've decided to move on.'

'Move on? Where?'

'I'm not quite sure yet. But I'll be needing a good recommendation if I'm to find a position elsewhere. Would you be willing to give me one?'

'Of course I would, I can't fault your work in all the years I've known you. So much so,' he added, voice tinged with regret, 'that I'd hoped you'd take over from me here one day.'

Cormac smiled. 'My da would've liked to hear that. And if circumstances were different... But Oakleigh's not the place for me anymore.'

John squinted at him. 'Why? What's happened?'

He tried very hard not to let his smile widen too much. 'I can't really say but 'tis a good reason so don't be troubled.'

John blew out his breath with puffed cheeks. 'Well, I'll be mighty sorry to see you go but my parting gift will be a character that'll knock the boots off any stable master in the country. Come back to me later and I'll have it for you.'

And he left the stall, shaking his head in woe.

In the afternoon, Cormac returned to the hay barn to persevere in his construction of the swing seat, even though in all likelihood Bridget would never have need of it. He kept grinning to himself as he worked, wondering at his own good luck. Behind him was their haystack, an innocuous mound with scattered blades of hay about it. He relived the details of that glorious experience, anticipating the impending bliss of waking next to her every morning and being able to call her his wife.

Liam entered the barn to gather some hay for the horses. He glanced over at Cormac as he dug his fork deep into a haystack beyond the lovers' nest. 'Why are you in such a good mood?'

'No reason,' said Cormac, still grinning.

Liam was silent for a minute or two, teasing out the hay into a smaller stack which he could carry to the stables.

Then he said calmly, 'I know she came to you last night.'

Cormac's head snapped up in surprise. 'What? How?'

'She was quiet, but not quiet enough. I woke when she crawled across the loft.'

Cormac shrugged and continued to saw at a length of wood.

'Be careful, Cormac.'

He heard the warning tone and screwed up his mouth in exasperation. 'Why do people keep saying that to me?'

''Cause you need to hear it, and it doesn't seem to be sinking in,' Liam said frankly.

Cormac stopped sawing and rested the blade on the floor of the barn. 'Enlighten me. Just what do I need to be careful about?'

Liam frowned. 'You've got to realise what you're doing. You groom horses and mend stools. She's a lady engaged to the heir of a huge fortune. She's a respected member of society. And she's the daughter of the meanest woman I know. How can it end any way other than badly?'

'That's one point of view,' Cormac acknowledged. 'But now try this one. I'm not rich and she won't be part of high society anymore, but she doesn't care about either of those things. And what harm can her mother cause us once we're gone? We'll start a new life somewhere else and she won't be able to do anything about it.'

'I wouldn't put it past her to find ways of hurting ye both. And what about your family? Are you going to leave them behind?'

He replied without missing a beat. 'Once I've found work and we've made a home for ourselves, we'll send for my family to come live with us. I've thought it all through.'

'I don't know about that,' said Liam, his doubt clear on his face. 'But I hope it turns out the way you think it will.'

'Thanks,' Cormac said, picking up his saw again. 'We're going to be fine.'

***

Bridget sat at her piano, her blank gaze fixed on the closed lid. She felt like she had aged ten years since the morning. The weight of the decision she still had to make rested heavily on her shoulders.

She heard the drawing room door open and shut. After a long time, she mustered the energy to look up. It was Garrett.

He did not seem angry or upset. In fact, the only expression she could discern on his face was something nearing apologetic. He took a seat by the fireplace and they stared at each other across the room.

Eventually, he pointed at her red cheek and said, 'You should put a salve on that. It will alleviate the stinging.'

She was bewildered. He ought to be furious with her, and yet Lady Courcey was the one who directed the finger of blame while he sat there with absurd equanimity.

'Why do you still want to marry me?' she asked, her voice husky from the many tears she had shed.

He pondered her question for a moment. 'Why do you think I wouldn't?'

She shot an incredulous look at him. 'Because I was unfaithful to you. I gave myself to another man while you and I were engaged. I told my mother I did not want to marry you and that I no longer love you. I am amazed you are not already on your way back to Dublin.'

Again, he cogitated before responding. 'I still love you. And I am certain that if you search hard enough inside yourself you could find a little love left for me too. That is my first reason.' He paused. 'The next is a shallow one but it still matters. Appearances are important and we are viewed as a model couple of society. You are not the only person in this relationship with a parent who values social status and reputation. It is too late to back out of the engagement now.'

He picked up a porcelain figurine from a low table beside him and twisted it in his hands, avoiding her eyes. 'And finally, you have not been honest with me but I have not been honest with you either. There have been other women, even while I courted you. I thought it might ease your guilt to learn that neither of us has been faithful.'

She had no right to reproach him but his confession left a bad taste in her mouth.

'I daresay we deserve each other,' he concluded, a noticeable slump in his customarily proud posture.

She grimaced, feeling like the worst kind of human being.

He replaced the figurine on the table. 'Have you decided what you are going to do?' he asked, assuming a more matter-of-fact manner now that he had unburdened his conscience. When she slowly shook her head, he said, 'May I offer some advice?'

She lifted her shoulders in an expression of weary acquiescence.

He leaned forwards, his gaze intent. 'I know the terms your mother has laid out before you. And I know you, better than you realise. You do not have it within you to inflict such pain on that family. Can you in all honesty tell me you would be able to sacrifice their home and livelihoods for the benefit of your own happiness? Such self-serving behaviour is beyond your capacity to allow.'

He spoke further but she stopped listening. She had been churning her tormenting thoughts over and over since Lady Courcey had delivered her ultimatum, trying to find a solution to her horrifying dilemma. She felt like she was drowning in a fathomless sea of anguish and uncertainty but, much as she yearned for aid, she would have to reach terra firma by herself; it would be cruelly unfair to ask Cormac to choose between his lover and his mother.

That, in effect, was what she had to do herself, for Lady Courcey's contemptible conduct had negated any obligation in Bridget's mind of calling *her* 'mother'. Dearest Maggie was the woman who stirred feelings of daughterhood within her, and it seemed like the greatest betrayal imaginable that she would repay her kindness by causing her to be ejected from the home where she and her husband had raised six children – and this on top of the losses she had already suffered. Recalling Cormac's heartbreaking description of Maggie's distressed state the day after Mary had been buried, Bridget knew that such a blow would terminate any hope of her attaining even a modicum of happiness on this earth again.

But ensuring that Maggie and her family remained in their cottage meant losing Cormac irrevocably. Bridget did not fool herself that she might be able to send him away in the short term and afterwards locate him by clandestine means. Lady Courcey intended for that bond to be severed and would do all in her power to guarantee that it could never be reconnected. And the lady's authority was absolute. It would be another year before Bridget came of age to inherit. She was as powerless as an infant in the nursery.

So if Cormac was banished he would disappear from her life forever. This was as inconceivable as choosing not to breathe. She had managed to bear their parting when she was taken to Dublin because she had known she would return to Oakleigh someday. But to be divided from him permanently, with no prospect of ever reuniting? Impossible. Furthermore, their previous separation had been as friends. Now, having joined with lovers' words and touches, the severance would be a thousand times worse. And, reinforcing that shattering loss, she would be required to marry Garrett. Her skin crawled at the thought of sharing that special, private experience with him.

Her body had been claimed by Cormac and none but he could have it.

In desperation, she wondered *could* they possibly survive? If she, Cormac, Maggie, the three girls and the baby fled from Oakleigh, what would happen? At the outset, they would have to sleep rough until they found means to support themselves. To her chagrin, she had little to offer in that regard – she boasted no skills useful for gaining viable employment and, if any money lay hidden in the manor house, she had no knowledge of its whereabouts and no notion how to appropriate it. While Margaret and Bronagh might be able to find maids' work, their wages would be a pittance, and in reality the family's hopes would lie in Cormac securing a good position. On his own, he would get by, but how far could the earnings of a stable hand or even a carpenter stretch when there were seven mouths to feed? They would be consigned to a level of poverty hitherto unknown to any of them.

She would do it in an instant if it were just she who would suffer. But to bring that misery upon innocent people whom she loved... An image swam into her mind of the family huddled together on a dirty roadside, cold and sick, begging for help from passersby. The little baby Patrick too weak even to cry. Though it was no more than her imagination, the distress of it was too much to stand.

She longed to feel Cormac's arms around her and hear him say that everything would be fine. But it was not within his control to salvage them from such a dire situation. And, if someone had to be wounded in this tragedy, it could only be the two of them and no one else.

Garrett was right. God help her, he was right.

Heart ripping from its mooring in quiet agony, she raised her eyes to meet his. After a moment or two of respectful silence, he said, 'Can Cormac read?'

She gaped at the unexpected question. 'Y-yes. Why?'

He drew a sealed note from his pocket. 'I am acquainted with a family in the city who recently had to dismiss a manservant. They discovered that he was stealing from them, a dreadful affair. But this means they have an opening and I have no doubt they would be pleased to appoint someone as hard-working as Cormac. They are a decent family and would treat him well. I have written their address on this paper. Perhaps you could pass it on to him, if you think he would consider the offer.'

She was stunned. He crossed the room and she accepted the slip of paper wordlessly.

'I shall write to the family with my highest recommendation that they take him into their employ. I am sure it will be a comfort to you to know he has somewhere to go when he leaves the estate.'

He kissed her on the forehead and left her alone.

She stared at the folded note, its plain wax seal a dull red. It astounded her that he could be so noble but she was very grateful to him for it. A measure of relief filled the cavity in her chest to know that Cormac would not have to be homeless or penniless after he was sent away from Oakleigh.

She contemplated breaking the seal and reading the address but resolved against it. She could not bear to know where he was going when he would be forever out of her reach.

It would only make it harder to forget him.

Chapter 26

Bridget left her cane behind when she went out to the stables. She saw no point in keeping up the pretence anymore; it was for nobody's benefit now that her motive for doing so had been so starkly laid bare.

John Corbett saluted her at the stable doors. Feigning cheerfulness, she returned the greeting and said, 'Could you tell me where I might find Cormac? I would like to see how the swing seat is coming along.'

Even that lie seemed redundant. The purpose of it was to prevent suspicion being raised, but soon Cormac would be gone and any question over their association would no longer exist.

'He's in the last hay barn, working on it as we speak. Shall I escort you there?'

'No, thank you. I know where it is.'

She certainly did. It was the place where mere hours ago she had experienced the most profound event of her life. But she needed to bury that memory and those feelings.

When she entered the barn, she found Cormac kneeling over the partly constructed wooden seat. His face lit up at the sight of her and she felt her insides shrivel with dread at what she was about to do to him. He laid his tools on the sawdust-coated floor and stood up, but she did not go any closer. If she allowed him to touch her, her resolve would disintegrate.

'There is something I need to tell you,' she began. Her teeth clamped down on the tip of her tongue. Did she have the strength to say it?

But he wasn't paying attention. 'What happened to your cheek?' he asked, concern changing to mounting anger. 'Did he strike you?'

She shook her head. 'My mother.'

His hands folded into fists. ''Cause of me?'

She took a breath, though it felt like the air did not reach her lungs. 'Yes.'

'Goddamn it,' he muttered, almost to himself. 'The sooner we get away from that woman, the better.' He let his fists unfurl with a conscious effort. 'So what happens now?'

It pained her to read the expectancy on his face. She had to force the words out of her clogged throat. 'I am going to stay with Garrett.'

He stared. 'What?'

'I cannot be with you, I'm sorry,' she said, and it tore at her heart to witness the crushing impact of that declaration.

'But last night—'

'I know,' she interrupted, keen to end the exchange as soon as she could. 'I know what we vowed to each other, but we were not thinking straight. It was just a silly fancy in our heads. It could never happen in reality.'

He was dazed but at this he lifted his chin boldly. 'Why not?'

'Because we come from different backgrounds. And because I am already engaged to someone else. And because we would have no money and nowhere to go. There are a hundred reasons.'

'I thought we'd decided none of those reasons mattered,' he countered.

'But they do. Of course they do. It was ridiculous of us to believe otherwise. Homelessness is not a minor inconvenience. We were being naïve.'

'We'd manage somehow,' he said with desperation in his voice. 'I promised I'd look after you.'

'And what about your mother and your three sisters and little Patrick?' she demanded. 'Would you be able to look after them too? Tell me, how do you provide for seven people when you have no income?'

He looked taken aback by her caustic tone. 'They wouldn't come with us straight away. They could stay here 'til we got settled somewhere ourselves.'

'My mother will throw them off the land if I go with you. She told me so herself.'

Realisation dawned on him. 'Is that why you're doing this? 'Cause she threatened to evict my family? Don't let her bully you. You're a grown woman, able to make your own choices. If you give in to her, you'll never forgive yourself.'

He stepped towards her and she backed out of his reach.

'Please don't,' she said.

His jaw clenched. 'She intimidated you. Well, I'm not afraid of her, or of him. I'll go to them right now—'

'No!' she exclaimed. If Lady Courcey or Garrett set eyes on him inside the manor house, they would send for the constabulary, a threat they had mercifully not made so far. 'That will only make this worse.' She hesitated. 'You won't do it if I do not want you to. If—if I do not want you.'

His bafflement was evident as he tried to reconcile the girl who had loved him so ardently with the fortress of resistance before him. 'Last night—' he tried again.

'Last night you bedded me on a stack of hay,' she said ruthlessly. 'That is not my idea of everlasting bliss.' She hated herself but could think of nothing else to say to persuade him they had no future together.

Her message had the desired brutal effect at last. The blood drained from his features and his body sagged as though the breath had been knocked out of him. She got the impression that she had just destroyed the happiest memory of his life. She felt wretched.

'I won't force you into an inferior situation,' he murmured, 'if you truly don't wish it.'

He searched her face and she pretended with all her might that the luxuries of her class were enough to surpass the desires of her heart. His air of abject resignation informed her that she had missed her calling on the stage.

'You have to leave the estate,' she said, her throat thick with emotion. 'Your family may stay but you must go. And you can never come back.' She produced the note from Garrett. 'Please take this. It is the address of a family in Dublin with a vacant position for a manservant. If you go to them, they will give you work.'

She decided not to tell him who the note was from in case he refused to accept the offer out of pride. He took it from her dumbly.

'You must be gone by nightfall,' she croaked, cast one last glance at his desolate blue eyes, and turned away.

As she left the barn, her whole body screamed at her to go back, to beg for forgiveness, but she kept walking. She felt a strange mixture of revulsion at the duty she had just performed, relief that it was over, and some consolation in the fact that at least he would have somewhere to go when he departed from Oakleigh for good.

***

Cormac was still standing immobile some minutes later when Liam came into the barn carrying a long length of rope wound in circles.

'I just found this in the stable loft. D'you think it'd be suitable for the swing—?' He stopped when he registered Cormac's frozen state. 'Something wrong?'

Cormac shook himself as though he were waking from a dream.

'I'm fine,' he said tonelessly.

He looked down at the note in his hand, paying no heed to Liam's curious expression. With sluggish fingers, he broke the seal and unfolded the paper.

There was no address but a short message written in a smooth script:

> Cormac,
>
> If you are reading this, then you know that Miss Muldowney has chosen to remain with me. I hope you will realise in time that this was the best decision for all concerned, most of all for the lady in question. I am sure you can appreciate how much she will benefit from the comfort and security which I can, and which you regrettably cannot, offer her.
>
> I do not mean to gloat. I take no pleasure in your current misfortune, and this coming so hard upon the recent, tragic death of your sister. I extend my commiserations that this lamentable situation did not transpire as you would have

wished and also my gratitude for allowing my fiancée to be returned to me.

Do not try to contact her again. Good luck wherever you go next.

Regards,
Garrett J. Lambourne

He read the note twice. Then he put it into his pocket, placed his saw and other implements in his father's tool chest, picked up the chest, and turned his back on the half-made swing seat which would now never be finished.

'Best of luck to you, Liam.' He held out his hand.

His friend shook it, mystified. 'What's going on?'

'You were right,' he said simply.

He left the barn and made for the stables where he found John Corbett closeted in his workspace, the tiny room barely able to accommodate the man, a stool and a narrow table covered with untidy stacks of papers.

'John,' he said and his tongue stuck.

The stable master stared at him. 'Are you not well, lad? You look like a ghost passed through you.'

He swallowed. 'I'm just looking for that character, if you have it.'

John came to the threshold and laid a hand on his shoulder. 'You were all smiles when you asked for it this morning. What's changed?'

'I need it for a different reason now.'

He watched John make the connections in his mind. Maybe he had glimpsed Bridget passing by a short while earlier. Or maybe he was shrewd enough to piece together all the little clues over the past few weeks. Either way, his eyes widened with sudden clarity.

'I think I see,' he said.

Cormac could only nod, again struggling for words. John didn't rebuke him and he was grateful for it.

'By rights, the order will come down to me not to give you a character. If your offence is serious enough' – one look at Cormac's face confirmed that it was – 'then you'll be expected to leave empty-handed.'

He squeezed his eyes shut and then opened them again. 'I understand.'

He tried to step away but John's grip on his shoulder held him back.

''Tisn't fair,' the stable master muttered. 'Whatever you might've done, you're a hard-working lad and deserve a decent position somewhere, if not at Oakleigh.'

He reached for a page lying on the messy table behind him.

'I already have it written. Take it. I can tell them I'd given it to you before...before anything was discovered.'

A lump obstructed Cormac's throat and for a moment he was afraid he would cry in front of the man. John clapped him on the back.

'Hurry on now,' he said gently, handing him the page, and Cormac turned away, his words of thanks unspoken but received.

He left the stables and headed for the kitchens, setting down the tool chest by the doorstep as he went inside. He located his two sisters in the scullery, where they were toiling over a mound of dirty dishes at the sink. They looked surprised to see him, even more so when he gave each of them a tight hug and a kiss on the cheek, disregarding their wet arms and flushed faces.

'What's the matter?' said Margaret, her brow furrowing.

'I have to go,' he replied. 'Look after our ma.'

They followed him back into the main kitchen where he took Mr Lambourne's note out of his pocket. Mrs Kavanagh grumbled something about idleness but the three of them ignored her.

'What's that?' Bronagh asked.

'Nothing.' He threw the paper into the cooking fire and watched it burn. Then, with a sad smile towards his sisters, he walked out the kitchen door.

He dragged his feet all the way across the fields, tool chest thumping heavily against his thigh, because he did not want to reach the cottage, did not want to face his mother in his disgrace. But the daylight would not last forever and his time was running short. He took a deep breath and pushed open the half door.

She was sitting at her spinning wheel, something which she had not done since Mary had died. This sign of progress cut through him like the blade of a knife; he suspected that what he was about to tell her would eradicate all her endeavours to revive herself. Patrick was sound asleep in his basket and Orlaith was nowhere to be seen.

Maggie twisted around at the sound of his arrival and her expression lifted.

'*A mhac*,' she said with just the slightest waver. 'I didn't know you were coming home this evening.'

He set the tool chest down. 'It was supposed to be Margaret and Bronagh but I expect they'll still be along later.'

She brightened even further. 'It'll be a rare pleasure to have ye all home together.'

His chest constricted. 'Where's Orlaith?'

'I let her go playing in the woods when the wet nurse visited a short while ago, but she promised to stay close to the cottage. Shall I call her?'

'No, don't.' This would be easier without the little girl present. His mother started to rise but he said, 'Please stay sitting. I've got to tell you something.'

She sat back down, looking puzzled. Feeling sick, he crossed the small room and knelt on the floor by her. He took her two hands in his own, just like the night after Mary's burial.

'Ma, I need you to listen and to be strong. This'll be hard for you to hear but I—I've got to leave you.'

Her eyes clouded over and he could tell she had not absorbed the meaning of his words.

He said distinctly, 'I have been ordered off Oakleigh land and I may never come back.'

'I-I don't understand. Wh-what's happened?'

Shame scalded his insides. Could he really tell his mother this? 'I've done—I've behaved—improperly...' And then he added, with an awful heaviness in his heart as he said her name, '...with Bridget.'

'Bridget?' she repeated, and her eyes cleared. She comprehended what he meant. She stared down at him. 'But she's engaged.'

'I know,' he said bitterly. 'We disregarded that fact.'

'Please tell me 'tisn't true. Such a dishonourable thing... She belongs to another man.'

'I *know*,' he said again. ''Tis too late for accusations now. We can't change what we did. The important detail is that Lady Courcey found out and she's commanded me to leave the estate before sundown tonight.'

A frightened look filled her face as the message sank in. 'No, you can't leave. Cormac, you cannot leave.'

'I have to. I've been dismissed from my position. And if I stay, the rest of ye will be thrown out too. I can't let that happen. 'Tis got to be this way.'

He stood and it was that action which caused his mother, so fragile now, to burst into terrified sobs.

'No!' she cried and clung to his hands. '*No*!'

Her weeping woke her grandson and he began to howl as well. Cormac tried to disengage himself from his mother's grip.

'I've got no choice. Please, you have to let me go.'

She just sobbed all the harder.

'Cormac?' came a small voice from the doorway. He spun about; Orlaith stood there, a posy of wildflowers clutched in one little fist. 'Why's Ma crying?'

Without waiting for an answer, she started to cry too.

He looked around at them all in desperation. How could he leave them when they needed him so badly?

How could he stay when to do so would hurt them even more?

Chapter 27

That evening, after dining in an atmosphere of glacial silence, Bridget, Garrett and Lady Courcey retired to the drawing room, which welcomed them with the comfortable glow of candlelight and a merry blaze from the fireplace. The room had a mellowing effect on the others and they took their seats in a more relaxed manner, but Bridget could not settle. She paced restlessly to the windows and twitched aside the curtains to peer outside. Night was descending, the sky tarnished a deep purple with only the last vestiges of daylight lingering on the western horizon. Shadows thrashed in the gloom: the trees on the edge of the avenue, whipped about by a strong wind which had begun to stir in the late afternoon. Now it blew around the manor in gusts, whistling through minute gaps in the windows and down the chimney.

An indefinable awfulness suffused every part of her, from her bones to her skin. However worthy her intentions, her decision today had inflicted the most grievous pain upon the man she loved. She pictured him preparing to leave his home, saying farewell to his mother, taking one last look at familiar surroundings, and felt a remorse beyond anything she had ever experienced. To save his family, she had ripped them from him. It was unpardonable but she had to believe she had made the right choice, or else succumb to an irreversible despair.

She had condemned herself too in the process, though she could not summon the energy to dread the rest of her life just yet, still too consumed by what she had lost to contemplate what she must face in the future. How could she come to terms with the heart-rending fact that she would never see Cormac again? It was as though he had died, and with him a significant portion of her. A sob threatened to erupt from her throat and she suppressed it with a desperate gulp. She had to continue to exist, one excruciating second at a time.

Turning back to the room, she found that Lady Courcey had become more loquacious since her taciturn performance at dinner and was now conversing with Garrett about the forthcoming wedding, all plans in that direction having been reinstated without opposition.

'If you obtain a licence and bring the date forwards to the beginning of October,' she was saying, 'I think you could indeed be in London by the end of that month. With such little time to prepare for it, it will need to be a much lesser affair, but that is all well and good considering recent events. We can say that Bridget was severely weakened by her illness this summer and that she would only be able for a small occasion. We shall just invite the most eminent guests. Everyone else will have to read about it in the paper.'

'That sounds acceptable to me,' said Garrett, with the blasé air of one who has got his own way on the most important matter and is not too bothered with the details.

Her spirits seeming to improve with every passing minute, Lady Courcey swivelled to her daughter and said in a positively chirpy voice, 'I think I should like some music. Why don't you play for us, Bridget?'

She obeyed because anything was preferable to joining that odious conversation. She seated herself at the piano, her fingers automatically seeking the keys, as her mother returned her attention to Garrett.

'While we are organising the wedding, you can be coordinating the travel arrangements for London. No doubt you are looking forward to going home.'

'I am, indeed. When we get there, I shall assume a larger role in the managing of my father's estate, so there will be many matters to attend to. Of course, I am also partial to the city itself. As you know, there is never a dull moment in London.'

'Quite true, it is a vibrant place. I thoroughly enjoyed the two seasons I spent there in my youth. I have a mind to take up residence at Oakleigh again after the wedding, but I hope to come and visit you and Bridget once you are settled.'

'For certain, you will always be welcome in our home.'

Bridget struck a discord on the piano but carried on.

'That is very kind, Mr Lambourne. I can see that family is important to you, which is as it should be. Family should always be the most imperative consideration in everything we do.' A deliberate pause. 'And I must say, I get a great deal of satisfaction from knowing that one particular family will be homeless by tomorrow morning.'

Both Bridget's heart and playing came to a standstill.

'What?' she exclaimed.

Her mother gave her a look of innocent enquiry. 'Why have you stopped? I do so enjoy Beethoven.'

'You promised they could stay! You said if Cormac left, then his family would not be evicted!'

Lady Courcey frowned. 'Yes, I did, didn't I?' She thought for a moment. 'Oh, well.'

Bridget wasted no more time. Eyes blazing, she slammed down the lid of the piano and dashed from the room. Neither her mother nor her fiancé made any move to stop her.

Out in the entrance hall, she took no notice of Mr Buttimer's appearance and sheer astonishment as she wrenched open the manor's front door. She raced around the side of the house, tearing through the courtyard, past the paddock, into the Gorteen and across the fields, the shortest way to Cormac's home. She ran as fast as she could, though her dainty shoes were no match for such a flight. The wind buffeted her, blowing her hair into her face, and she leaned forwards into it, struggling to make headway against its brute force. The giant's claw materialised out of the shadows, beckoning to her in menacing greeting as she passed, but for once she paid it no mind.

If homelessness was to be that family's fate no matter her decision, then of course she was going to go with Cormac, despite the hardships they would have to endure. There was no advantage to remaining with Garrett – she would not be saving any lives and she would be committing herself to a lifetime of restraint under his and her mother's command. She did not know how she and the McGoverns might survive the coming months of poverty, but at least she and Cormac would be together.

She glanced up at the dark sky. Night had fallen fully which meant that Cormac ought to have left the estate by now. But maybe he had lingered a little longer, perhaps in defiance of the order he had been given, or because he found it difficult to part from his family. She clung to these hopes, urging her body on even though her legs protested and her lungs burned. The wind whistled in her ears and her heart beat uncontrollably in her chest.

At last, she reached the McGoverns' little cottage, gasping for breath. She spared a fleeting look for the horse shoe above the door – what sort of luck had it brought the family within tonight? The door was closed but a faint light glowed through the crack underneath it. She burst in without knocking.

'Cormac!' she cried.

A pitiful sight met her eyes by a sputtering rushlight on the table. Cormac's mother sat on the bench, her face buried in her hands, her rosary beads twined between her fingers, her body shaking with sobs. Orlaith stood beside her, arms around her shoulders, trying to comfort her. The baby lay crying in his basket in the corner. There was no one else in the room.

Bridget's heart leapt into her mouth. Cormac was gone from the cottage but he might not be gone long. She ran back outside and screamed his name. The wind whisked her voice away as if she had never spoken. She darted down the lane, calling out to him again and again, but even if he had been just around the corner he would not have been able to hear her. And she had little expectation of catching up to him in the darkness; she could not even be sure which way he had taken.

But she did not give up yet.

She tore back the way she had come, forcing herself to breathe in short, painful wheezes. Twice she tripped over in the fields but she picked herself up and kept going, paying no heed to her filthy dress. All she cared about was undoing the tremendous mistake she had made.

She barrelled into the drawing room where Garrett and Lady Courcey still sat in an environment of tranquillity. Her mother tutted at her dishevelled state but Bridget ignored her and went straight to Garrett, who got to his feet at her approach.

'What is the address?' She clutched at his lapels. 'The address you gave to Cormac. Please tell me!'

He looked blank but then he understood what she meant and chuckled.

'Oh, my darling,' he said, patting her hands. 'Your naïveté is truly charming.'

'What do you mean?' she demanded, throat strangling with fear.

'There was no address. Did you really believe I would help him after he nearly broke up our engagement?' He snorted. 'I have learned that he did manage to depart the estate in possession of a character reference—John Corbett swears he was unaware of the situation until too late—but it will not stand to him in the long run. Be assured, I will take every action within my power to counteract its worth and guarantee his downfall.'

She was still for all of five seconds. Then her shock was overcome by rage and she shrieked at him and pounded his chest with her fists. She dimly registered her mother's sharp reprimand at her conduct but flouted the warning, shedding the ladylike exterior she had cultivated for so long and invoking the spirited nature repressed inside her as she attempted to take out all her fury on the man who had misled her into making the greatest error of her life. When he grabbed her wrists and held her at arm's length, she started kicking out at him. He forced her back with a little push and she lost her balance and fell over in front of the hearth. All at once, the fight drained out of her and she collapsed on the rug in floods of tears.

She had no means of locating Cormac. He had been sent away from the estate with nowhere to go and with a gentleman's revenge on his heels. What would he do? Wander around the countryside until he died of starvation? Make his way to Dublin where his prospects might be better? But, in his destitute circumstances, how could he gain honest employment anywhere? She allowed herself to imagine what might happen to him and recoiled from the devastating vision, weeping all the harder.

And his family were to be subjected to a similar fate. Whatever hope Cormac had of finding a way to support himself, they had none at all, for now they would be facing poverty without a man to provide for them. It was coming into the winter season, the worst time of year to be without shelter. Could they even survive until Christmas?

The hatred she felt for her mother in that moment was overpowering in its intensity. Lady Courcey had brought about the suffering of every person involved in this sickening power play. They were nothing but pawns in her quest to control and further her family's fortunes. And Bridget had played her part to perfection. If only she had gone with her heart instead of being ruled by her mother, everything could have turned out differently.

Utter desolation engulfed her and she whimpered in physical and emotional pain. Her whole existence was reduced to this crushing sphere of anguish; the voices beyond it signified nothing. It was not until a pair of tender arms encircled her that she returned to reality, believing for one irrational moment that Cormac had come back to her. Then she realised that the arms belonged to Garrett.

'Hush,' he murmured. 'Please do not cry. This is not the end of the world.'

She tried to push him away from her, though she felt as weak as if the fever were upon her again.

'Take care of her,' he commanded to someone over his shoulder, and then Ellen was crouching beside her, tugging at her hands.

'Please, miss, come upstairs.'

Still crying, she stumbled to her feet and allowed herself to be guided up the staircase to her bedchamber. Ellen changed her into a clean nightdress, washed her hands and feet, and helped her into bed, tucking the bedcovers around her. At last, the tears stopped.

'Oh, dear God,' she said, her voice hollow. 'What have I done?'

Ellen's freckled face was fearful. She didn't know what had happened yet but she soon would. By tomorrow, everyone at Oakleigh would learn that the McGoverns had lost their positions and their home. How quickly would they ascertain the reason why? Bridget and Cormac, however innocent of these terrible ramifications, were responsible for the sequence of events that had brought them about. The shame was nearly unendurable.

'Can I do anything else for you, miss?'

She shook her head and Ellen slipped out of the room. At once, her hand slithered under her pillow and withdrew the little wooden bird, fingers curling around the one thing she had left of Cormac. She pressed it to her breast, mourning its creator with a speechless grief.

Ellen had left a candle lighting on the bedside table; Bridget turned onto her side and stared at it, calling to mind the heartbreaking scene lit by rushlight at the cottage. Her eyes became wet again as she recalled the depth of Maggie's distress. That poor woman did not deserve this. She had never been anything but kind to Bridget in all the years she had known her, embodying the role of mother much more than Lady Courcey had ever tried to. Apart from her beloved father, Bridget's real family had always been the McGoverns.

She gulped. Yes, that was so true. Then why would she stay here? She may have lost Cormac – and the agony of it choked her – but she still had a surrogate mother and three almost-sisters and there was a sweet baby too. She would leave Oakleigh with them and they would find a way to survive together. That would be a far better alternative to remaining with her own evil mother and manipulative fiancé.

For the second night in a row, she decided to sneak out of the house after dark. She flung back the covers and climbed out of bed, then pulled the burgundy curtains around it to deter anyone who might check on her from probing further. She groped in the drawer of her dressing table for a pocket to tie around her waist – into this she placed the precious bird and a few trinkets from her jewellery box, judging the value of these latter items to be sufficient enough that they might be pawned for the purpose of the family's subsistence. In her haste, she did not give thought to dressing properly; she just hauled on her boots and a cloak over her nightdress and headed to the bedchamber door.

She could not risk descending the mahogany staircase and passing the drawing room where Garrett and Lady Courcey were likely congratulating each other on a task well accomplished. It would be wiser to take the servants' stairs down to the kitchens. She stuck her head out of her bedchamber, looked up and down the deserted corridor, and then darted for the inconspicuous door across the way. Beyond it was the narrow servants' staircase which snaked through the belly of the house, with an access on each upper floor to allow the servants to come and go. She had explored these hidden stairs as a child but otherwise had never had any need of them.

Though there was nobody on the stairs, she still made her way down on tiptoe. Would the kitchens at the bottom be empty, the clean-up after dinner already finished? With any luck, that would be the case.

She reached the last step and pushed open the door into the kitchens.

She caught a glimpse of Mrs Kavanagh first, her face confused.

Then she saw her fiancé sitting on the bench by the kitchen table, his hazel eyes sad.

And there was her mother standing in the centre of the room, her arms folded.

'Foolish girl,' the lady said.

Bridget threw away all caution and ran for the outer door. She tried to wrench it open but it was locked. She twisted to grab the key from its hook but it wasn't there.

'No!' she screamed. 'Let me out!'

She had to get to Maggie, she wanted to be with the McGoverns. She banged on the door in desperation. Two strong hands grabbed her from behind.

'I have no wish to manhandle you,' came Garrett's voice, 'but I will use force if you do not come with me now.'

He wanted her to go quietly but she would not. She made it as difficult for him as she could, jerking away from him and digging her heels into the floor. He swept her up into his arms, as far from the romantic gesture Cormac had made in the orchard – had that only been the day before yesterday? – as it was possible to be. He carried her struggling back up the servants' staircase to her bedchamber, thrust aside the curtains, and deposited her on top of the bed with rather more gentleness than she had anticipated. For one terrified moment, she wondered whether he would choose to exert his rights as her future husband right there and then, but he spun around and strode from the room without looking at her.

A faint jangling signified the presence of Mrs Walsh, and it was followed by the sound of a key turning in the lock.

It did not turn again until the next morning when she was immediately bundled from her bedchamber into a carriage waiting at the front of the house. She saw nobody on the way, not a single soul to whom she could appeal for help. The door of the carriage slammed shut, the coachman whipped the horses, and the warm red bricks of Oakleigh receded rapidly from view.

Garrett and Lady Courcey shared the carriage with her, both on edge as though they expected her to launch herself out the door while they were moving. But she made no more effort to resist.

She had not slept at all and fatigue threatened to consume her. However, her thoughts were clear and in the nadir of her sorrow she knew that she had been defeated. The McGoverns were beyond her reach. It was no use vowing that she would overturn her mother's eviction notice as soon as she came into her inheritance; that was still over a year from now, by which stage all trace of them would have disappeared. They were as lost to her as Cormac was.

She felt like her passionate outburst of the night before had caused every drop of energy and enthusiasm to seep out of her, leaving a void inside. She was now a husk, submissive and primed for marriage. The appalling realisation had finally come to her that she had been very naïve to believe she had any real say in the choices she made. She understood now that she had no free will and that Garrett and her mother would direct her life in every respect from now on.

And she resigned herself to her lot. What else could she do?

The wedding in Dublin the following month was a quiet affair. Miss Madeleine Wallace and Lord Newby performed the honour of attending the bride and groom. Madeleine was Bridget's closest friend in the city but Bridget did not breathe a word to her of what had happened at Oakleigh that autumn. It was an unspoken agreement that those events would never be mentioned again within the Muldowney or Lambourne families.

Bridget and Garrett informed their guests that they would be postponing their official honeymoon until a later period, as Garrett had urgent business to attend to which expedited his return to England. But both of them knew there would never be a honeymoon.

However, their wedding night was an inevitability. She was unsure what to expect but in the end he came to her without spite. Still, there could be no pleasure for her in it. She merely performed her duty as a good wife should.

They were in London by the end of October.

CHAPTER 28

On a bright morning in late May, there was a knock on Bridget's bedchamber door and the midwife opened it to admit Garrett.

'Come in, sir. You have a beautiful, healthy baby girl.'

He approached the bed and stared at the sturdy bundle in Bridget's arms. Such bright, blue eyes. And a head of soft, golden curls, so fair they were nearly white. Bridget's gaze met his. They both fully comprehended.

He leaned over and placed a cold kiss on his wife's forehead. 'Congratulations, my darling,' he said and left the room, shutting the door behind him.

In the midst of her exhaustion, Bridget held her baby close. The midwife fussed around, plumping the pillows and chattering about Bridget's good fortune.

'You're blessed that the child is healthy. Born a whole month too soon! I feared for you both, that's the God's honest truth. There can be so many complications with early birth. Naturally, I didn't say any of that to you before, but all is well now so it's fine. Who do you think she favours more, her mother or her father?'

Bridget started and a tear squeezed out of the corner of her eye.

'Now, now,' said the midwife, patting her shoulder. 'Don't you worry, he'll be back. He's just disappointed that it's a girl. The men always are. Wait until he gets to know her.' She laughed. 'And remember to bring him a son next time.'

She packed her various intimidating-looking implements into a leather case and cast a kindly look at Bridget. 'Shall I send your maid up to you now?'

'Please wait a few minutes before you do. I would like to be alone with my baby for a little while.'

Nodding understandingly, the midwife left the bedchamber.

Bridget stared down at the bundle she cradled and her daughter stared back, wide-eyed. The midwife had wrapped her in a blanket so only her head was visible above its folds. Bridget absorbed every minute detail: the delicate curve of her ears, the plump cheeks, the dainty mouth, the button nose. She had no eyelashes yet but her eyes... According to the midwife, a baby's eye colour could change, but Bridget somehow knew that that familiar shade of blue was here to stay.

She inhaled the sweet fragrance of clean newborn skin. Touching the top of her daughter's head, she felt the swelling on the scalp. Although the midwife said it had been caused during the delivery and would fade in a few days, Bridget couldn't help feeling anxious; she wanted no harm to befall this tiny, perfect person. She kissed the bruised spot. The fine, fair hair was like silk against her lips.

The emotion inside her became too much to contain and tears of joy spilled over. She held a part of Cormac in her arms. He was not completely lost to her after all. A tear splashed onto her daughter's cheek and the little girl blinked in surprise. Bridget pressed her to her chest in the fiercest hug she could manage while not crushing the small body. God, how she cherished every single bit of her. How she wished Cormac could too. How she wished the girl could cherish him.

Her crying halted in a short, stuttering sob. She hiccupped and looked over at the dressing table. A distance of ten feet. Her legs felt like water and she was in a good deal of pain after the birth, but she could make it.

She pushed back the bedcovers and, reinforcing her tight grasp on her daughter, eased herself out of the bed. Letting out a low moan, she stumbled over to the dressing table and lowered herself onto the stool before it. With her baby nestled in one elbow, she used her other hand to grope in one of the drawers of the dressing table.

She withdrew the wooden bird from the back of the drawer. Every morning and every night, she took it out and pressed a kiss to its carved beak. Now she loosened the blanket wrapped around her baby, freed one of her arms, and touched the wooden bird to her daughter's miniature fist. The fingers wouldn't unfurl but a tiny thumbnail scraped the bird's wing.

'You *shall* know your father,' Bridget whispered fiercely. 'I will tell you about the land where he and I grew up and you shall learn his tongue and speak his prayers.'

She made the sign of the cross over the baby's forehead.

'*Emily is ainm duit*,' she said. 'I have named you and I promise, my precious Emily, that you shall know your father.' A fountain of unfounded yet unshakeable hope surged up inside her. 'And I pray with all my heart that you shall meet him someday.'

What's Next

Thank you for reading! Would you like to spend more time in Bridget and Cormac's world? Join the **Susie Murphy Readers' Club** on www.susiemurphywrites.com, where you will receive a collection of five free short stories which are prequels to the whole series. You will see exactly how Bridget and Cormac became friends, how they were first torn asunder, and the tumultuous events that brought about their transition from childhood to adulthood. By joining, you will also be the first to get updates about A Matter of Class, including book release details and other bonus content.

Did you enjoy this book? If you did, please help other readers discover Bridget and Cormac's story by leaving an honest review about A Class Apart on Amazon and/or Goodreads. A short review will make a huge difference in spreading the word about A Matter of Class.

The next novel in the series is A Class Entwined, available now.

Acknowledgements

Thanks first of all must go to Averill Buchanan for her excellent editorial advice and Andrew Brown for designing such a beautiful cover. They helped shape this book inside and out, and I am so grateful for their expertise.

Next I wish to thank all the people who helped me at various stages along my publishing journey: Mary Arrigan, Sr Cecilia O'Dwyer, Eoin Purcell, Catherine Ryan Howard, Robert Doran, Vanessa O'Loughlin, and Corinne DeMaagd. Most of these people won't even know why they are on this list, but believe me when I say their generosity did not go unappreciated.

Huge hugs go to my early readers and cheerleaders: Miriam Lanigan, Claire Moloney, Grace Noon, Noreen Shanahan, and Laura Mason. They read my unpolished manuscript, offered invaluable feedback (especially that important piece of advice, Miriam!), and never wavered in their belief that I would make it someday. Thanks so much also to Petra Hanlon, TL Harty, and all those who have engaged with me about my book online or in person.

I want to say a massive thank you to my amazing parents and to the rest of my family who have been so supportive of my dream to become a published author. Words cannot express how much it has meant to me.

Lastly, my unending gratitude goes to my husband, Bob, who has had to endure countless discussions about grammar rules and the 19th century over the past few years. He has continued to encourage me when at times I might otherwise have stumbled. All my love.

Get in Touch

www.susiemurphywrites.com
www.facebook.com/susiemurphywrites
www.twitter.com/susiemwrites
www.instagram.com/susiemurphywrites
www.tiktok.com/@susiemurphywrites

Printed in the USA
CPSIA information can be obtained
at www.ICGtesting.com
LVHW090727270424
778634LV00010B/366